'His chariots of wrath the deep thunder-clouds form,
And dark is his path on the wings of the storm.'

Sir Robert Grant

Part One
Messing About in Boats

'Believe me, my young friend, there is *nothing* –
absolutely nothing – half as much worth doing as
simply messing about in boats.'

Kenneth Grahame

The Race

'I have the Casquets light,' Bryan called. He had just come on deck from his watch below, and was amidships, with his arm wrapped round a foremast stay.

'Good show,' said the Honourable Duncan Morant 'Bearing and distance?'

Bryan levelled his hand-bearing compass and waited for the next series of flashes. 'One six five. I estimate ten miles.'

'That sounds about right.' Morant looked at the luminous dial of his watch. It was just coming up to two; the schooner had left Cowes at six o'clock the previous evening. 'Now, if only we could get a bit of that breeze we were promised . . .'

'It's going,' Bryan said.

'What? Where are the others, Billy?'

Billy was aft with the skipper. Now he peered into the starboard darkness. Half an hour ago it had been easy to pick out the white sails of the other yachts. Now . . . 'They've gone, sir.'

'Shit!' Morant commented. He was a powerfully built young man, looking heavier than normal in his thick blue turtle-necked sweater; even in August the middle of the night could be cold at sea. He had ruggedly handsome features and a mop of black hair, half-concealed beneath his woolly hat. Twenty-five years old, both because of his birth and upbringing and the physical health and athletic prowess he had enjoyed throughout his life, he did not take kindly to opposition, especially when it was provided by nature rather than a physical force with which he could get to grips. But now he could clearly see the wisps of white mist closing around the schooner; there remained just enough wind to keep the sails full, but it seemed to be sucking the moisture towards them rather than blowing it away from them.

And now even the topmast and the burgee were obscured. *Kristin*, named after his mother, was his most precious possession; he valued it, emotionally – it was obviously his most expensive possession – above his Bugatti and even above Lucinda Browning, to whom he was getting married the following March. Forty-five feet long overall, with a twelve-foot beam and six and a half feet of draft, she was an excellent sea boat, and her eight hundred and fifty feet of sail could push her along at better than eight knots with any sort of breeze. As she had an eighty-horsepower Perkins Diesel and eight berths she was a very comfortable cruising yacht, and although Duncan's friends and fellow competitors scoffed at the idea of modern racing under a schooner rig and with such a heavy engine, she had proved very useful in offshore events over the past year, one of her great assets being that because the schooner rig was so much easier than most others to handle, she only required a crew of four, apart from the skipper and a boy to cook, thus reducing the constant problems and disappointments of trying to keep a large crew together throughout the season. He had had some hopes of doing well in this Cowes–Dinard Race, which had become an annual event over the past few years. But fog! Though this entire summer of 1939 had been pretty miserable, the annoying thing being that the way things were going politically this could be the last such fixture for some time.

'Well,' he said. 'I'm going below for a nap.' He had been on the helm since the start, conning the ship down the Solent and through the Needles Channel out into the broad reach of the Channel itself. Then there had been other boats all around them; now *Kristin* was alone in the suddenly damp gloom. 'She's all yours, Johnnie. Billy, one nine zero, and keep a sharp lookout.'

'I have it, sir.' Billy was a West Country fisherman, hatchet-faced and thin, with a cautious approach to problems at sea.

Bryan came aft. 'I think two hundred would be better.' Dapper and spruce, his clothes as neat as his hair, John Bryan was assistant manager in a bank. More importantly in this context, he was, like Duncan, a sub-lieutenant in the Royal Naval Volunteer Reserve, and so could treat the skipper on equal terms and more than that; as he had specialized in navigation, where Duncan was a gunnery officer, he could generally keep control.

'Surely not,' Duncan protested. 'The rule says we have to

leave the Channel Islands to port, not necessarily give them a wide berth.'

'With respect, Duncan, in these conditions we're only just making four knots, and the tides around Guernsey run at pretty near that on a spring. We could get sucked in. And it has outliers, maybe a mile offshore.'

'Well . . . just remember that we're bound for Dinard, not Brest. You heard the man, Billy. I'll be up at six, but call me the moment there's a change in the weather.' He swung down the hatchway in the low doghouse to land in the saloon.

'Cup of cocoa, sir?' asked Jamie Goring.

'That sounds just right.' Duncan sat on one of the settee berths; although *Kristin* had six-foot headroom, generous for a yacht, he was six two. He contemplated the boy pouring the hot drink. Jamie was a youthfully slim fellow, although his shoulders were powerful enough. He had relaxed features and somewhat untidy fair hair. This was the first time he had crewed on *Kristin*, 'How old are you, now?' Duncan asked.

'Eighteen tomorrow, sir. Good heavens! It's today.'

'Are you, now. We'll celebrate in St Malo. So what do you think of offshore racing?'

'Can't complain, sir. We seem to be being lucky with the weather.'

'Of course, you've sailed these waters before.'

'Yes, sir. With my dad. But you must know them like the back of your hand.'

'I've never actually sailed off the west coast, before.'

'But . . . I thought Lord Eversham had a house on the island.'

'He does. And we used to spend most summers there when I was a kid. But by then he was into motorboats rather than sail. Nipping across to Herm or Sark was all he ever did in these waters. How many times have you been out here?'

'Every year for the last seven, except when we went up-Channel to Belgium and Holland, or last year when we went down to Biscay and up the Gironde. Mind you, the old *Tamara* isn't quite in this class.'

Peter Goring owned a successful garage business outside Lymington, and serviced the Eversham cars, which was how Duncan had come to know the family.

'A Bristol pilot cutter, isn't she? Good old gaff rig.'

'Yes, sir.'

Duncan sipped his cocoa. 'Tastes good. Where'd he get the name?'

'Tamara was a queen of Georgia, sir. Seven hundred years ago.'

'Georgia? You mean she was a Red Indian? I didn't know they had queens.'

'No, sir. This wasn't the state of Georgia. This was an independent country in the Caucasus. It was actually known to antiquity as Colchis, and was the Land of the Golden Fleece. That story is legend. Tamara was its most famous factually historical queen, and by all accounts was no woman to rub up the wrong way. I beg your pardon, sir. I didn't mean to be rude. The kingdom was finally destroyed by Genghis Khan, a few years after her death.'

'How did your dad find out about this woman?'

'He reads a lot of history, sir. So do I.'

'Hm. Is that what you're going to do when you leave school? – teach history?'

'I left school two years ago, sir.'

'At sixteen? Good God! I didn't leave school until I was nineteen.'

'Yes, sir. But with respect, my school wasn't Eton.'

Duncan gave him an old-fashioned look, then let the riposte go. 'Then what are you doing now? For the past two years?'

'I work for my dad, sir. As a mechanic. I've just got my certificate as a diesel engineer.'

'Well done. But diesel? What about petrol?'

'Oh, I know petrol engines, sir. We deal with them all the time.'

Duncan jerked his thumb at the engine box, the lid of which formed part of the companion down from the deck. 'But diesel . . . they're a complete mystery to me. You mean that if something went wrong with the Perkins, you could fix it?'

'I should think so, sir.'

'Well, well. That's interesting. None of us can. I'm going to turn in. Can't do a damned thing till this fog lifts.' He made his way aft, past the companionway, kicked off his sea boots, rolled into his bunk, and was apparently asleep in seconds.

Billy came down a few minutes later, together with Harry, Duncan's valet, who accompanied him everywhere, while Bob, the burly Southampton policeman, replaced them on deck to join Bryan for the morning watch. Like the skipper, Billy and Harry accepted a cup of cocoa each and then retired forward.

Jamie had no desire to sleep. Although, as he had told Duncan, he was an experienced deep-water sailor, this was the first time he had taken part in an offshore race. He had been overwhelmed at the atmosphere in and around the Royal Yacht Club in Cowes, the protocol and the famous names he had almost rubbed shoulders with: the adrenaline was still flowing, even if thus far the passage had been so uneventful as to be boring.

He pushed his head through the hatch. 'Anyone for cocoa?'

'That sounds like a very good idea, young Jamie,' Bryan said.

Jamie slipped back down, made the drinks and passed them up, then followed to stand behind the helm.

'Tastes good,' Bob commented. 'Like to take her for a spell?'

'May I?'

'Well, don't jerk it about. We don't want the boss back up. Course is two hundred.'

Jamie peered into the binnacle light. 'Two hundred it is.'

Looking forward, for the first time he realized how thick it had become; the bow seemed shrouded in white soup. 'Gosh!' he commented.

'Yes,' Bryan agreed. 'It's not lifting. I think we need to make a noise. Bob.'

'Right you are, Mr Bryan.' Bob opened one of the lockers along the rail and took out the trumpet.

Jamie could not resist the temptation. 'What are you going to play?'

'Mind your manners, young Jamie.' Bob blew a long blast.

'Now what?' Jamie asked.

'We wait, and listen for a reply.'

'And there isn't one,' Bryan commented. 'Every three minutes, Bob.'

The yacht slipped through the fog, accompanied by the mournful wail of the horn.

'What do you think we're making, Mr Bryan?' Jamie asked.

'Two and a half, maybe three.'

'Then we won't be in Dinard until the day after tomorrow.'

'It's the same for the others,' Bryan pointed out.

'The tide runs faster than that, sir. We could be going back-wards, over the ground.'

Bryan looked at his watch. 'Not right now: it's slack. And when it turns at three it'll be running with us.'

'Listen,' Bob said.

They turned their heads.

'What?' Bryan asked.

'Ah . . . There it is again.'

They heard what sounded like a huge gasp from out of the mist.

'That's an explosive fog signal,' Bryan said. 'I'll go down and get the book.'

'That was the Platte Fougère,' Jamie said.

Both men turned their heads to look at him.

'It marks the northern extremity of the reefs off Guernsey.'

'You sure?'

'Yes, sir. I've heard it often.'

Bryan brought up his hand-bearing compass and waited for the next report. 'One three two. How far do you reckon?'

It was Jamie's turn to wait the few minutes to the next bang. 'Ten miles, maybe.'

'Who needs charts with you on board,' Bob remarked.

Bryan was still concerned. 'How far is it from the Casquets to the Platte?'

'Twelve miles,' Jamie answered without hesitation.

'Then surely we should have heard that signal sooner?'

'We should, sir. But you know what it's like in fog. You get areas of null sound.'

'Hm. Take the helm, Bob. Keep her on course. Jamie, come below.'

They dropped down the companionway into the warm glow of the cabin, and Bryan spread the chart on the table, using his slide rule to draw a line along the bearing from the Platte Fougère light tower, using his dividers to mark off ten miles, then made a small pencilled 'X' on the stiff paper. 'You reckon?'

'Should be about right, sir.' Jamie touched an earlier mark. 'When was that?'

'An hour or so back. We confirmed it when we saw the Casquets light.'

'That shows an offing of about ten miles, sir. In that case

and on two hundred we should be more than ten miles off the Platte.'

Bryan regarded him for several seconds. 'So one of our estimates is, or was, wrong. You think we're being carried in?'

'Well, sir . . .'

Bryan surveyed the west coast of Guernsey, littered for a good distance offshore with marked rocks. 'What a mess. But even if we are here, with the tide just turning, on two hundred, we should clear it all comfortably enough.'

He was looking for reassurance, which Jamie was unable to provide. 'When the tide turns, sir, it will be running mainly south-easterly, at a steadily increasing speed. It's quite a big one, too. On this coast it can get up to five knots or more.'

'So we'll make better time over the ground.'

'To the south-east, sir. Into that mess, as you call it.'

Bryan stroked his chin. 'You'd like us one two one oh? That really is OTT. The skipper wasn't happy about two hundred.'

'Maybe we should wake him up, sir. And let him make the decision.'

'I think we'll let him sleep a while longer. He's had a pretty exhausting day. We're in no danger at the moment. You turn in, Jamie. We may need your local knowledge later; this'll burn off when the sun gets up.'

Jamie was tempted to remark that if this had been his father's ship, and there was some uncertainty as to exactly where they were, Dad would have wanted to be wakened up, no matter how little sleep he had had. But he felt that perhaps he had been sticking his oar in far too much already, even if he suspected that at this moment and in these waters he was more experienced than any of them. So he said, 'OK, sir. I'll see you at dawn.'

As the junior member of the crew, Jamie was required to use one of the settee berths in the saloon, but despite the lights being on he was asleep in seconds. When he awoke it was to the sound of snoring from the forward cabin, so it could not yet be six, although the cabin ports were light. He sat up, vaguely concerned. The ship was involved in a long, slow roll, but there did not seem to have been any increase in wind.

He pulled on his boots and sweater, switched off the lamp and went up. It was just on dawn, and the fog seemed to have lifted a little: it was possible to see some fifty feet to either side. As he had surmised, the wind remained light, but on the beam; the yacht heeled only slightly as it sailed on, through a flat-calm sea, except for that long swell, also coming out of the west. As it was just past dawn, the Blue Ensign – which denoted either that the yacht skipper was a member of the armed services or that he had a special warrant from the Admiralty – had been set on the staff and stirred gently.

'Good morning, Jamie,' Duncan said. 'Going to make us some breakfast?'

He wasn't due on watch until six, but Jamie could tell he was uneasy with the situation. With good reason, he reckoned. 'Yes, sir. May I ask where we are?'

'Haven't a clue. Mr Bryan told me you heard the Platte Fougère signal, but that was some hours ago. We must be pretty well down the west coast of Guernsey by now. We've got the tide. Anyway, the fog is lifting. When the sun gets up in another hour or so we should be able to get a bearing on something.'

'Yes, sir. This swell . . .'

'It must be a forerunner of that weather they promised us for this afternoon, coming out of the Atlantic. It can't come too soon for me.'

'May I make an observation, sir?'

'Go right ahead. You know these waters better than I.'

'This is an inshore swell, sir.'

'What?'

'Have you cast the line recently, sir?'

'We're in deep water.'

'From the size and shape of the swell, I don't think we have much more than five fathoms under us, sir. That means there could well be heads only a few feet under the surface.'

Duncan looked over the side at the slow-moving water, gently picking the schooner up and letting her slide sideways down the other side. 'You serious?'

'Yes, sir.'

'Won't they mark?'

'Not from any distance when it is this calm, sir. You might get a slight swirl, but nothing you could see until you're up to it.'

'Shit! Harden that sheet, Bob. We'll alter course two one oh.'

Jamie gave a sigh of relief as the ship turned slowly closer to the wind. 'I'll get breakfast.'

He slid down the companionway, placed a saucepan on the stove, opened the locker beside it to take out the carton of eggs, and there was a resounding crash which threw him right across the cabin, accompanied by both saucepan and eggs. *Kristin* went right over on to her beam ends for a moment, before coming upright as she slid off the obstruction.

'Get that canvas down,' Duncan was shouting. 'Ahoy, below!'

Bryan emerged from aft and Bob from forward, while Jamie sat up to claw a mess of broken eggs from his sweater; there was no time to consider the various bruises he had suddenly accumulated. 'What the hell happened?' the navigator demanded.

'Threw me out of my bunk,' Bob complained.

'I think we hit something,' Jamie said, giving up and taking the sweater off.

'We hit a rock, that's what,' Duncan said down the hatch. 'Get those floorboards up and see if we're making water. Start forward.'

Bryan and Bob began lifting the boards to peer into the bilges, where the lead ingots of ballast were stowed.

Jamie went on deck. Looking aft he could see a swirl of water behind them, rapidly disappearing as it settled, and even without the sails, which lay in a cluster of canvas on the deck, they were carried away from it by the tide. To either side of the disturbed patch everything remained calm.

Bryan emerged. 'Dry as a bone. Must have been the keel. Shall we anchor? Could be a reef.'

Duncan hesitated.

'I don't think it was a reef, sir,' Jamie ventured. 'There's no marking, anywhere. I think it was an isolated head.'

'Where there's one there could be others.'

'If we stand straight out to sea, under foresail alone to keep our speed down, we should be all right.'

A last hesitation, then Duncan nodded. 'Harry, Billy, get that jib back up. Any damage below?'

'The eggs are all gone, sir. But there's still bacon.'

The two officers looked at each other. 'I think we should leave breakfast for an hour or so,' Bryan suggested.

'Then I'll make coffee,' Jamie said, and dropped down the hatch.

'Nothing seems to upset that kid,' Bryan remarked.

'He has a lot of spunk,' Duncan agreed. 'Comes from experience. I'd say he has more than us, even if he is only eighteen.'

'Maybe you should make him a regular.'

'You know, Johnnie, I might just do that.'

Bryan looked forward. 'Well, glory be; here comes the sun. And . . . what the hell is that?'

The mist was still only slowly clearing, although the sun was now burning it off. And to the east there was suddenly a huge blaze of ordered rows of lights.

'God Almighty!' Duncan cried. 'That's a liner!'

'Amongst those rocks?'

Duncan took off his woolly hat to scratch his head, and Jamie came up the companion with two steaming mugs of coffee. 'You ever seen anything like that before?'

'Why, yes, sir.'

'What?'

'You see that every dawn out here. That's the sun shining on all the glasshouses. As you know, sir, Guernsey's industry is tomatoes, grown under glass.'

'I never knew they looked like that!'

Jamie reflected that not only had the skipper never sailed out here, but when he had holidayed here as a schoolboy he would never have been up at dawn.

'And there's the land,' Bryan said, as the island itself came into view, rising steeply into low green hills, dotted with houses.

'So where are we?' Duncan inquired. 'Good God! Isn't that Lihou?'

He pointed at the small island no more than a mile away on the port bow, separated from Guernsey itself by a causeway, presently covered by the south-running tide.

'Yes, sir,' Jamie agreed. We're too close in.' By a hell of a long way, he thought.

'And it's about two-thirds of the way down the coast,' Duncan mused. 'So we've only a few miles to clear. We've made pretty good time, fog or no fog.'

'There's a lot of muck ahead of us, sir,' Harry said.

They looked forward, at the rocks and the flurries of white; the breeze had freshened to ten knots, Force Three on the Beaufort scale.

'That's the Hanois Reef,' Jamie said. 'Stretches a good couple of miles to the south-west.' He pointed. 'That lighthouse marks the end of it.'

'What's it doing outside us?'

'We've been sucked in too far by the tide.'

'You mean we have to get round that, from here?' Duncan demanded, and looked up at the burgee, fully extended by the breeze. 'Wind just north of west. We'll have to beat.'

'You're talking about two hours minimum,' Bryan pointed out. 'If those other fellows are out there already . . .'

'There they are, sir,' Harry said.

The morning was now quite clear, with at least ten miles visibility, and some six miles to the west there was a cluster of sails.

'They're not round it yet,' Duncan growled.

'But they will be, long before we can get there,' Bryan said. 'Shit!'

'Excuse me, sir,' Jamie ventured.

'Yes, boy? What is it?'

'There is a passage through the reef.'

'Eh?' Duncan levelled his binoculars. 'That's nothing but black rock and white water.'

'It's there, sir. You'd see it if we got closer. It's only about a cable's length wide, but it carries two fathoms even at dead low.'

'Twelve feet,' Bryan muttered.

'There's no big surge at the moment, sir. And it won't be dead low for another couple of hours. And right now the tide is still running with us.'

The two officers looked at each other.

'It'd put us a couple of miles ahead of the rest, sir,' Harry commented.

'Or swimming for our lives,' Bryan countered. 'Anyway, is it legal?'

Duncan snapped his fingers. 'Check that out, Johnnie. Meanwhile, we'll hold our course. Billy, Harry, get the main and the staysail back up.'

The wind was freshening all the time, and with the two big sails again set the schooner began to heel as she steered straight for the reef. Bryan slid down the companion and came back a moment later with the booklet of terms and conditions. He riffled the pages. 'Here we are. "The Casquets Bank, the islands of Guernsey and Jersey, the north-west Minkies buoy, and the south-west Minkies buoy shall all be left to port."'

'No mention of the Hanois Reef?'

'No. That's probably because they didn't reckon anyone would be crazy enough to try to go inside it.'

Duncan looked at Jamie. 'Can you do it?'

'I've done it before, sir.'

'In a thirty-footer, with your dad on the helm, right?'

'There's room, sir. And I have helmed the passage myself. Although Dad was standing at my elbow.'

Duncan looked at Bryan.

'She's your boat,' Bryan said.

Duncan stared ahead using his binoculars again to study the reef.

'The passage is just coming into view now, sir,' Jamie said. He could see the terribly narrow-looking piece of blue water, with the breakers to either side.

'It's a bit late to change our minds,' Billy muttered. They were within a mile of the rocks, being driven onwards by both wind and tide. There was now no chance of beating out of it; if they wanted to get round the reef they would have to use the engine, which meant officially abandoning the race.

'She's yours,' Duncan said, and stepped away from the helm.

Jamie wrapped his hands round the spokes and stared ahead. There were no marks, but the slight chop made it easier; where there was no white there were no rocks. On the other hand, they were now travelling quite fast, making a good five knots through the water and another two at least over the ground; he had to get it just right.

The crew were all on their feet, holding on to the shrouds as if expecting to hit. To their left, the hilly promontory of Pleinmont rose some three hundred feet, bright green in the morning sunlight and appearing perilously close. To either side the rocks showed, their bulk increasing with every second as the tide fell. But in front of them was the slow surge of blue water.

The sun was now shining over the hills and across the passage; Jamie had to squint to maintain full visibility. None of the men spoke; they were all holding their breaths. Then the schooner was in the passage, the rocks to either side looking close enough to touch but actually more than fifty feet away. And ahead of them was the broad expanse of open sea.

'By God!' Duncan said. 'You've a berth on my boats, any time you feel like it, Jamie boy.'

'What's the verdict?' Bryan asked, as Duncan strode along the dock and swung his leg over the rail. It was late afternoon, and *Kristin* lay snugly alongside in the inner pool of St Malo Harbour, separated from the increasingly boisterous weather outside by the lock gates, although the wind was now thrumming the rigging.

'We broke no rules,' Duncan announced, 'even if the committee consider our action to have been foolhardy in the extreme. I suspect that passage may be out of bounds next year. But they want to meet you, Jamie.'

'Sir?'

'I think they want to congratulate you. But I told them they'd have to wait. Smarten up, lads. Everyone ashore to shower and shave. Then it's lobster and champagne. There's Jamie's birthday to celebrate, and . . . we've won our class.'

'Hooray!' Bryan said. 'But shouldn't we have a look underneath?'

Duncan peered over the side. The water inside the pool was more brown than blue, and there were some forty yachts on the various pontoons, not to mention some larger ships alongside . . . all with heads being continually used. 'Anyone who goes in there will wind up in hospital with galloping impetigo at the very least. As you said, Johnnie, it can only have been the keel that struck. We'll check her out when we get back to Lymington.'

They went ashore to use the showers, then shore-going gear was brought out, blazers and ties for the officers, smart jumpers and clean trousers for the crew. Jamie had visited St Malo often enough before, with his father, but he always found the romantic battlements, and the narrow, crowded streets they guarded, fascinating. And this was a special occasion for him, less because of their success in the race than because Duncan, unlike Peter Goring, saw no reason why his youngest crew member should stop at one glass of wine.

In fact the wine and champagne flowed very freely, as did the lobster and crab and oysters. The bar/restaurant was crowded, the men all in high spirits, and the waitresses willingly took part in the fun, allowing their bottoms to be squeezed as they bent over the tables, and giggling girlishly as they were propositioned.

There was the possibility of a punch-up when they were joined by some of the other crews, one of whose skippers decided to make a speech. 'Ladies and gentlemen,' he bawled across the crowded room, swaying on his feet, 'I wish to congratulate the *Kristin* and her gallant crew on their success. *Kristin*, as we all know, is owned and skippered by Duncan Morant, whose mate is Johnnie Bryan. And we know the secret of their success: they are both officers in the Royal Naval Volunteer Reserve. Well now, we have all heard the saying, eh? An officer in the Royal Navy is a sailor trying to be a gentleman. An officer in the Royal Naval Reserve is a gentleman trying to be a sailor. While an officer in the Royal Naval Volunteer Reserve is neither trying to be both. Haw, haw, haw.'

'Oh, Christ,' Bryan muttered, 'here's where we all wind up in the calaboose.'

But Duncan took the ribbing in good heart and did not swing a punch. It was midnight before the six drunken men staggered back to the dock and stumbled on board. The wind seemed to be stronger than ever, but that meant nothing to them; they were asleep in seconds.

Jamie awoke to daylight and a gonging head, surrounded by snores. He rolled out of his bunk and went on deck, inhaling great gulps of fresh air and the delicious smell of baking bread rising from the city. That reminded him that he would be required to serve breakfast when the crew started waking up and that he was entirely out of eggs; also that, as they were in France, they would probably want croissants. He turned to go back below and see if he could locate some money and was halted by a peremptory summons. 'You!'

It hadn't been '*Vous*'. Jamie turned and did a double take. The woman standing on the dockside above him was tall, with shoulder-length wavy auburn air, boldly handsome features and undoubtedly long legs. Prosaically she wore a brown calf-length skirt and a loose green blouse, but her watch was gold, there was a string of pearls resting on her very ample bodice, and he didn't care to estimate the value of the two rings on her fingers; neither indicated that she might be married or even engaged. 'Me?' he countered, feeling inane.

'You are crewing on that boat?' She had a faintly foreign accent.

'Yes, mademoiselle.' His father had laid down an inflexible rule when addressing strange Frenchwomen: if you estimate they are under thirty, it is an insult to call them madame, as that suggests they are older than they are trying to appear; but if you reckon they are over thirty, it is an insult to call them mademoiselle, as that suggests they are incapable of getting married. This woman was definitely well over thirty, if not forty, and despite the absence of any evidence he could not believe anyone as good looking would not be married, or have been married. But despite all of that, for some reason he could not immediately define, he chose mademoiselle.

She did not appear to take offence. 'It belongs to Mr Morant. Is he aboard?'

'Well, yes, mademoiselle. But he's asleep.'

'You mean he's sleeping it off. I stopped by last night, but there was no one aboard. What were you celebrating?'

'We won our class.'

'Did you?' She seemed to be both surprised and pleased. 'I suppose it's a shambles down there.'

'Well . . .'

'Don't tell me. We can deal with that later.'

We? he wondered, now definitely alarmed.

'What is your name?'

'James Goring.'

'Goring. Don't tell me. Your father owns that garage.'

'Yes, he does,' Jamie said. 'Ah . . .'

'Have you breakfasted?'

'Well, no.'

'Neither have I. Come along.'

'I was going to get something for the crew.'

'Let them wallow in their booze for another hour. It'll do them good.'

'You don't understand. The skipper . . .'

'Oh, come along,' she said. 'Fuck the skipper.'

Jamie was left speechless. He had never heard a woman, much less a lady, as she certainly appeared to be, use that word. He had not been aware it was even known to the female sex.

'I'll take the responsibility,' she said kindly. 'Don't worry about it.'

Jamie found himself standing on the dock beside her. 'What . . . I mean, well, who *are* you?'

'My name is Kristin Eversham.'

'Oh, my God! You're . . .'

'Yes,' she agreed. 'I'm his mother.'

Lady Eversham selected a table outside another popular bar/restaurant, and ordered in fluent French, delivered too rapidly for Jamie to follow. 'One of the great delights of France is that one can breakfast out of doors, at least in summer. You wouldn't believe that we are only a hundred miles south of England.' She rested her chin on her hand to inspect him. 'Mind you, it is better when one's companion looks a little less dishevelled and bleary-eyed.'

'I'm sorry. You didn't give me the time to do anything.'

'Of course. I am a dreadful woman. I kidnapped you. You should beat me.'

'What?'

'Don't you like beating women? My husband used to like beating me. Until I decided to beat him back. Then he divorced me instead. Ah, smell this.' The coffee and croissants had arrived. 'Isn't it a shame the French just cannot make coffee.'

'What's wrong with French coffee?'

'Coffee,' Lady Eversham said severely, 'should be as hot as hell, as black as night, and as sweet as sin. This brown stuff falls short on every count. Have a croissant. They *can* make croissants, like nobody else in the world.'

Jamie munched, while he tried to get his brain under control. He had actually seen Lady Eversham before, at the garage, but only from a distance, as he wasn't a forecourt attendant; thus he had not immediately recognized her. Certainly he had never spoken with her before. Now he wasn't sure he was in condition to cope with a whirling dervish, especially when it manifested itself as a beautiful woman. 'Do you live in France?' he asked, conversationally.

'Sometimes. I have a house outside Bordeaux.'

'And you came all the way up here to see the end of the race?'

'I came across from England, by ferry, yesterday. Not to see the end of the race. I have something important to give to Duncan. Do you like him?'

Another unanswerable question, at short notice, certainly when coming from such a source. 'I don't really know him, milady. He's a good skipper.'

'I'm glad you said that.' Lady Eversham daintily wiped her fingers on her paper napkin. 'So you spent last night celebrating. How old are you?'

'Oh! Good Lord! I'd forgotten. I was eighteen yesterday.'

'You forgot your birthday?'

'Well, there's been rather a lot on . . .'

'And you are a Leo. That means you are a lion. Are you a lion?'

'I don't know.'

'You have never grabbed life by the throat? Were you expelled from school?'

'Well, of course not.'

'What do you mean, "of course not"? Duncan was expelled from Eton.'

'What?'

'Oh, we managed to pull strings, make a few donations, and they took him back. No one was prepared to pull strings for me,' she added darkly.

'You were . . .'

'I was expelled from my convent in Madrid, yes. I was sixteen. My father was very angry. He beat me.'

'Until you beat him back,' Jamie said, absent-mindedly, registering that she appeared to be Spanish, although from her name there had to be something else involved. Lady Eversham arched her eyebrows 'I do apologize,' he said. 'It just slipped out. What I meant was, you seem to have been beaten by an awful lot of men.'

'I did not beat my father back,' Lady Eversham said with dignity, 'because he was bigger than I. But you are right: men do like to beat me. Or at least, spank me. I have been told that I have the most spankable ass in the world.'

Jamie choked on his second croissant, and hastily drank some coffee.

'Do you like spanking girls?'

'No.' He flushed. 'Well, I don't know. I've never tried it.'

'Well, perhaps one day I will show you my ass and you will decide whether you'd like to spank it.'

Jamie dropped his coffee cup. He caught it before it hit the pavement, but coffee splattered everywhere. 'Oh, I'm terribly sorry.'

'It missed me,' she pointed out.

'I do think we should be getting back. They'll be awake by now.'

'As soon as I have finished my coffee. You'll be telling me next that you're a virgin.'

Jamie stared at her with his mouth open.

'You have had a singularly uneventful life, Mr Goring. That's why I was expelled from my convent at the age of sixteen: for no longer being a virgin. Actually, I don't suppose it would have made much difference if I had been eighteen. The nuns didn't go in for that sort of thing.' She opened her bag, placed a five-franc note on the table – according to the chit they only owed two – and stood up. 'Take me to your leader.'

Predictably, Duncan was on deck, gazing at them with his hands of his hips. 'Mother! What in the name of God . . .?'

'I do like sons who greet their mothers affectionately,' Lady Eversham remarked. 'Lucinda sends her love She didn't feel up to coming over with me. She hates boats.'

'I know,' Duncan said sadly. 'I'm sorry things are in a bit of a mess. We were celebrating.'

'This young man's birthday, yes. Permission to come on board?'

Duncan looked at his mother's low-heeled shoes. 'Of course you may come on board. We were actually celebrating winning our class. Didn't he tell you that?'

'Yes he did. Hold my hand,' Lady Eversham commanded, and when Jamie did so, hitched up her skirt with the other and swung her leg over the rail, revealing an expanse of very shapely stocking.

In the midst of this operation, Bryan appeared on deck. 'Good Lord!' he remarked. 'Lady Eversham! How nice to see you.'

'I don't think either of you is the least pleased to see me,' Kristin said, swinging her other leg over without releasing Jamie's hand, so that he nearly went with her. 'Fortunately, Mr Goring has been a perfect gentleman. He even took me out to breakfast?'

'Did he?' Duncan inquired.

Kristin released Jamie's hand. 'However, Jamie . . . I wish you to make me a promise.'

'Ah . . .' Jamie desperately tried to avoid catching Duncan's eye 'Yes, milady?'

'Promise me that you will never apologize, never say, "I'm sorry", to anyone, ever again.'

'Ah . . . yes, milady. Not *anyone*?'

'Not anyone,' she said firmly.

Duncan was showing signs of impatience. 'May I ask why you are here, Mother? I mean, it's splendid to see you, but . . .'

'One should never lie to one's mother. I am here because I have something for you.' She opened her shoulder bag, took out a stiff manila envelope.

Duncan snatched it, gazed at the huge black letters along the top: OHMS. 'My call-up papers! But . . .' He turned the envelope over. 'This has been opened.'

'Of course. I opened it.'

'You opened my personal letter? And an official communication from the Admiralty? That makes you—'

'A spy? Don't be absurd. That arrived a couple of hours after you left the house the day before yesterday. I knew you'd be very busy once you got to Cowes, and that you would be totally preoccupied with the race. So I thought I had better find out just how important it was. When I had done that, I realized that it would only distract you from the race, so I decided to come over and meet you here. I think I acted in a most responsible manner.'

Jamie reckoned she was speaking as if she knew that she did not always do that.

Now she asked, 'Aren't you going to read it?'

Duncan had been gazing at her with undisguised hostility.

'You may as well tell me. I suppose I've been appointed to
a ship. I hope it's one of the new battleships.'

'You have been given a command,' Kristin announced
triumphantly.

'What? Me? A command?' He looked at Bryan, as if for
confirmation that that could possibly happen when he had
never served apart from during the yearly fortnight's manoeuvres, and certainly never in a responsible position. He tore
open the envelope, read aloud. 'Report to Portsmouth immediately to assume command of . . . *MTB 20?*' He raised his
head. 'What the devil is that?'

'It's a motorboat, darling – a small motorboat.'

Heavy Weather

D uncan sank on to the transom, the letter trailing from his
fingers. 'A small motorboat? I have been given command
of some smelly organ-grinder? Something smaller than this?'
His mother sat beside him. 'Actually, I think it's a bit bigger.'
He turned his head. 'How do you know?'
'Before coming across, I went down to Portsmouth myself,
and saw Jimmy Lonsdale. You remember Jimmy Lonsdale?'
Duncan sighed. 'I met Rear Admiral Lonsdale at one of
your cocktail parties, two years ago. You told him you had
opened my letter?'
'I told him the truth: that the letter had arrived just after
you had left for the race, and that I felt obliged to open it
because it might have been important, but I had decided not
to stop you, and that you would be with him the moment the
race was over . . .'
'You told the commander-in-chief, Portsmouth, that you did
not consider his letter to be important?'
'One has to keep a sense of perspective. A day or two
cannot make any difference. Your new boat isn't going anywhere.'
'You also told him that I would come to see him when I
had finished a yacht race?'
'As you didn't know you had been called up, he can't blame
you. He doesn't.'
'I'm surprised he didn't lock you up.'
'Or beat you,' Jamie said without thinking. Both mother
and son turned their heads to look at him. 'I'm sorry. It just
slipped out.'
'You are breaking the promise you just made me,' Kristin
pointed out. 'Jimmy and I are old friends,' she added, enigmatically. 'Aren't you interested in your new ship?'
'You mean you know about that too?'

'He showed me over her. She's sixty feet long, but of course there is so much gear and things there's not a great deal of comfort. But he says she's very fast. More than thirty knots.'

Duncan looked around his crew. 'Anyone here ever sailed at more than thirty knots? Or motored?'

'Sounds like it might be fun,' Bryan suggested.

'Anyway, what am I supposed to do, rushing about at thirty knots?' Duncan inquired, looking at his mother, as she seemed to have obtained the answers to everything.

'I don't think they know yet. The whole idea appears to be a bit experimental. The thing is that the Germans have apparently developed whole squadrons of these fast motorboats, and the Admiralty feels that we should have some too.'

'I see.'

'And someone like you,' Kristin went on, winningly, 'a yachtsman who knows the Channel waters like the back of his hand – well, you're a natural. You'll probably get one too, Mr Bryan.'

Duncan looked at Jamie, remembering who had virtually taken command on the crossing they had just made. Jamie felt it best to continue looking po-faced. 'Well,' Duncan said. 'I obviously have to get back, immediately. I suppose it means leaving the ship here . . .'

'Why?' Bryan asked. 'It may be a long time before you can pick her up, and this is a very open harbour when it comes to pilfering. We can take her back far quicker than if you tried to catch the ferry to Guernsey and then another ferry to England.'

'Mr Bryan is right, sir,' Billy said. 'We don't want to abandon *Kristin*. Begging your pardon, milady.'

'I agree with you entirely,' Kristin said.

'With respect, Mother, it's blowing Six out there now, with a forecast of maybe Eight later.'

'It'll be fun.'

'*What* did you say?'

'I said, it'll be fun; I'm coming with you, of course.'

There was a collective dropping of jaws. 'You can't do that,' Duncan protested.

'I have to come with you. I have no clothes.'

'What?'

'You are starting to sound like a broken record,' Kristin

pointed out. 'I just had the time to catch the ferry out of Southampton yesterday after seeing the admiral. So I did. I didn't have the time to go all the way home and pack a bag. So I got into Guernsey just after lunch and came on here in the afternoon. I came down here as quickly as I could, but the yacht was locked up.'

'Well, we'd gone ashore to celebrate.'

'I worked that out for myself.'

'So where did you spend the night?'

'I had brought some money with me, so I took a room at the Café Central.'

'But . . . you had no clothes? No nightclothes?'

'Silly boy. I don't wear nightclothes. But I do like to change my knickers every day.'

'Ahem,' Duncan said. 'Couldn't you have picked up a change from the Guernsey house?'

'Of course I could not. Don't you remember that your father changed all the locks so I couldn't get in? Anyway, I don't have any clothes there now. There is nothing there of mine, except my painting.'

'Yes, yes, yes,' Duncan said hastily. 'I take your point.'

'So, I have now been wearing these for thirty-six hours – as well as everything else. So I wish you to take me home as rapidly as possible so that I can have a bath and change.'

Again Duncan looked at his crew, but they were trying to pretend they weren't really there. 'Mother,' he explained, speaking as reasonably as he could. 'This is an overnight trip.'

'So? You have eight berths, haven't you?'

'But there are no private cabins, except aft.'

'Oh, I'll move into the saloon,' Bryan volunteered.

Duncan glared at him. 'And only one heads,' he shouted.

'I'm sure I'll manage.' She looked across the harbour. 'I think we should leave as soon as possible.'

'Mother, it is blowing thirty plus knots of wind out there, and is supposed to increase.'

'You just said that. Won't *Kristin* take it?'

'Well, of course she will. But—'

'If one Kristin can take it, so can the other. What does that green light mean?'

'Eh?' Duncan turned his head. 'It means that the lock is operating.'

'Then hadn't we better get a move on? We'll need fresh food. I interrupted Jamie when he was setting off this morning. Come along, Jamie. We'll make a quick trip to the shops.'

'Jamie stays here,' Duncan said. 'You go with her, Johnnie.' He looked at his watch. 'Don't be too long; it only has about another hour to go before it shuts until the next tide.' He handed over his wallet.

'Right.' Bryan assisted Kristin over the rail.

'Come below, Jamie,' Duncan said. 'Billy, Harry, prepare for sea. Storm canvas.'

Oh, Lord! Jamie thought, as he went down the companion. I'm for the high jump. 'She took me by surprise, sir,' he explained.

'She takes everyone by surprise,' Duncan agreed, spreading the chart on the table. 'She used to do a lot of sailing when she was a girl. That's how she met my father. But I'm not sure how up to it she still is. So . . . wind south-west. You know these waters. Plot me a course which will be the least uncomfortable.'

'Ah . . .' Jamie considered a moment, not because he didn't know what to say, but in relief that he was not going to get a roasting for his apparent intimacy with her ladyship. 'It's behind us. That's a help for a start.'

'But the tide is running south,' Duncan argued. 'We'll have wind across tide. It's going to be brick walls.'

'Only for the first couple of hours. It'll turn again about eleven. By that time we should be off the north-west Minkies. Then we should carry a fair tide for over six hours. If we're out of here by eight, we should be able to make Gros Nez by one. Then with a good fair wind and the tide we should be able to make the Race of Alderney before the tide turns back. It's only about forty miles from Jersey to the Race. If we go inside Sark we should have a relatively smooth passage.'

'Have you gone completely bonkers?' Duncan demanded. 'Are you suggesting that we should try to take *Kristin* through the Race of Alderney in a gale? That is just about the most dangerous stretch of water in Europe.'

'With respect, sir, it is *the* most dangerous stretch of water in Europe when the wind is across the tide. Even Force Four can push up a lethal chop. But it's a different matter when wind and tide are together, and if there's a south-westerly gale blowing, there'll be much bigger seas off the Casquets.'

Duncan tapped the channel between Alderney and Burhou. 'Why can't we try the Swinge?'

'We can if you like, but I think we'd get to the Race quicker; there's a lot of muck off the west coast of Alderney that would need circumnavigating, and there's no shelter from the south-west. The Race is in the lee of Alderney itself. As I said, we should get there just about slack water. We'll be through it in half an hour.'

'I suppose this is something else you've done with your dad?'

'Yes, sir, it is. Twice in these conditions.'

Duncan remained staring at the chart for several seconds. Then he shrugged. 'You knew what you were talking about yesterday. What happens if we're late, and get there after the tide turns?'

'I think we need to make sure we're not late, sir.'

Duncan gazed at him for several more seconds, then went back on deck to supervise preparations, having the crew stow the big racing genoa and replace it with the much smaller storm canvas. While this was going on he was accosted by the skipper of one of the other yachts, walking along the dockside 'You putting out, Duncan old boy? It's a bit nasty out there, isn't it?'

'Not too bad, I don't think. And I have to get back.'

'Well, rather you than me.' He looked at the nearest town gate, through which Kristin and Bryan were hurrying with bags of groceries. 'Good God! Isn't that your mother?'

'That's right.'

'And she's going with you?'

'That's what she says. She likes a bit of fresh air.'

His friend scratched his head, then arranged his features into a smile. 'Good morning, Lady Eversham. Bit choppy out there today, what?'

'I have no idea,' Kristin said, clearly with no recollection of having ever met him before. 'I haven't been out in it yet.'

'Oh. Ah. Yes, of course. Well, bon voyage.'

He watched her hand her burden to the waiting Jamie.

'Cretin,' Kristin remarked. 'Now, Jamie, these poor fellows have had no breakfast. You and I will prepare a meal while they get ready. When are we putting to sea?'

'Now,' Duncan said. 'The lock had already opened and closed twice.'

'Very good. You can eat under way. Come along, Jamie.'

Jamie looked at Duncan; having two skippers was confusing.

'Oh, go ahead. Jamie,' Duncan said. 'I'm beginning to get quite peckish.'

Jamie slid down the companion ladder; Kristin was already breaking eggs. 'You certainly seem to know your way around a galley, milady,' he remarked.

'I should. I have spent a lot of time in one. I used to crew Duncan's father when I was a girl.'

'He told me.' Jamie started slicing bread, while the engine growled into life behind him and he felt the ship start to move. 'You said . . .'

'I told you, I was expelled from my convent because I was pregnant. That was by Duncan's father. He hadn't inherited the title yet, and spent every summer sailing in the Med. We met at a party during the holidays, he asked me to crew for him as cook, and – well, one thing led to another. He was a good-looking man – then. That was 1913. Before the war. Life was really worth living, then.'

Jamie nearly sliced off the end of his finger. He found it hard to believe that he was having such an intimate conversation with a woman who was both old enough to be his mother and so far above him in the social scale. 'But . . . But . . .' he ventured.

'Oh, yes,' she agreed. 'As soon as I was expelled Donald did the decent thing and married me. So Duncan was a few months premature. But he wasn't a bastard. Mind you, I wouldn't mention the matter to him. The fact that he *was* so premature still rankles. I mean, everyone knew what had to have happened. Doesn't that look good?' She ladled eggs and bacon on to plates. 'Smells good too. Come and get it,' she called up the hatch.

Jamie went up; they were just entering the lock and the warps were being passed up; the steadily falling tide meant that this would be the last opening. 'I can take one of these, sir,' he volunteered.

'Good lad,' Duncan agreed, switching off the engine as the ship came to a halt. 'Go down and eat, lads. Tell Mother to keep mine hot. You have about fifteen minutes.'

The lock gates were still open to the yacht basin, but only one more boat came in, and she was a small launch, clearly intending to do nothing more than cross to Dinard or go up the Rance. Duncan regarded it with disfavour, clearly envisaging a future confined to such a contraption.

The same thought occurred to Jamie. 'So will you now be in the Navy permanently, sir?' he asked, with some regret; he had thoroughly enjoyed these few days.

'Sounds like it. Certainly now there's going to be a war.'

'Will there be a war, sir? I thought Mr Chamberlain said there wouldn't be.'

'You're about eight months out of date, Jamie. That was last November. The moment he gave those guarantees to Poland and Rumania there was going to be a war. Now they must feel it's pretty close. Will you join up?'

'Well, I know that now I'm eighteen I have to register. I'll do that as soon as we get back. Then I suppose it'll be a matter of waiting to be called.'

'Why? You could volunteer now. That way you'd have more chance of getting what you want.'

What do I want? Jamie wondered. Certainly . . . 'I wouldn't much care to be stuck in the Navy if there is no war, sir.'

'There's going to be a war,' Duncan assured him. 'Take my word for it. Listen, join up now and I'll see if I can get you on board this beastly motorboat with me. You tell me you're a qualified motor engineer? We'll have to have an engineer.'

'That would be great, sir.' But his tone was doubtful.

'Those things can't have much range,' Duncan said. 'That means we'll based on a home port. That means you'll probably be able to get home every weekend. Take the bow.'

The gates were closing. Jamie hurried forward, unhitched the bow warp, and fed it under a cleat; when in a lock, certainly when it was a falling one, mooring warps could not be secured or there was a risk of tearing the cleats out of the deck as the strain tightened. The water level was already dropping, and he paid out the warp as it did so. Duncan was doing the same thing aft. The schooner went down some twelve feet, until her first crosstrees were level with the dockside.

One of the keepers looked down at them. 'It is blowing Force Six out there, monsieur,' he said, 'Maybe more, later on.'

'I know,' Duncan said. 'But we have to get on. Will you cast off, monsieur.'

The dock-master flicked the warps over the bollards around which they had been looped. Jamie coiled his and then hurried aft to do the same for Duncan, who had left it lying on the deck to take the helm. The engine growled into life, and the crew emerged on deck. 'I'll take her,' Bryan said. 'You go and eat.'

'We'll put sail on in the estuary,' Duncan said. 'Two reefs in the main. We can shake them out later if conditions improve.'

'And the staysail?'

'Leave it till we see how things are.'

'You have it.' Bryan grasped the wheel and the schooner moved slowly out of the lock, while Jamie, having coiled the after warp, took in the fenders. Immediately they entered the outer pool there was movement beneath them, although the harbour was completely sheltered from the south-west; other small craft bobbed to their moorings and the wail of the wind became louder. Bryan expertly steered his way through the various obstructions until they were in the broad estuary of the Rance, then he turned into the river flow, which also happened to be mainly the wind direction, and held the yacht there on just enough power to maintain her station. 'Mainsail first,' he told the crew.

Billy and Harry worked the winch and the great sail climbed the mast. Jamie looked aft at the passage to the sea. It was well protected by several high rocky islets, and on these the seas were breaking with clouds of spray. 'Exciting,' Bryan commented. 'Good enough,' he shouted. 'Now two reefs.'

Billy held the tension on the winch while Harry and Bob clawed the canvas down. Jamie went up to stand by the still-secured boom, although it was jerking to and fro on its sheets, removing each batten as it came within reach, and then folding the sail inside itself to make it fast.

'That's far enough,' Bryan called. 'Now the foresail.'

The small jib climbed the fore halyard.

'Slacken the mainsheet, Jamie,' Bryan said quietly.

Jamie paid out the line, and the sail filled. Immediately the schooner started to sail. 'Lee-oh!' Bryan switched off the engine and the only sound was the whine of the wind as he brought her round.

Duncan came on deck, 'Nice work. I'd better take her out.'

Bryan let him have the wheel. Even under reduced canvas the ship was moving fast, driven by both the wind and the river flow. Already they were into the main passage, with spray-smothered rocks to either side and the Jardin light tower looming in front of them.

Kristin appeared, her head bound up in a scarf, but she remained wedged in the hatch rather than coming on deck. 'What are we making?'

Duncan had not yet had the log streamed . . . He looked over his shoulder at the wake. 'Eight knots, I'd say. But we won't be so fast over the ground until the tide turns.'

'Whee!' she said. 'We'll be home for dinner.'

By the time they lost the river and were well out to sea, although still sheltered by the land only a few miles behind them, the seas began to build, the wind pushing the waves into the south-running tide to create steep, eight-foot valleys and breaking crests. As the wind was astern, little water came on deck, except right forward when the bow dipped into the slope of a wave in front, but for the most part the little ship bounced from crest to trough and back again with bone-juddering force. Duncan's face was rigid with concentration. He had two main tasks, closely connected: to keep the sails filled so as to maintain his speed, and at the same time to make sure he did not plough into the base of the wave in front of him, which would not only knock way off the ship but as a result risk her being caught by the one behind before she could recover, and thus broaching, being driven over on her beam ends, which for a ship under sail could be dangerous. 'In fact,' he said. 'We're going too fast, Johnnie. We'll need another tuck.'

Bryan, standing by to assist on the helm if necessary, signalled the crew, and a third reef was taken in the main. Under sail and before the wind, this was an extremely slow business, as the sail was full. Duncan helped them by allowing short yaws to spill the wind, but they had to be very quick every time so as not to lose too much way. 'Good lads,' he said, as the exhausted crew came aft.

Bryan was levelling the binoculars. 'I have the south-west Minkies buoy.'

'Spot on. It's going to be a good day. Jamie, nip below and see if Mother is all right.'

Kristin had disappeared from the hatch. Jamie slid down the ladder, but she was not in the saloon. Cautiously he opened the door to the aft cabin, and gulped. She lay on the port bunk, half concealed beneath a blanket. As far as he could see she was still fully dressed, but her eyes were closed, and her face was contorted in an expression he had never seen before.

Holding on to the grab rail he moved closer. 'Milady?'

Her eyes flopped open, and her cheeks suffused in a deep flush.

'Are you all right?'

For a moment she did not reply; then she gave a little sigh, and her hands emerged from beneath the blanket. 'Yes, I am all right.'

'Mr Morant thought you might be unwell.'

'He should know better than anyone that I do not suffer from seasickness.' She sat up and threw off the blanket. Duncan stared at her exposed legs, and she straightened her skirt as she swung them out of the bunk. 'Have you never seen a woman's legs before?'

'Not a *lady*'s legs, milady.'

'Who has a quick little wit, then? Well, you wouldn't have seen them now, if you hadn't come barging in like that. Don't you know that one should never enter a lady's bedroom un-invited? Even if it is only a cabin?'

'I'm sorry, milady. I—'

'Uh-uh!' She held up her finger. 'Now you've broken your promise again. You are not having a good day. I know: Duncan sent you. And you arrived at a very inopportune moment. Do you know what I am talking about?'

'Ah . . . you were sleeping.'

She gave a delicious gurgle of amusement. 'Jamie Goring, I could love you. I probably shall. No, definitely. Come and sit beside me.'

Now he was in a quandary. 'Can I get you something?'

'I said, come and sit here beside me.'

Cautiously Jamie crossed the cabin and sat down. Almost as if it was on cue, the yacht lurched, and he was in her arms. Before he could stop either himself or her, she had kissed him on the mouth. 'Oh!' she said, 'When did you last shave?'

Jamie was gasping for breath. 'Last night, before going ashore.'

'Hm. Well, you're all man. But that's what I wanted you to be.'

'Milady . . .'

'Do you know what the judge said at my divorce? I can remember it word for word. He said, "Lady Eversham is clearly a woman of excessive sexual requirements, who, unfortunately, lacks the willpower to control those requirements. She has admitted to eight counts of adultery, and the three she has denied appeared to have been proved." Can you imagine having to listen to that in open court?'

'It must have been awful But—'

'Oh, it was all true. The ones I denied were because they weren't very good. I hate being associated with inferior performances. And it was all rather amusing, actually, watching the faces of those who had pretended to be my friends. They were all there, you know. They wanted to learn all the gory details. But they also wanted to see me come crashing down in flames. Certainly the women did. They had never forgiven me – a Spanish adventuress, they called me, for marrying Donald when he could have married one of them. Me, an adventuress! I am an Ojeda de Santos Lopez. Do you know those names?'

'Ah . . . there was a famous conquistador named Alonso de Ojeda. He sailed with Columbus, and did a lot of exploring on his own.'

Kristin seemed impressed. 'How did you know that?'

'I read a lot of history.'

'And you obviously have a very good memory. Our relationship to Alonso de Ojeda is tenuous. But my family is far older, aristocratically, than the Evershams. The men were mostly titillated. But they all decided to drop me like a hot potato.'

'It must have been terrible for you,' Jamie murmured, terribly conscious of the arm round his shoulders and the breast pressed against his arm.

'I survived. I said to myself, if they want to ostracize me – well, fuck them. Their problem was, nobody wanted to do that, while everyone wanted to fuck me. Do you know, as I left the court after the nisi had been issued, one of the ushers asked if he could take me out to dinner? Now I have new friends, people like Jimmy Lonsdale, who know all about me and still want to know me.'

'And . . . ah . . . Mr Morant . . .'

'Oh, he knows all about it – all about me. And he still prefers to live with me than with his father. I think that's rather sweet. Mind you, he doesn't know what I do in private. On the other hand, I don't know what he does in private. Although I imagine it's the same thing. But, you see, having stumbled on me in a private moment, I'd prefer it if you kept it private. Our secret. Won't you enjoy sharing a secret with me?'

'Ah . . . yes.' But my God, he thought, if Morant does know all about his mother's proclivities, he's liable to come down here himself at any moment to find out what's going on. But there was a question he had to ask. 'But how . . . I mean, what . . . well, you say you have two houses?'

'I have four houses, Jamie. As well as the properties in England and France, I have the mansion in Madrid and the villa in Denia. But I see what you are wondering. As I was clearly the guilty party, Donald was not required to pay me a penny in alimony, and he never did. Daddy supported me.'

'You mean he didn't – well . . .'

'Oh, he was very angry.'

'I'll bet he beat you,' Jamie said, absently.

'Yes, he did. I told you he liked doing that. But I was his only child. And Mother was on my side; she never liked Donald. She was Swedish, you know.' Which explained her name, Jamie supposed. 'So he kept me in funds, and then, three years ago, he died. I think the civil war got him down. I mean, he wasn't a Communist or anything, but he didn't like Franco. So there I was: free, forty and a millionairess. Donald,' she added, with some satisfaction, 'has never got to be a millionaire. His various partners have seen to that.'

'But Duncan – Mr Morant – seems to have done pretty well.'

'You mean this boat?'

'And the Bugatti? And – well . . .'

'Duncan has a job in the city, but I don't think he does an awful lot of work. I bought him this boat, and the car. But I would not like you to remind him of that either. It is our secret, remember.'

'Of course. Well . . .' Gently he disengaged himself; she was stroking her hand up and down his arm. 'I really must get back on deck, or they will think something has happened to me.'

'Just don't forget to come back down in a couple of hours to help me get lunch.'

When Jamie returned on deck they were rounding the north-west Minkies buoy, but because of the heavy seas were half an hour behind schedule. The low-lying group of rocks and islets had presented as spectacular a sight as the approaches to St Malo, equally smothered in spray and breaking water. Now the ship was totally exposed and it was really rough as they neared the Corbière light tower, which, like the Hanois off Guernsey, marked the end of the reef running south-west from Jersey. But Jamie recalled it was always rough off the Corbière.

'I don't suppose there's an inshore passage through this lot,' Duncan remarked. Steering in these conditions was hard work and required maximum concentration, so to Jamie's relief the skipper had done nothing more than ask if his mother was all right when he had reappeared, and had made no comment about the length of time he had been below.

But then, Kristin had said that he knew all about her. So much that he might suspect she would attempt to seduce someone young enough to be her son? Because that was what she had been doing, he realized, feeling hot all over. Of course it had to be simply because, as she had said, being at sea sexed her up. But it was not an experience he had ever had before, even with someone of his own age. He had no idea how to handle it, how to face her when he next went below.

But he couldn't afford to let any of his emotional upheaval show. 'I believe there is an inshore passage, sir. But I don't know it.'

'Then we'll have to take the rough stuff.'

Fortunately, as the tide slackened, so the seas became less steep. Corbière behind them, they made their way up the west coast of Jersey, staying two miles off shore in steadily improving conditions.

Duncan pointed to the cliffs at the north-west corner of the island. 'Gros Nez!' Visibility was excellent, and Guernsey was big on their port bow, some twenty miles away, with Sark dead ahead. He looked at his watch. 'We should be there about half past one. You still reckon we can make the Race in time?'

'We should make it by half past five, anyway, sir. That should do it.'

'And you want us to alter course when we round the headland and leave Sark to port.'

'I think it would be most comfortable, yes, sir. And the most direct route up to the Race.'

'And it'll put the wind dead astern for a while. I think the pressure's off, lads. Ah, Mother! Lunch ready?'

'No, it is not ready,' Kristin said. 'Nobody came down to help me.' She glared at Jamie.

'Well, we'll all help you, as soon as we've set the staysail.' He grinned at them. 'We can stand it, and an extra knot will help.'

They hoisted the staysail, between main and foremast, and the yacht seemed to bound ahead.

'There we go,' Duncan said. 'Normal watches, Johnnie; we're not going to need any more sail changes for a while. Can you and Bob take a couple of hours?'

'Will do.'

'Gros Nez on the present course, and then oh four five. You've got the tide, so just remember not to get pushed into any of that muck off the south coast of Sark. I'll be up as soon as we've eaten so you can have yours.'

'Take your time.'

Duncan dropped through the hatch, followed by Jamie, Harry and Billy. 'Ah, this is nice.' The cabin was warm and wind-free, although the howl above and the slapping of the sea beneath meant that they had to shout. 'Tell us what you want us to do, Mother.'

Kristin placed a large bowl in front of him. 'You and Jamie can peel those potatoes. I am making a stew.'

That earlier hour might never have been. Perhaps, Jamie thought, it hadn't really happened after all.

Duncan winked at him and got to work. 'Tell me, with your knowledge of history: have you ever heard of motor torpedo boats being used in action? – I mean, worthwhile action.'

'Oh, yes, sir. In 1904 the Japanese launched an attack on the Russian naval base at Port Arthur. The base was supposed to be impregnable, because of the difficult entrance – they called it the Tiger's Tail. But the Japanese took them by surprise – they hadn't even declared war as yet – sneaked in and caused havoc. A couple of battleships were sunk and most of the rest put out of action. The Russian Pacific Fleet virtually ceased to exist. Mind you, sir, I think the Japanese ships were a bit bigger than sixty feet. But they weren't as fast as thirty-plus knots.'

'You've cheered me up no end,' Duncan remarked. 'Maybe, when the shooting starts, we will see some worthwhile action. On the other hand, as you say, sixty feet . . . How do you think a fast motorboat would behave in these seas?'

'I've never been on a fast motorboat, sir. I imagine it could be tricky.'

'Thirty knots,' Duncan mused. 'What do you estimate the present wind strength?'

'Not far off forty, sir.'

'Therefore, it wouldn't feel much more than ten. That's a balmy breeze.'

'Yes, sir, but the sea state wouldn't relate. Supposing *Kristin* could make thirty knots' – as if, he thought, she doesn't appear habitually to be making at least thirty knots through life – 'can you imagine driving her at that speed through these seas? If you didn't tear the bottom out of her, you'd certainly tear the backbone out of the crew.'

'Hm. A lot would depend on what she's made of. I don't suppose you managed to find that out, did you, Mother?'

'Oh, yes,' Kristin said from the galley. 'They are made of plywood.'

That was an effective conversation-stopper, as Duncan went into some obviously deep reflections. Jamie had to wonder if he was actually thinking of declining the posting. But no officer in the Royal Navy – and no seaman either – could possibly refuse to go wherever he was sent. Besides, to be offered a command, however small, at the very start of a career was hardly something to be sniffed at; he knew he certainly would not hesitate for a moment. And he had been offered a berth!

But first they had to get home. Actually, conditions improved all afternoon, sheltered as they were by Sark for the next couple of hours. But the wind was steadily increasing until it was blowing a full gale. While they were carrying the north-west-running tide this was hardly more than exhilarating, although as the wind freshened Duncan had the crew hand the staysail just to be safe. But when they left Sark behind, and levelled their binoculars to the north-west, the view was frightening. Alderney was now big on the port bow, and with excellent visibility the Casquets were well in sight. But the seas around the light tower were enormous, a mass of heaving white, dashing against the rocks in clouds of spray. Nor did the entrance to the narrow Swinge Channel look much better even if it was still carrying the north-east-running tide.

'I reckon we made the right choice in following Jamie's advice,' Bryan remarked.

'Try looking forward,' Duncan suggested.

Bryan turned his glasses, and gulped. The Race appeared to be absolutely molten. 'We could put back to St Peter Port for the night,' he suggested. 'This'll have blown itself out by tomorrow.'

'Um.' Duncan looked at the hatch, in which Kristin had just appeared. 'What do you reckon, Mother? Give her the glasses, John.'

Kristin remained wedged in the hatch, for the ship was both rolling and pitching, although still taking very little water on deck. She levelled the glasses. 'You are going through the Race?'

'As opposed to going round the Casquets, yes.'

Kristin swung the glasses, studied the distant seas for some minutes. 'I see what you mean,' she said at last. 'Either will be exciting.'

'Jamie's idea. He's done a lot of sailing in these waters.'

Kristin studied the Race again. 'And I would say he's right. Those seas are smaller.'

'We could turn back to St Peter Port for the night. It'll be choppy, beating, but we should be there in a couple of hours.'

'Don't you think the ship will take it?'

'Oh, the ship will take it all right.'

'And the crew?'

'Where I go, they go. I was thinking of you.'

'I told you,' Kristin reminded him: 'I have no change of

clothing. I am getting as tired of them as they are of me. I want to be in my own bath first thing tomorrow morning.'

'It could be lunch,' Duncan said with a grin.

All hands were on deck, clustered aft, as they approached the narrows. Everyone knew they had not entirely made up the half-hour they had lost at the beginning and it was past five; the sun was low in the west, but visibility was sharper than ever, with the wind now stronger than ever, although Jamie knew that it should soon start to decrease, as it invariably did for a couple of hours over dusk. Alderney was now wide to port, the French cliffs of Flamanville behind them to starboard and the Cap de la Hague light tower dead ahead.

Duncan was back on the helm. 'Best water?' he asked.

'Alderney provides the only lee, sir,' Jamie said. 'But you don't want to get too close. There are outliers.'

'As there are in all these goddamned islands. Do you want her?'

'Only if you would like me to, sir.'

'You've been through here before?'

'Several times, sir.'

'Then she's yours.'

Jamie wrapped his hands round the wooden spokes, feeling a surge of exhilaration as the ship beneath him responded like a living creature, to a far greater extent than the previous morning, when there had been so little wind. But a ship under sail at sea in a gale *was* a living thing, responding to an expert helmsman as a thoroughbred horse will respond to an expert rider and, by the same token, ready to punish any loss of concentration.

'Adjusting course to oh one oh, sir,' he said. Now *Kristin was* travelling very fast through the water, but less so over the ground as the tide began to slacken before turning. Jamie felt that the approach of slack water was actually flattening the waves, to a certain extent, but could do nothing about the sudden whorls depicting the uneven bottom, nor could he prevent the occasional lurch into unexpected holes in the sea. It required very little imagination to envisage what conditions might be like had they arrived an hour late, after the tide had turned to crash against the booming wind; conditions would be at least double what they had experienced that morning off the Minkies Reef, with the added, and dangerous, complication of the unseeable, and thus unavoidable, holes. As he had told Duncan, he had come through here with his father several times, and he recalled one occasion when they had had a fair wind, not strong – about twenty knots – but against the tide. It had been a neap, and they had been in a hurry, as now, but the waves had been the steepest he had yet known, and the holes twice as deep; when *Tamara* had dropped into one of them, she had been entirely submerged save for her mast, for what had seemed an eternity, but could not have been more than a few seconds.

He stared forward, along the length of the deck, his vision blocked only by the two masts, and the low cabin roof ... and Kristin, who, now that the most critical moment of the voyage was at hand, had resumed her position in the hatch; she had abandoned her headscarf and was letting her hair scatter in the wind.

She also had been looking forward, but now she turned her head, saw him looking in her direction and blew him a kiss. He could only hope that none of the others had noticed, or perhaps that each would suppose it was meant for him. But talk about concentration! He had to avoid looking at her. But if she was the most startling, and frightening, woman he had ever known, he had to give her ten out of ten for guts.

As he had promised, however, the passage through the Race was mercifully quick. In half an hour the seas began to lengthen and, although higher than before as they left the shelter of the land, rapidly became even.

'Well done, Jamie,' Duncan said. 'If this keeps up we'll be home for breakfast. Mother, I think the crew deserves a tot.'

'Coming right up,' Kristin said.

Billy went to the hatch to receive the tin cups of rum and pass them round. Kristin brought the last two, and herself gave Jamie his. 'The hero of the hour,' she said. 'You will have to take him off the helm now, Duncan, so that he can come below and help me prepare supper.' She went down the companion.

'My mother,' Duncan said enigmatically, 'always gets her own way.'

A Lesson in Speed

'Jamie?' Mary Goring peered at her son. 'We didn't expect you back until tomorrow, what with that storm.'

Jamie put down his duffel bag, took her in his arms for a hug and a kiss, reflecting that, as she was forty-one, she was actually two years younger than Kristin Eversham, but she could have been Kristin's mother. Which was grotesquely unfair, and unforgivable: Mary Goring had had none of the privileges of wealth. 'The skipper was in a hurry to get home.'

'Well,' she kissed him again. 'Many happy returns of the day before yesterday. I hope you celebrated.'

'Oh, I did indeed – in style.'

Peter Goring came in. 'The number of blokes who get into trouble at sea by being in a hurry to get home . . .'

Jamie grinned. 'It wasn't too bad. She's a good sea boat. And we had an experienced crew.' In every way, he thought.

'So how did the race go?'

'We won our class.'

'Brilliant. His nibs must be pleased.'

'He is and he isn't. He's happy about the race but he's been called up.'

Peter Goring frowned. 'It's a bit early for manoeuvres; they don't usually start for another fortnight.'

'Seems there's a flap on. Everyone expects there to be a war at any moment.'

'Hm. What about "peace in our time"?'

'Seems that's out of date. In fact . . .' Jamie drew a deep breath. 'Can you spare me from the garage?'

'Where are you going?'

'Well, now that I'm eighteen, I thought I'd go down to the recruiting office tomorrow.'

'Well, of course. You must put your name down. But if

you're expecting an immediate call-up . . . government departments don't work that way.'

'I wasn't going to put my name down, Dad. I was going to enlist.'

Both senior Gorings stared at him. 'But . . . that'll mean signing up for at least five years,' Mary protested.

'Well, you never know. I could wind up an admiral.'

'You could wind up being sent overseas,' his father pointed out, more realistically.

'I've always wanted to see the world. The important thing is if there is to be a war, I want to be in on the ground floor.'

Peter Goring gazed at his wife for several seconds. Then he turned back to his son and held out his hand.

'Captain Fitzsimmons will see you now, Lieutenant Morant,' said the Wren, very smart in her uniform.

Duncan stood up, glanced in the mirror to make sure his tie was straight – he clearly wore his uniform less regularly than the girl, at least so far – and entered the inner office, standing to attention. 'Sub-Lieutenant Morant, reporting for duty, sir.'

Captain Fitzsimmons looked up. He was a small man with sharp features, at this moment not registering pleasure. 'You received your papers three days ago.'

'That is not correct, sir.'

Fitzsimmons raised his eyebrows.

'The papers were delivered to my mother's house, sir,' Duncan explained.

'That is the address we possess as being your residence.'

'That is where I live, sir, yes – when I am in England. However, I was at sea when the papers arrived' – he assumed Fitzsimmons could not know the truth of the matter – 'and did not receive them until yesterday morning. I returned immediately, and docked just after dawn.'

'What were you doing at sea?'

'Racing, sir. Cowes–Dinard. We won our class.'

If he had hoped to impress the captain, he failed. 'So you were back in . . .?'

'Lymington, sir.'

'Lymington. At dawn. And it has taken you eight hours to travel the thirty miles to Portsmouth?'

'Well, sir, it was a fairly choppy crossing. I had to clean

up the ship and make sure she was secure. And we had touched a rock during the race, and I had to make sure there was no serious damage below. There wasn't, fortunately – just a nick on the keel which will be fixed when she's taken out. Then I had to inform my business associates that I would not be coming in for the foreseeable future. Then I felt I should return home and have a bath and a shave and put on uniform, and have lunch . . .' He paused, hopefully.

'Something that you are going to have to learn, Lieutenant Morant, is that when the Royal Navy says immediately, it means, immediately.'

'Yes, sir. I did not realize the matter was so urgent.'

'Any command is to be regarded as urgent.' He pressed his intercom. 'Miss Brodie, is Mr Leeming in the building?'

'Yes, sir. He is standing by as you required.'

'Very good. Ask him to come in, will you?' He switched off. 'Lieutenant Leeming will show you over your new craft. He is your flotilla leader.'

'Yes, sir. Can you tell me where we will be posted, sir?'

'You will receive your orders in due course. As I have said, you are under the command of Lieutenant Leeming. Come in,' he called, as there was a tap on the door. 'Ah, Leeming. You know Sub-Lieutenant Morant?'

'We have met, sir.'

As Duncan remembered, shaking hands; they had encountered each other at last year's manoeuvres. Leeming was a tall, lean young man with a long nose; the two stripes on each sleeve were straight-edged as opposed to the wave on Duncan's, to indicate that he was a regular.

'Welcome aboard.'

'Thank you.'

'Well,' Fitzsimmons said, 'show him the ropes.'

'Aye aye, sir.'

Leeming saluted, as did Duncan, then the two officers left the office and went down the stairs.

'I seem to have put up a bit of a black,' Duncan said.

'It's not difficult to do, with old Fitz. Cowes–Dinard, was it?'

'You mean you knew? He knew?'

'I think everyone knew. Your mother lunched in our mess, with Lonsdale. Caused a bit of a sensation.'

'I can imagine,' Duncan said grimly.

'Very rare for an admiral to lunch in the mess,' Leeming pointed out. 'But it seems she insisted. A very positive woman, your mother.'

'Yes,' Duncan agreed. As long, he thought, as it was masculine and not *too* old. If once he had resented her promiscuity, he had long got used to it. His sympathy was all with her victims, who if, as was usual, they were careless enough to form a genuine attachment to the glamorous, amoral and still amazingly youthful divorcee, were liable to a severe shock when she became bored and moved her affections on.

In that regard he was just happy that young Jamie had had too much to do to spare the time to be seduced; they were hardly likely to meet at a cocktail party.

The command building overlooked the inner harbour, the mass of pontoons and mooring, with ships' boats coming and going from the larger craft anchored off Spithead. 'There we are,' Leeming said. 'They are sleek.'

There were three apparently identical motorboats moored alongside a single long pontoon, and whatever his reservations Duncan had to agree with his superior. The boats were long and slender and certainly looked fast, with a low exposed bridge positioned halfway from bow to stern, out of which rose a thin mast from which there flew the White Ensign, above which was a wireless aerial. And on the foredeck . . . He frowned. 'Are those torpedo tubes?'

'Two eighteen-inch bow tubes. That's why they're called MTBs: motor torpedo boats. Originally they were aft-facing, I suppose the idea being that one would only fire them when trying to escape an enemy. Facing forward, now – well, they haven't actually told us yet, but it raises all kinds of possibilities. Sure as hell they can only be fired when *approaching* an enemy.'

'So we're not just to be messenger boys or admiral's barges.'

Leeming led him along the pontoon to the end boat. 'I would say not. Do you know what those things on the after deck are?'

'Ah . . . not depth charges?'

'Four. Just remember not to hang around if you have to fire one: no one knows how this hull will stand up to blast. You'll see you also have four machine guns for close work.'

'Close work against what?'

'Against any enemy who gets close enough to be – well, close.'

'At sea?'

'You never can tell. They are actually intended for anti-aircraft protection. I'm sorry, old boy, the fact is that so far no one has given us the slightest idea as to what we will actually be doing when the shooting starts. Which leads one to believe that they don't know.'

'I'm told Jerry has a whole fleet of these things.'

'So I believe. But then, he doesn't have much of anything else, save for a few subs.' Leeming grinned. 'And of course those three heavy cruisers that he calls pocket battleships.'

'He must have some ideas. Didn't the Japs use a flotilla of fast MTBs to get into Port Arthur in 1904 and destroy the Russian Pacific Fleet?'

'Who's been boning up on history, then?'

'It's our business, isn't it?' Duncan said modestly, with a mental vote of thanks to Jamie. 'Naval history, anyway.'

'Good point. Maybe they should have you on the staff instead of messing about in boats. But seriously, old man, I can't see a bunch of German torpedo boats getting into Scapa Flow to destroy the Home Fleet; they'd be spotted long before they could negotiate the narrows, even if the tide didn't put them ashore. Those tides run stronger than anywhere save perhaps the Channel Islands.'

'Yes,' Duncan agreed, thoughtfully.

'So, do you want to have a look at her?'

'Can't wait.'

'Good man. Petty Officer Carling.'

'Sir!' There was a gangway aft, and this Carling, heavy-set and blue-chinned, held open for the two officers. 'Welcome aboard, sir.'

'Thank you, Mr Carling. Are you part of my crew?'

'Ah . . .' Carling looked at Leeming.

'Mr Carling is at this moment acting as caretaker. Carry on, Petty Officer.'

'Aye aye, sir.' Carling led them to the door into what would have been the saloon on a yacht but here was simply a mess. There was not a lot of headroom because the deck seemed disproportionately high. 'Galley down here, sir.' He went down a short ladder. 'Crew's cabin forward. Eight berths.'

'But no one is on board yet.'

Again Carling looked at Leeming.

'Crews haven't been assigned yet. We feel that, if possible, they should be volunteers, and that, again if possible, they should have some knowledge of small boats.'

'Were we invited to volunteer?' Duncan asked. 'That must have been in the fine print I didn't read.'

'We were not invited to volunteer,' Leeming said. 'We are officers.'

'Your cabin is aft, sir,' Carling said, anxious to defuse any tension between his superiors.

This was quite a comfortable cabin, although with insufficient headroom for Duncan, which contained a small desk as well as a bookcase, and its own heads.

'Do you approve?' Leeming inquired, with a touch of sarcasm.

'Oh, absolutely.'

'Good. Now come and look at what matters.'

There was a door beside the after companionway, which led into the engine room; this only had five-foot height, and contained the biggest piece of machinery Duncan had ever seen. But . . . 'That's a diesel?'

'That is a one thousand, six hundred and fifty brake horse-power Napier three-shaft petrol engine. It will give you thirty-five knots, if pushed.'

'Wow! But did you say, petrol?'

'A comparative diesel would have to be twice the size and weigh at least twice as much.'

'I take your point. But you are taking us to sea, hopefully to fight an enemy, sitting on top of . . .?

Leeming indicated the two large tanks, one let into each hull. 'You have nine hundred and fifty gallons of petrol. At full speed you will burn twenty gallons an hour, so you will have over a thousand miles capability. When speed is reduced, the fuel consumption of course comes down.'

'Sounds tremendous. But I shall still be driving a floating bomb, contained in a plywood hull.'

'Five-ply. It's stronger than most woods.'

'Will it survive a hit?'

'No.'

Duncan gazed at him.

'The plan,' Leeming explained, 'is not to get hit. Preferably by anything – even a rifle bullet. With the speed at your command, this should be perfectly feasible. Now as regards your concern about petrol: supposing you manage to avoid being hit' – his tone suggested that he was beginning to have doubts about that – 'the only real danger lies not in the petrol itself, but in the fumes it gives off, which are inclined to gather in the bilges and are highly explosive. Obviously, smoking is strictly forbidden . . .' He paused.

'I don't,' Duncan said.

'Excellent. Still, it is a rule that must be enforced amongst your crew. However, if those fumes are allowed to accumulate, there is always the chance of a spark when the ignition is turned on, in which case, bingo, and out come the harps. Therefore the drill – and it must be adhered to – is that first thing every morning the bilges are pumped. Whether there is any water to be expelled or not, the pump will expel petrol fumes. Follow that rule and there should be no problem.'

'I take your point, sir. But I'm beginning to appreciate why you feel the crew should be volunteers. Am I allowed to look for them myself?'

Leeming frowned. 'I'm not sure I follow you.'

'Well, as you know, I do a bit of yacht racing, and over the past couple of years I have built up a good crew, men who know they can trust me, and on whom I know I can rely.'

'These are all Navy personnel?'

'At this moment, I doubt it. But if they were to join up . . .'

'They would still need several months training to become seamen.'

'With respect, sir, they are already seamen – with, I would say, more experience than most of your chaps.'

'But they are not Royal Navy seamen, Mr Morant. I doubt our superiors would go for that idea.' Leeming decided to get on to a more congenial subject. 'Would you like to take her out?'

'Oh, indeed. Now?'

'That's the idea. Come up.'

They climbed on to the bridge, and Duncan surveyed the console and the rows of instruments.

'Do you understand all of those?' Leeming asked.

'I'm sure they'll come to me. Are they all necessary?'

'They all serve a purpose. Now, as it's a petrol engine, it doesn't require a heat start. Just turn the key. Petty Officer!'

'Aye aye, sir.' The wind was southerly, and blowing into the harbour. Carling freed the stern warp and coiled it, so that the ship was held by the bow only moving slightly to and fro.

'She's yours,' Leeming said.

'I take it the actual controls are the same as for a diesel?'

'Probably more responsive.'

Duncan grasped the single lever, and pulled it sideways to disengage the gears. Then he turned the ignition key with considerable trepidation, but the engine burst into reassuring life.

'There is just one thing,' Leeming said: 'if you're a racing yachtsman, I imagine you're used to deep-keeled boats. This has very little in the water: two foot ten inches to be precise. She will respond instantly at speed, but when manoeuvring at low speed she's very sluggish. Needs a lot of helm. So mind how you go; we don't want to hit anything.'

'How do I know how fast I'm going?' Duncan scanned the console; surely something that appeared to be a seagoing version of his Bugatti should have a speedometer. But there was nothing that he could see amongst the oil gauges and pressure gauges and temperature gauges . . . The only instantly recognizable instrument was the large compass mounted in the centre.

'You'll pick that up as you go along,' Leeming said. 'You relate it to the rev counter, there. Fifteen hundred revs will be about right for normal cruising. But you'll get the hang of it when we go out as a flotilla, when I'll set the speed. Shall we go?'

Duncan realized that quite a few officers and ratings, and even one or two Wrens, had gathered on the dock above the pontoon, no doubt all aware that he was a tyro having his first outing; he didn't doubt that even Fitzsimmons would be watching from his office window. This had to be good. 'Let go forward, Petty Officer,' he called.

'Aye aye, sir.' Carling brought in the warp and then moved along the deck to ship the fenders; normally, with a full crew, this would be done in seconds, but being on his own he would need several minutes, during which he would not appreciate any great speed with the resultant spray and loss of balance. Not, Duncan thought, that there was going to be any great speed for a while yet.

He clicked the lever into gear and the engine tone changed from a hum to a murmur as the ship slipped gently forward. The next pontoon was about two hundred feet away. Duncan turned the wheel to port, gently, as he would have done with *Kristin*, and nothing happened; the MTB kept moving resolutely if still slowly, towards the next row of boats.

'You need a lot more helm than that,' Leeming suggested. 'And you could do with a bit more power. Not that much,' he hastily added, as Duncan pushed the throttle forward and rotated the wheel violently at the same time. The ship turned virtually in her own length, and Carling had hastily to grab a stanchion to avoid being pitched overboard.

'Oops!' Duncan commented.

'Slow down,' Leeming commanded, and Duncan closed the throttle. 'And straighten up, for God's sake.'

Duncan sent the helm spinning to starboard and the MTB lost speed as her bows pointed at the gap between the pontoons.

'Steady as she goes,' Leeming said. 'You'll get the hang of it.'

Duncan, having spent so much of his life on various helms, from sailing dinghies up to *Kristin*, very soon did get the hang of it, as he proceeded slowly out of the harbour and into the Solent.

'Take her up to a thousand revs,' Leeming said. 'We're going out through the forts.'

'Aye aye,' Duncan said, and glanced at Carling, who had joined them on the bridge. 'Sorry about just now, Petty Officer.'

'She takes getting used to, sir.'

'Absolutely.' Duncan eased the throttle forward, and the murmur below him became a growl. The MTB started to move through the calm water with smooth speed, leaving a broad wake behind her. 'What's she like in heavy weather?'

'I have no idea. We're not allowed to take them out in heavy weather.'

'You mean you weren't out yesterday?'

'Certainly not.' Leeming glanced at him. 'I suppose you were.'

'Last night I was crossing the Channel.'

'I'm glad you got here.'

'But . . . if push comes to shove, we may have to use them, regardless of the weather.'

'That's for the big boys to decide. These are expensive toys.' He watched the two forts that guarded the eastern exit of the Solent come abeam and then drop astern. In front of them, at a distance of some miles, was the solid bulk of the Nab Tower, marking the deep-water channel used by battle-ships and ocean liners, while to their right the Isle of Wight fell away to St Helens and Bembridge Harbour. 'We'll go inside,' Leeming said. 'But keep your speed down.' He pointed at the beach, crowded with August holidaymakers. 'We don't want to spoil their tea.'

'Happens whenever the *Queen Mary* comes into Southampton,' Carling remarked. 'It's a miracle no one has got drowned.'

At fifteen knots the MTB responded readily to the helm, but even at half-speed and several hundred yards from the shore she created little wavelets to break on the sand. A few moments later they were out in the open waters of the Channel. There was still a swell remaining from yesterday's blow, but the wind was light.

'You happy?' Leeming asked.

'You bet.'

'Well, then . . . I think we should weather up, and then, let's go.'

He brought the thin leather strap down from above the brim of his cap and secured it under his chin, then pulled on an oilskin top over his uniform tunic. Carling and Duncan did the same, and then Duncan eased the throttle forward, and the growl became a roar. The ship gathered speed very quickly, and was soon racing along, up and down the slow mounds of water as if on a roller coaster, spray spuming away from her flared bows and flying high enough to scatter across the three men on the bridge, while astern the wake became huge, spreading out for perhaps a mile to crash into the distant beach of Sandown and the rocks below St Catherine's Point.

'Now this is something,' Duncan shouted, as the wind whis-tled about his ears. 'We're on two thousand. What do you reckon?'

Leeming was hanging on to the mast. 'Thirty-odd. That's fast enough.'

'Oh. let's see what she can really do,' Duncan protested, and pushed the throttle right forward. Now he had a wild animal in his hands, and he realized that if for any reason he were to let go of the wheel the ship would probably broach and roll over several times before sinking.

'Two two,' he yelled.

'Enough,' Leeming bawled. 'That's an order.'

Reluctantly Duncan closed the throttle, and the MTB slowed.

'Bring her round,' Leeming commanded. 'Petty Officer, you'd better go below and see if we're making any water.'

'Aye aye, sir.' Carling left the bridge.

'I thought you said that five-ply was as tough as several inches of solid wood,' Duncan remarked.

'I'd say we're about to find out.'

'You mean you've never opened yours up?'

'Not quite so violently. Now, as I said, next time we go out, it'll be as a flotilla, supposing she is still seaworthy. You'll conform to flotilla speed and my orders.'

'Aye aye, *sir*.'

Carling emerged from below. 'Tight as a drum, sir.'

'Looks as if you were right after all, sir,' Duncan said.

The Bugatti scraped to a halt on the drive before the house, sending gravel in every direction, some of it splattering against the Austin Seven already parked there.

That brought a comment from an upstairs window. 'Really, Duncan – must you always drive like a bat out of hell? I hope you haven't marked it.'

'I was in a hurry to see you, my sweet.' Duncan ran into the house, handed his cap to the waiting Harry, and fielded the large white Pyrenean mountain dog who bounded at him. 'Easy, Lucifer, easy. I'm in uniform.' He gave the massive head a loving caress, and started up the stairs; the open window had been that of his mother's sitting room.

'But you didn't know I was here,' said the woman standing at the top. Lucinda Browning was an unlikely fiancée for Duncan Morant. She was small, barely five feet tall, petite in every way, and wore her blonde hair short. This, and her dress, were invariably untidy; Lucinda considered herself to be an artist – not that she had ever, to Duncan's knowledge, sold a painting. But she had a wealthy and indulgent father, as he had a wealthy and indulgent, if somewhat scandalous, mother, and she was also, as he had discovered, capable of being quite congenial from time to time, when encouraged by either the company or the amount of alcohol she had recently consumed. Sadly, at five o'clock in the afternoon and in this house, neither applied, and for most of the rest of the time she operated off a very short fuse.

'I had a hunch,' he suggested.

'You are a lying toad.'

He got up to her and swept her from the floor for a hug and a kiss, allowing his hand to slip down her back to find her knicker elastic.

'Stop that,' she said. 'Krissy tells me you've been called up. Is that why you're wearing uniform?'

He set her on the floor again. 'Sherlock Holmes, roll over.'

'And you have your own ship.'

'In a manner of speaking.'

'She also tells me you came back from France in a gale.'

'It was there and so were we.'

He held her hand as they entered the room, where Kristin was pouring tea. She was not looking terribly pleased, but then, she never did when closeted for any period of time with her prospective daughter-in-law. 'How was it?'

Duncan released Lucinda to hug her instead. 'You won't believe this, Mother, but it was, actually, superb. She was fast, furious and – wait for it – she has two torpedo tubes.'

'Whatever for?' Lucinda asked.

'Well, my darling, hopefully, to shoot at the enemy.'

'You're not serious. We don't have an enemy.'

'Not right this moment. But you never know your luck.'

Kristin stirred and handed him his cup. 'So when do you take command?'

'Officially, first thing tomorrow morning. I don't have a crew yet, but I gather they will be turning up over the next few days. I have to be on the spot to meet them. So . . . this is my last night in the old homestead for a while.'

'What?' Lucinda squeaked. 'How long a while?'

'I have no idea. Until this flap is over.'

'But you'll be coming to Jennie's party? On Thursday.'

'I don't think that's on.'

'Oh, really, Duncan. You're taking me.'

'Ah. Well . . . you'll have to go on your own. Or press-gang some other bloke.'

'I think that is absolutely hateful.'

'My dear Cindy,' Kristin said, 'this appears to be a national emergency. You cannot possibly put a party in front of that.'

'National emergency,' Lucinda said contemptuously. 'It's just an excuse, like these ridiculous yacht races, to allow lads to get together and do their own thing. It's positively obscene. Well, thanks for the tea, Krissy. You can call me when next you're free, Duncan, and we'll see if *I'm* free.'

'Aren't you going to stay for dinner?' Duncan asked. 'And, well . . . I may not be available for some time.'

'Don't be ridiculous,' Lucinda snapped, and flounced down the stairs.

'One day,' Kristin remarked. 'I am going to strangle that girl.'

'Oh, I suppose she can't help being frivolous.'

'I was talking about the way she calls me Krissy. She knows I can't stand it.'

'Actually, I don't think she cares for being called Cindy. She thinks it's common. What do you think she meant by her last remark – that it's ridiculous to suggest that I might not be available for some time? or that she should stay to dinner so that we might have a bit of nookie afterwards?'

'I would say the second. I'm quite sure she regards having a bit of nookie as common, too. I cannot understand why you wish to marry her.'

'It's just one of those things. I asked her, and she said yes.'

'And you immediately felt bound by your code of honour. I should never have let Donald send you to Eton. I suppose you were drunk when you made this absurd proposal?'

'It was at a party, yes.'

'And have you ever taken her to bed?'

'Good heavens, no, Mother. Lucinda is a very well brought up young lady.'

'Are you trying to tell me something?'

'Oh! Gosh! I didn't mean . . .'

'I was far better brought up than Lucinda ever was,' Kristin pointed out, 'which is why I got bored and decided to fuck the whole thing. Only then I decided to fuck your father instead. He was a real go-getter in those days. And you know what being on a small boat at sea does to me.'

'Yes, Mother. I do know that.'

'Do you *want* to take her to bed?'

'Of course I do. I'm going to marry her.'

'You have just told me that you were virtually inveigled into that. But you don't seem to be actually champing at the bit. Now tell me . . .' The telephone jangled. Kristin picked it up. '*Digame*. How absolutely lovely to hear your voice.' She waggled her eyebrows at her son. 'Do you actually have something to say? Oh, certainly. He's right here.'

She handed Duncan the receiver. 'Your father!'

'Look here,' Lord Eversham declared. He always spoke as if he were declaring something. 'I've just heard about this call-up business. I'll arrange a deferment, of course.'

'Why should I want to be deferred, Father?'

'My dear fellow, you have your life to live, and this is some aimless flap. It's sure to blow over.'

'You are starting to remind me of Lucinda.'

'Sensible girl. How is she?'

'At this moment, not too well.'

'I'm sorry to hear that. Not contagious, is it?'

'Do you know, Dad, I think it is. It's a disease, called burying one's head in the sand.'

'Eh? What?'

'It's been lovely talking to you, Dad, but I really have a lot to do. Would you like another word with Mother?'

'What? Still there, is she?'

'Well, it's her house, you see.' Duncan winked at Kristin, who turned her thumb down. 'But actually, she's just stepped outside for a moment.'

'Oh, right. Well . . . You're determined to go through with this business?'

'Yes, I am. Why don't you come down to Portsmouth and have a look at my ship?'

'I might just do that. A battleship, is it?'

'Not exactly. It's a small, fast motorboat. You'll love it. ''Bye for now.'

He hung up.

'Pompous prick,' Kristin growled. 'I was going to ask you about this crew of yours. Are they any good?'

'I told you that I had no idea; I haven't seen them yet.'

'But they'll be regulars.'

'Somehow I doubt that. You must get it through your head, Mother, that we are very small beer. The fact is, no one quite seems to have worked out why we are there at all.'

'Service prejudice against anything new.'

'Actually, apparently we did have quite a few in the last show. They called them CMBs – Coastal Motor Boats – but they did have a torpedo tube. They don't seem to have been put to much use then, and at least three of them caught fire and sank. Petrol engines, you see.'

'You are making my day.'

'Oh, things have developed a bit since then. Regular checks etc., etc. However, I still don't think the powers that be altogether trust them. Do you remember those old German battleships in that war, the ones they called ten-minute ships?'

'Because it was estimated that they would not last ten minutes in battle with a dreadnought? All of which makes it the more important that you have a good crew. Can't you use *Kristin*'s people?'

'I could apply for them, if they happened to be in the service. But none of them are. I checked. Not even the reserve. And even if they put their names down now, it'd be weeks, maybe months, before they got their papers. Anyway, it's not as if there was a war on. I can't ask Billy or Bob to give up their jobs to join the Navy just for the fun of it.'

'There's Harry. He could go on being your valet.'

'Mother, Harry is forty-five years old. MTBs are a young man's game.'

'What about Johnnie Bryan! He's RNVR just like you.'

'Oh, he's in. But he has an appointment. In a battleship,' he added, bitterly.

'And Jamie Goring?'

'Eighteen last Saturday? He's only just eligible for service. Even if he put his name down tomorrow, he'd be at the very bottom of the list to be called up.'

'He could volunteer, and be in straight away.'

'He'd still have to be trained from scratch.'

'Balls! He probably knows more about small ships and the

sea than anyone in the Navy. He can pilot you anywhere in
the Channel. And he's a qualified motor mechanic. Aren't
those the qualities you are going to need?'

'Yes, Mother. But he knows nothing about drill, about naval
etiquette, about—'

'If you have to go into action, are drill and naval etiquette
going to matter a damn? He'll deliver what you want him to
deliver, without question.'

'That may well be. But the Navy just doesn't work like
that. It's an institution – a very old institution. I know you
don't give a damn for institutions, but they are there, and they
are what has made this country great. Anyway, you know, I
did put that idea to him, yesterday – that he should volunteer.
He wasn't very enthusiastic. I mean, why should he be?
Working for his dad he has an absolutely secure job, doing
what he likes best, either messing about in boats or messing
about with engines.'

'Hm,' Kristin commented.

'Now, Mother . . .'

'I think it's time for a gin. No more shop tonight.'

Duncan had experienced his mother's sudden decisions to
terminate a conversation before. It invariably meant that she
had had an idea . . . on the subject just under discussion. 'Now,
Mother,' he said again.

Kristin blew him a kiss.

Kristin used the Sunbeam in preference to the Bentley, stopped
in the forecourt of Goring's Garage. 'Fill her up,' she told the
attendant. 'And is Mr Goring about?'

'He's in the office, milady.' Everyone in the garage knew
Lady Eversham.

'I meant, Mr Jamie.'

'I'm here, milady.'

Just getting out of the car, Kristin turned in surprise; she
had taken the man in the doorway for a customer and not
looked very closely. Instead of the usual overalls, or the sweater
and canvas trousers he had worn on the yacht, Jamie was in
a smart suit, with a tie, and carried a small suitcase, but he
looked more attractive than she remembered; his fair wavy
hair was combed back from his bronzed forehead, his eyes
intensely blue. 'Jamie!' she cried.

'You just caught me,' he explained, coming towards her. 'I was on my way to catch the bus.'

'Where are you going?'

'Portsmouth.'

'What are you going to do in Portsmouth?'

'I'm going to join the Navy. Actually, I signed on yesterday, but they told me to go home and think about it for a night, and if I didn't change my mind to go back this morning.'

'And you didn't change your mind. Jamie, I could fall in love with you. In fact, I think I will. I have. Get in.'

'Milady?' Jamie cast an embarrassed glance at the attendant, who was unsuccessfully trying not to grin. 'I have to go to Portsmouth. This morning.'

'I know. That's where I'm going, too.'

'Oh. Ah . . .'

'I can get you there much quicker than any bus.'

'Oh. Well, that's very kind of you, milady.'

'So get in. Put that petrol on the account, will you?' she told the attendant, and sat behind the wheel.

A few moments later they were hurtling down the country road. 'This is very kind of you, milady,' Jamie said.

'It is my duty,' Kristin asserted. 'England needs you. Duncan needs you. *I* need you.'

She glanced at him, and he flushed. 'Anything I can do, milady.'

Did he mean that? She was an incredibly attractive woman and she was throwing herself at him. Never look a gift horse in the mouth? But he had no idea what to do to or with a woman, what she might want him to do; a few kisses and mutual fumbles after a Saturday night dance in the village hardly comprised a sex education. And she was Duncan's mother! How could he ever go sailing with Duncan again if he . . . what?

'You see,' Kristin explained, 'I was actually coming to the garage to persuade you to join up. And you'd already gone and done it. That is fantastic, don't you think? It shows we share a mental telepathy.'

'Well, actually, milady, it was Mr Duncan's idea.'

'I know. He told me he'd put it to you. But he said you hadn't been very enthusiastic.'

'Well, it's been quite a big step. I mean, it's the biggest

thing I've ever done. I didn't know what Mum and Dad would say. But then I got thinking about it . . . Oh, mind that cart . . . I do apologize, milady.'

Kristin swerved round the horse and cart with expert confidence. 'Those goddamned things take up the entire road,' she growled. 'Of course, you started thinking about it just about the time I also started thinking about it. That is a clear case of mental telepathy. And what did your parents say?'

'They weren't all that happy, at first. They seemed to think it was a bit of a dead-end job. I mean, it's not as if there was a war on.'

'There will be a war, soon enough. So you persuaded them.'

'When they saw that I really was keen . . .'

'Absolutely. Why are you really keen, Jamie?'

'I . . . well . . . I'm not sure, really. It was a sort of gut feeling.'

'I knew it. I planted that feeling, Jamie.'

They were now on a deserted stretch of road, and to his consternation she pulled into a lay-by and braked.

'Portsmouth,' he protested feebly.

'It's still there, and we are at least an hour ahead of the bus.' She switched off the ignition and turned to him, leaning her head on her arm, which was now resting on the back of the seat. 'Did I embarrass you on board the yacht?'

'Ah . . .'

'I told you, I get very turned on when at sea, especially if there's weather. I wish I could be going to sea with you and Duncan.'

He decided to take refuge in certainties. 'We won't be together, you know, milady.'

'Don't you want to serve with him?'

'Well, of course I would like that, milady. But I have to be trained, and then I will have to go wherever I'm posted.'

'You will be posted to Duncan's MTB. I will see to it.'

'You?'

'I have friends in high places. I want you to be with Duncan, because I think he needs you, and because I want to know where you are.'

'I don't really think—'

'Sssh. Just trust me. And now, kiss me.'

*   *   *

'Lady Eversham is here, sir,' said the Wren, disapprovingly.

'Kristin?' Rear Admiral Lonsdale rose from behind his desk, rather like a startled pheasant. He was a stockily built man of medium height, with blunt features and close-cut iron-grey hair. His staff were all somewhat afraid of him, which the Wren felt was as it should be; she had seldom before seen her boss looking alarmed, but she remembered him looking like this only a couple of days ago, when similarly invaded by this ghastly woman. 'What brings you back to Portsmouth so soon?'

'You, Jimmy.'

Kristin presented her cheek for a kiss, and after an embarrassed glance at the waiting young woman he obliged. 'That will be all, thank you, Miss Williams.'

'Aye aye, sir.' Miss Williams withdrew, tactfully closing the door behind her.

'Do you have sex with her?' Kristin asked, sitting down before the desk.

'Oh, for God's, Kristin. Of course I do not.'

'If I was a man, and had total control over all these nubile young women, and wearing uniform, too, I'd be quite unable to keep my hands off them.'

'In which case you'd be cashiered and locked up.'

'If I were to join the Navy, would I have a uniform?'

'I don't think the Navy – this Navy at any rate – is quite up to coping with someone like you. And, well . . .'

'I am too old. Do I look old?'

'Of course you do not. You do not look a day over . . . well . . .'

'Thirty?' she suggested helpfully.

'Definitely.'

'I don't feel old at all,' she said. 'I feel eighteen. I would love to have a uniform. I have never had one, you know.'

'Kristin,' he said uneasily. 'I really am quite a busy man. So—'

'I know,' she said. 'But you do eat, don't you?'

'Of course I do.'

'I do too.' She looked at her diamond-studded Cartier lapel watch. 'I would like you to take me out to lunch. Not the mess, this time. Somewhere private. I have something I wish to discuss with you.'

Part Two
First Blood

'Ye Mariners of England,
That guard our native seas.'

Thomas Campbell

Casual Heroics

The Austin Seven braked in a flurry of gravel and Lucinda ran into the house. 'Oh, get away, do,' she shouted at Lucifer, who, as was his custom, was attempting to embrace her. 'Krissy!' she shouted. 'Krissy! Have you heard the news?'

Kristin stood at the head of the stairs. 'Of course I have heard the news. Are you staying to lunch?'

'Lunch?'

'It is a meal,' Kristin explained, 'which is normally eaten between one and two in the afternoon. It is now half past twelve. If you are staying to lunch, I need to let Lucia know, immediately.'

'Lunch? Food? How can you think about food at a time like this?'

'I cannot believe Herr Hitler will be so rude as to interfere with lunch on the first day of a war.'

'But there'll be bombers over here at any moment. Everyone says so.'

'Then everyone is almost certainly wrong, which is not unusual. In any event, he must have an awful lot of bombs if he can spare a few to drop on such an irrelevant part of the country as Lymington. Lucia,' she called, 'Miss Browning will be lunching. Come upstairs, Cindy. You need a glass of sherry.'

Lucinda stumbled up the stairs. 'What are we going to do?'

Kristin poured. 'Do about what?'

'Well . . .' Lucinda spilled amontillado on its way to her lips. 'Duncan! He's at war.'

'I think we are all at war.' Kristin sat down and crossed her legs. Including that gorgeous little boy, she thought. And all I have had from him is a brief kiss and cuddle. She didn't even know if her plan to get him into the same ship as Duncan had worked, or was going to work: Jimmy Lonsdale had seemed to think she was asking him to go above and beyond the bounds of his command.

'But he'll be killed.'

'Not for a few days. After that, we'll just have to keep our fingers crossed.'

'Oh, you – you are a cold-blooded monster.'

Kristin regarded her for some moments, then said, 'I think you need another drink.' She poured, and raised her glass. 'Here's to the Royal Navy, and all who serve in her . . . even in small motorboats.'

'But what about the wedding?'

Kristin raised her eyebrows. 'I was under the impression you had called that off.'

'Of course I haven't called it off. I just don't like being stood up, that's all.'

'Ah,' Kristin said. 'Well, you may have to get used to that for a few weeks. On the other hand,' she added sadly, 'as today is the third of September, and the wedding is set for the ninth of March, I very much fear that the war will be over by then, and so there should not be a problem.' She refilled her glass, morosely.

'Flotilla will reduce speed.' Leeming's voice over the VHF radio was, as always, quiet. Duncan reflected that he was actually a very good commanding officer, although he had no doubt that the lieutenant was as frustrated as the rest of them. In another week it would be Christmas, which meant that it was now well over three months since Great Britain had declared war on Germany, and the MTBs had not fired a shot in anger, much less a torpedo. In fact, they had not seen an enemy, save high above them in the sky.

He obediently closed the throttle, and the little ship slowed in unison with her two companions. St Alban's Head was behind them now, and their routine sweep to the west along the south coast was just about completed. Ahead of them lay the Needles lighthouse, with the cliffs of the western point of the Isle of Wight rising behind it, and the channel leading up to Hurst Castle at its foot. As was their usual procedure, they would enter the narrow passage in line ahead, and then proceed through the Solent at half-speed. This was tedious, but any other way would send shock waves of wake through all the other shipping using the virtually landlocked stretch of water.

MTB 20 was last in the line, positioned so that the wake of the boat in front of her went to either side and left her with a reasonably comfortable passage. But on this cold, grey December day the sea was in any event lumpy: there had been a wind during the night. Duncan and both the men on the bridge with him were wearing heavy greatcoats and thick gloves. Still, Duncan thought, even at half-speed they'd be in Portsmouth in time for tea and then a warm evening in the mess.

'Looks like a spot of bother over there, sir,' remarked Petty Officer Harris, his second in command.

Duncan turned his head: there was certainly smoke just over the horizon, far too much smoke for a funnel. He checked the compass bearing then thumbed the radio mike. '*Twenty* to Commander. There is a ship on fire, bearing one eight seven, estimated distance six miles. Permission to investigate.'

'I'm sure it is already being investigated, *Twenty*,' Leeming replied. 'But you may have a look. Just don't get yourself into any trouble. Remember that wood burns.'

'Aye aye, sir.' Duncan closed the mike. 'He seems to think we're halfwits. Action stations, Mr Harris. I am about to implement full speed.'

'Aye aye, sir,' Harris acknowledged, and rang the bell several times.

Duncan turned away from the course followed by the other two boats, lined himself up with the distant smoke, and pushed the throttle forward. The little ship seemed to leap out of the water and then raced across the sea, bumping and slamming in the chop. Duncan had both hands on the helm, but Harris wedged himself against the mast to level the binoculars. 'A coaster,' he said. 'She is properly ablaze. I don't think she has more than a few minutes.'

'We'll be there in five,' Duncan promised. 'People?'

'Heads in the water, yes.'

Duncan could see them also, as the MTB raced at the now definitely sinking ship. He throttled back and she came off the plane to coast towards the swimming men, who were waving and shouting. 'Get a net over the side,' he called to the two seamen on the foredeck.

Then he reduced speed still further, cautiously approaching the victims at dead slow, and bringing the little ship to a halt a few yards away. 'Anyone hurt?' he shouted.

'No one serious,' came the reply. 'We'll make it.'

All the other six members of the crew were now on deck to assist in bringing the men on board. 'Tell Wilson to get below and prepare something hot to drink, Mr Harris. They'll need blankets, too.'

'Aye aye, sir.' Harris left the bridge.

Duncan gazed at the coaster, still blazing as her stern went below the surface with a huge sizzling sound. The radio was crackling. He thumbed the switch. '*MTB Twenty*.'

'*Penelope*. Report. There was no Mayday.'

'I think it must have been rather sudden.'

'Can you cope? We are four miles away.'

Duncan saw the destroyer; he had been concentrating so hard he had not noticed its approach. 'I can cope, sir.'

'Good man,' the lieutenant-commander acknowledged. 'We're around if you need us.'

The coaster's skipper arrived on the bridge, wrapped in a borrowed greatcoat and sipping a cup of cocoa. 'Thank God you were nearby. That water is perishing. We never saw you until you arrived.'

'Well, we weren't actually around,' Duncan said. 'But we can travel pretty fast when pushed. What happened?'

The skipper gazed at the glowing mass of wreckage that was all that was left of his ship. 'We were torpedoed, that's what happened. Went up like a bloody torch.'

'What? In our Channel? Within six miles of the coast?'

'Yeah. Bloody cheek, ain't it? And the bugger's still around.'

'What?' Duncan began to feel like a parrot, as he looked left and right.

'Saw his periscope while we was in the water. Looking at us! Probably laughing his head off.'

Harris had joined them and was using the binoculars, sweeping the surface.

'See anything?' Duncan asked.

'No, sir. He's probably got the hell out of there since we turned up.'

'On the other hand,' the skipper put in, 'you're a sitting duck, still like this.'

'Good point.' Duncan reached for the throttle.

'I doubt he'd waste a torpedo on us, sir,' Harris said. 'He might try gunfire.'

'He won't surface while that destroyer is about,' the skipper argued.

'There's something in the water, sir,' said one of the crew. 'Three points off the port bow, maybe a cable's length. It's moving, like . . .' His voice was excited.

Harris handed Duncan the glasses, and he studied the ripple. 'That's a periscope. But we're too close for a torpedo.'

'He's moving away, sir,' the seaman said.

'Running like hell,' Harris commented.

'If he was running,' the skipper said, 'he'd submerge totally. He's going off to get the right range.'

'Well,' Duncan said. 'I think we should do something about the bugger. You game, skipper?'

'Yes, sir.'

'Mr Harris, make to Portsmouth and to *Penelope*, "Am engaging enemy U-boat six miles south by west of the Needles tower. *MTB 20*. Then get aft and prepare the depth charges for firing.'

'Aye aye, *sir.*'

'Permission to stay on the bridge?' the skipper asked.

'You have it. This is as much your show as ours.' He eased the throttle forward and the MTB gathered way. 'Clarke, keep your eyes on that periscope.'

'Aye aye, sir,' came the response from the seaman on the foredeck. 'But it's gone.'

'He's seen that we're after him,' the skipper grumbled. 'Damn and blast.'

'We'll get him back up,' Duncan promised. He could clearly see the swirl in the water where the submarine had dived. The question was, which way would he move once he was down. But he couldn't be very far, and now they were right over the mark. It occurred to Duncan that the German was probably unaware that a ship this small could carry depth charges. 'Fire one, fire two,' he called, then remembered Leeming's warning, and thrust the throttle forward.

The MTB leapt through the water, but they were only fifty yards away when the sea behind them heaved upwards. The entire little ship trembled and bucked beneath his hands.

'Someone told me these things are made of wood,' the skipper remarked.

'Absolutely correct,' Duncan agreed. 'Plywood.'

The skipper gulped.

Duncan slowed, and turned the ship. 'Anything?' he called to Clarke.

The seaman was using his glasses. 'Nothing there, sir.'

'That destroyer is coming back,' the skipper said. 'She got your signal.'

But as she had actually been steaming away from the casualty she was still several miles off.

'It's our show,' Duncan declared. 'Anything, Mr Harris?'

'No, sir. But . . . there's something over there.' He pointed.

Duncan levelled the glasses. There was certainly a disturbance under the surface. Rather like that rock off Guernsey, he thought. And of course, he remembered, the sea out here was not all that deep. It had been a pretty risky, if no doubt admirably courageous act, for a U-boat to enter these waters at all – but then, only a few weeks ago, for all Leeming's contemptuous dismissal of the possibility, one had actually penetrated the supposedly impenetrable approaches to Scapa Flow in the Orkneys, and sunk the battleship *Royal Oak*. That blighter had got away; he was damned if he was going to let this one escape.

'We'll target that,' he decided. 'Prepare three and four.'

'Aye aye, sir.'

'How many of those things have you got?' the skipper inquired.

'Four.'

'You mean you've nothing after these last two?'

'If we can damage him, the destroyer should be able to finish him off. Hang on. Fire three!' he shouted, pushing the throttle forward. 'Fire four!'

This time the thrust of the engine took them a cable's length clear before the two explosions. He reduced speed and turned the helm, gently, to bring her round. 'Anything?'

Clarke had been kneeling and holding the grab rail, both to resist the shock waves and to prevent himself being tossed about by the sudden surges; he had in any event been soaked by the water coming over the bow. Now he wiped the glasses as clean as possible on his sleeve before levelling them. 'Nothing, sir.'

'Damn, damn, damn,' Duncan growled. 'In these shallow waters he must have felt that.'

'Look there, sir,' Harris shouted. 'There, there, there! He's coming up.'

Duncan swung his own glasses, saw the conning tower breaking the surface. The U-boat was further away than he had supposed; he estimated at least four cables lengths – say eight hundred yards. She must have been well away from where he was targeting. But even so, as he had thought, because of the shallowness of the sea she must have felt the blasts. Eight hundred yards, he mused. Was it possible?

In any event, he had to do something. The submarine was now fully surfaced, and men were clambering down the conning tower to serve the gun, while the destroyer was still three miles away – a long shot for her four point seven, even if she would risk damaging, or even sinking, the MTB by a near miss. That lieutenant-commander must be fuming.

Duncan could also read the mind of the U-boat commander: if he could sink the MTB, the destroyer would surely stop to pick up survivors, and give him a chance to get away.

Of course, *he* could get away, by simply turning his ship and opening the throttle. But that went against his every instinct.

The skipper seemed able to understand his dilemma, and he was also out for revenge for the loss of his ship. 'You think your machine guns can reach her?'

'She's in range. But I reckon she can sink us before we can hurt her. Going round, Mr Harris,' he shouted. 'Prepare your tubes.'

The MTB had been moving slowly forward, and was now within three cables, which was far too close. Duncan spun the helm and increased speed to full. The boat roared away, just as the submarine's gun exploded, the shell landing precisely where the MTB had been a couple of seconds earlier.

'Good shooting,' he muttered.

'You're not going away?' the skipper asked, anxiously.

'Just getting the range right.' He was now racing straight at the destroyer.

'She's signalling with the lamp, sir.' Harris had joined them. 'And the radio's spluttering.'

'And I can tell you exactly what they're both saying,' Duncan said. 'Get out of it. Range?'

The U-boat's gun had exploded again, but this time the shot fell well short of the fast-moving MTB.

Harris was checking his range-finder. 'One thousand yards.'

'Then here we go. Stand by your torpedoes.'

The destroyer was now within two miles, and closing rapidly. The gun on her foredeck exploded, but the shot was well wide. The U-boat in turn fired again, but Duncan was again swinging the helm to bring the MTB round, and again his sudden manoeuvre disconcerted the enemy aim.

'She's diving!' the skipper said.

White water foamed as the U-boat skipper realized that his plan was not going to work, and that he was no match on the surface for the destroyer. The gun crew were running for the conning-tower ladder.

'Fire one,' Duncan shouted. 'Fire two.'

The ship seemed to jerk as the loud hisses cut across the afternoon. Duncan reduced speed and the MTB came off the plane.

'What happens if you miss?' the skipper asked.

'I get reprimanded for wasting two expensive torpedoes. Come on, come on!'

The twin streaks were clearly visible, just below the surface, but the gun crew had all been recovered, and Duncan could see only the captain left on the tower; as he watched, that head also disappeared. Now the hull was submerged, with only the tower left visible.

'Damnation,' Duncan growled, but as he spoke there was a huge bang and a pillar of smoke and water shot skywards. The torpedo hadn't struck the conning tower but the hull, still only a few feet below the surface.

'Yippee!' the skipper shouted. 'You got the bastard.'

The crew were also cheering.

Duncan put the engine in neutral and let the MTB coast to a stop. Then he picked up the radio mike. '*MTB 20*, sir. Sorry I didn't reply before. I was a little busy.'

'So we saw. You took a bit of a chance, but well done. Any survivors?'

'I'm going to have a look now, sir. But I'm doubtful. Everyone was below when she was hit.'

'They had it coming. It'll be a good headline: "U-boat torpedoed by MTB". Are you damaged?'

'I don't think so, sir.'

'Very good. Again, congratulations. *Penelope* out.'

'You'll be famous,' the skipper said.

'Ah,' Duncan said. He wondered if Lucinda would be pleased about that.

Harris returned to the bridge; he had been below, checking up. 'With respect, sir. We are making water.'

'Oh, damnation. Where?'

'Aft, sir.'

'A lot?'

'Quite a lot, sir. I think some seams opened in those depth-charge explosions.'

'Right. Get the pumps working We have to make sure there are no survivors from that U-boat. Think you can keep us afloat long enough to get home?'

'The admiral will see you now, Sub-Lieutenant.' Miss Williams was as severe as ever.

'Thank you.'

She was holding the door open and Duncan entered the inner office, saluted. 'Sub-Lieutenant Morant, sir. Reporting as ordered.' If he was apprehensive, he kept telling himself that this man was a close friend of his mother's, and in the context of Mother's close friends, that might mean quite a lot.

Lonsdale did not look terribly pleased to see him, but then he did not look terribly displeased, either. 'Ah, yes, Lieutenant. Captain Fitzsimmons tells me your MTB has had to be taken out.'

'I'm afraid that is correct, sir. We strained some seams.'

'I assume you were taught to get well away from depth charges before they explode?'

'Yes, sir. I take full responsibility for the slowness of my response. I was too interested in where the target was, or might be.'

'I imagine you were. But your boat is repairable? My information is that you reached Portsmouth in a sinking condition.'

'There again, sir, I must take responsibility. I underestimated the seriousness of the damage. And of course we were heavily laden with the crew of the coaster we picked up. So the water was gaining on the pumps when we reached our berth, yes. But a crane was waiting to lift us out, and the yard tells me she'll be back in the water in a fortnight.'

'Hm.' Lonsdale picked up the newspaper lying on his desk. 'Good headline. MTB TAKES ON U-BOAT . . . AND WINS. One for your scrapbook, eh?'

'Yes, sir.'

'Coming on top of the news from Montevideo, the sinking of the *Graf Spee*, it is a boost not only for the Navy but for the country.' Lonsdale stood up and came round the desk to shake Duncan's hand. 'Congratulations, Lieutenant. That was a bit of the Nelsons. I intend to recommend you for a gong.'

'Thank you, sir. Mother will be delighted.'

'Ah, yes. Well, she should be.' He returned behind his desk and sat down. 'Speaking of your mother: a couple of months ago she asked a favour of me. I take it you are going home, some time soon?'

'With your permission, sir.'

'As your boat is out of action, you, and all your crew, have a week's leave. When you go home, will you tell Lady Eversham that I have now been able to comply with her wishes. Dismissed, Lieutenant, and again, congratulations. And to your crew.'

Now, what was the old bugger referring to? Duncan wondered, as he returned to the dock. The MTB was up on the hard, on legs, while the yard manager was peering at the hull. The crew were peering at him, but they came to attention as the officer appeared. 'Ah . . . is all well, sir?' ventured Petty Officer Harris.

'All is very well, Petty Officer. The admiral sends his congratulations to all of you.'

They chorused their approval. All except Moultree, the engineer. 'They don't seem too happy with me, sir.'

'What?'

Moultree showed him the paper. 'Got this an hour ago, sir.'

Duncan scanned the sheet of foolscap. 'Transferred to the *Barham*? My dear fellow, that's a big step up. She's a battle-ship. My best congratulations.'

'I'd rather remain with the *Twenty*, sir.'

'And I'd rather you were remaining, too. But there it is. Man proposes and their Lordships of the Admiralty disposes.

Not very good grammar, but you know what I mean. I expect you to do great things on that bigger stage, Moultree.'

Harris accompanied him to the yard superintendent. 'Odd, that, sir, replacing one of our crew, after only a couple of months and one action. May I ask – well . . .?'

'No, I did not, Petty Officer. I am as mystified as you.'

'Moultree's a good man. I hope his replacement is in his class.'

'So do I. Well, Mr Hawkins?'

Hawkins indicated the plywood planking, which was split in several places. 'She took a battering, Mr Morant. In fact I'd say that had you been ten miles further out you might not have got her home.'

'But she can be repaired? I told the admiral she'd be in the water in a fortnight.'

Hawkins had a rather long nose, which he now pulled. 'Aye, well, that could be. Providing nothing more serious comes along. I think Mr Leeming wants to have a look.'

Leeming joined them. 'What a mess. Still, it's a salutary lesson.' He shook Duncan's hand. 'Congratulations. I wish you'd called us back to help you.'

'Well, I didn't realize that I needed help, until I needed help, if you follow me.'

Leeming did not look convinced. 'How long are you out for?'

'No more than a fortnight, hopefully.'

'Hm. We may have to part company.' Duncan got the impression that he would not be altogether sorry about that. 'Meanwhile, I have a replacement engineer for you. He'll have time to shake down before actually going to sea.'

Duncan looked past him at the sailor, who had respectfully remained standing some distance away while the officers chatted. 'Jamie? Good God!' He hurried forward, hand outstretched. 'It's good to see you. Welcome aboard.'

'Thank you, sir. It's good to be here.'

'Do I gather that you've completed your shore training?'

'Well, I don't know, sir. I understood I had another month to go, when I received orders to report here. I don't think my CO was very pleased.'

'I can imagine. But you had put your name down to serve on MTBs?'

'Well no, sir. I didn't think it was my place to do that. I thought perhaps you had – well, requested my presence.'

Duncan regarded him for several moments, while the penny dropped and he finally understood what had lain behind the admiral's cryptic message to his mother. 'I'm just glad to have you.'

'Do I gather that you know this rating?' Leeming asked, tone redolent of disapproval.

'Ordinary seaman . . . but I suppose you're an artificer, now?'

'I suppose I am, sir.' He was wearing the appropriate badges.

'Goring sailed with me on the Cowes–Dinard.'

'Ah,' Leeming said, more disapproving yet. 'Then I'll leave you to it.'

'Pompous prig,' Duncan muttered as the lieutenant went off. 'Come and meet your shipmates.'

'The papers are full of what you did yesterday, sir.'

'Apparently. But it's what *we* did, not me, personally. Even more than on the yacht, we're all part of a team. Petty Officer Harris, Goring is our new engineer.'

'Yes, sir.' Harris shook hands, although he clearly disapproved of the new arrival as much as had Leeming. But equally clearly, his disapproval was based on Jamie's obvious youth.

'Goring is a qualified motor mechanic,' Duncan explained. 'Introduce him to the other crew members, will you, Mr Harris. And then, as the old girl won't be fit for at least another fortnight, we all have a week's leave. You'll be home for Christmas. Everyone is to report here on Thursday week. We'll have to fit her out all over again.'

'Aye aye, sir.'

'With respect, sir,' Jamie said, 'am I allowed to go on board now and look at the engine?'

'Certainly. She's your baby. And she probably needs more work than anything else; some of the water we took on board got to her. But it can wait until next week, you know.'

'I'd like to take a look now, sir, if I may – see what needs doing.'

'Very good. Carry on.' Duncan faced the rest of the patiently waiting crew. 'I wish to thank you all for your support yesterday. We seem to have made ourselves famous. All we have to do in the future is maintain that standard. But right now, we all have a week's leave.'

'Three cheers for the captain,' Harris called. 'Hip hip . . .'

The crew responded with a will, and Duncan stood to attention. 'Thank you. Ship's company will stand down.' He saluted and walked away.

'Known the skipper long, have you?' Harris asked.

'A few years,' Jamie said. 'I've crewed in his yacht.'

'And he seems able to pull strings. I suppose that can't be bad, if you happen to be one of the strings. But he's a good officer, if a little wild. He's going to finish this war – if he survives – either as a hero or cashiered.'

'And if he doesn't survive?'

Harris gave him an old-fashioned look. 'If he doesn't survive, neither will we. So it won't matter. Come and meet your shipmates.'

'Her ladyship in?' Duncan demanded of the maid.

He knew she was, because both cars were in the garage. As the young woman now acknowledged, with one of her habitual simpers, 'She is, 'ow you say, Mr Duncan, pooting.' She was Spanish, as Duncan reckoned was reasonable enough, as she had a Spanish mistress.

'Right.' Duncan strode through the hall and out of the door into the garden. Lucifer, who had already been barking as he had recognized the sound of the Bugatti's engine, bounded forward. Duncan scooped him from the ground as he reared on his hind legs to place both paws on his master's chest, and carried him to the putting green, where his mother, wearing a twin-set and pearls, was concentrating on getting the ball into the cup. But at the sight of him, she dropped her putter to come towards him.

'Duncan! You are a hero. Oh, do put him down. You have no idea how ridiculous you look walking about with that huge beast in your arms like a toy.'

Duncan obeyed, placing the dog on the ground and accepting her instead.

'You are in all the papers,' she said, kissing him on both cheeks. 'The photographs were not very good. But I am so proud.'

He held her away from him. 'Mother! What did you do to have Jamie Goring assigned to my ship?'

Kristin clapped her hands. 'You mean he *has* been? Oh, I am so pleased.' She peered at him. 'Are you not?'

'I am embarrassed, and so is he.'

Kristin frowned. 'Why should you be embarrassed?'

'Mother, he has only been in the Navy just over three months. He has not yet completed his basic training.'

Kristin held his hand to lead him back to the house. 'We will have champagne,' she announced, 'to toast your success.'

'It wasn't *my* success. It was the ship's success – the crew's success.'

'The crew had to be led. Lucia, bring up a bottle of the Clicquot, will you? Your father has been on the phone,' she said as they climbed the stairs. 'He wants you to call him. And Cindy has been calling also. She wants you to call her.'

'Do you mean I'm forgiven? – simply for sinking a German U-boat?'

'It's not something everyone does, every day,' Kristin pointed out. 'They've made Commodore Harwood a KCB and promoted him admiral.'

'Mother, he sank a battleship.'

'A pocket battleship. And he had a lot of help. What are you going to get?'

'I have absolutely no idea.'

'But you are going to get something?'

'Well, the admiral did mention the possibility . . .'

'Possibility? I will have to give him a ring.'

'*Mother!* You do not run the Royal Navy. And you have done quite enough interfering.'

Kristin regarded him for some moments, then smiled at her maid. 'Thank you, Lucia.' She uncorked the bottle with considerable expertise. 'I assume I am allowed to toast your success.'

'Oh, Mother! Please behave.'

'And to drink to your next triumph.'

'Seeing that this one was the most utter fluke, that may be a long time coming.'

She blew him a kiss.

Behave, Kristin thought, always behave. She did not wish to behave; there was too much behaviour as it was – too much convention, too many rules and regulations.

She wished she could stand on the bridge of a warship and

give the command to open fire. Not that she had any desire to be a man – only to be able to do what men did, without being regarded as a freak. As for behaving herself as a lady should . . . 'Fill her up,' she told the forecourt attendant.

'Yes, milady. Ah . . . I'll need the coupons.'

'Coupons?'

'You must have coupons to buy petrol, milady. It's the rationing, you see. You should have received a little booklet, with tickets that you tear out as you purchase petrol.'

'Oh, that thing. Yes. I did receive one of those.'

'Well, then . . .'

'I have no idea where it is.'

The attendant scratched his head. 'It's against the law for me to put petrol in your car without a coupon.'

'Well, then, as my tank is showing empty, I will have to leave my car here, and you will have to drive me home in one of your cars. Then we will find the coupons, and you can bring them back here and fill my tank. Then you can deliver my car.'

'Milady, I can't leave the forecourt unattended.'

'So, are you inviting me to spend the morning here? I am certainly not walking home. It is three miles.'

Some more head scratching.

'Milady! How nice to see you.'

Jamie hadn't meant to go out at all. She was an embarrassment and was setting up to be a catastrophe. He had not seen her since the day she had driven him into Portsmouth to join the Navy. He had not wanted to. Those frantic ten minutes in the lay-by when she had searched his mouth with a passion he had not known it was possible for a woman to feel – or a man, for that matter – and searched his body too, her hand slipping inside his shirt to caress his chest and then sliding down the front of his pants . . . He had not known what to do, what he would do if she started unbuttoning his flies. But at the same time she had taken his hand and placed it on her breast, allowing his fingers to sink into the soft flesh beneath her blouse.

So he had got his fingers inside as well, and found paradise. Briefly. Because suddenly she had seemed to remember who and what she was, and what she was doing. She had sat up straight, cheeks pink but showing no other sign of embarrassment. 'Now we share another secret,' she had said, between deep breaths. 'Will you keep this secret as well?'

'Of course, milady,' he had promised, having problems with his own breathing, and terribly conscious of his erection, which she surely had felt and now could probably see.

'And you will forgive the foibles of a lonely, passionate old lady.'

He had not known how to reply to that, so she had asked, 'Do you think I am old, Jamie?'

'Oh, good Lord, no, milady.'

'You are a convincing liar. I am old enough to be your mother. But I want to have sex with you. Am I not terrible?'

'Milady . . .'

'Would you like to have sex with me?'

He remembered licking his lips, whether in anticipation or blind terror he had not been sure.

She had smiled. 'But you are like the cat in the adage.'

'Milady?'

'Shakespeare, Jamie. The cat who let "I would", wait upon "I dare not". You must let me know when you feel up to daring. But now you have a war to win. And I have things to do. So, let us go to Portsmouth. And remember that we share secrets.'

So, never again. But to see her sitting there, calmly irritated . . .

'Jamie!' Kristin cried. 'My knight in shining armour . . .' She frowned at him. 'Why aren't you in uniform? I have never seen you in uniform.'

'I'm on leave, milady – while the ship is being fixed.'

'So you're home for Christmas. You are more fortunate than I appear to be.'

'Milady?'

'Mr Probert will not sell me any petrol, so I can't get home.'

'Tim?'

'There has to be a coupon, Mr Jamie. Your father said that no one is to be served without a coupon. We'd be breaking the law.'

'Don't you have coupons, milady?'

'Of course I have coupons. But I don't travel with the damned things. They're somewhere at home. I offered to give them to him when he took me home, but he won't do that either.'

Jamie looked at Probert.

'Your dad said there were to be absolutely no exceptions, Mr Jamie. I'd lose my job. And you know I can't leave the forecourt unattended.'

'But *you* can drive me home, Jamie,' Kristin said.

'Well . . .'

'And I can give you the coupons to bring back.' She opened the door and got out. 'Which is your car?'

'I'm afraid I don't have a car, milady.'

'No car? Good Lord!'

'I have a bicycle.'

'A . . .?' She turned to look at the BSA. 'I have never ridden on a bicycle. Is there room for two?'

'Well, you'd have to sit on the crossbar . . .'

'You will have to show me.'

'You mean you will?'

'Of course I will. I love new experiences.' She walked across and inspected the bike. 'Where do I put my legs?'

She was wearing a skirt.

'Well, you sit sort of side-saddle.'

Kristin considered. 'My legs would freeze.'

He hadn't been thinking of that aspect of the situation. 'Yes, milady. They probably would.'

'But it will only be a short ride. Do I get on first or do you?'

'You should get on first, milady. But . . .'

'Jamie,' she said severely. 'Remember the cat. Let's go.'

Jamie cast an anxious glance at the clearly scandalized Probert, then held the bike steady, while Kristin hitched her bottom on to the crossbar. 'You hold on to the handlebars,' he explained, putting his arms round her to do the same as he swung his leg over the saddle, while he looked down at a long length of stockinged leg, surmounted by the clips of a suspender belt; she had lifted her skirt above her thighs. This had clearly made Probert's day, the bastard. Jamie peddled out of the yard.

'Whee!' Kristin commented, as the bicycle came to a halt before her front door. 'I must look a sight.'

Jamie moved his head, which had been resting on her hair
– she had not been wearing a hat – to look at her; it was not
a sight he was ever likely to forget. Now she slid off the
crossbar, pulling down her skirt as she stood, a little uncer-
tainly.

'Do you know,' she said. 'I nearly had an orgasm. We must
do that again. Come inside.'

Jamie was not sure he knew what she meant; he was not
sure he wanted to. But he was very conscious of his arms
being round her for the fifteen-minute ride, of the feel of her
back against his chest. 'I should be getting back,' he protested.

'Why? You are on leave. Do you have somewhere to go?'

'Well, no, milady. But Lieutenant Morant—'

'Duncan is not here. He is out shagging his fiancée. At
least, I hope that is what he's doing. I told him if he didn't
do it on this leave he never would.' She opened her handbag,
took out her key and unlocked the door. Instantly there was
a loud, deep barking. 'Don't let him alarm you. He only makes
a lot of noise. Lucifer! Behave.'

The huge white dog stood on its hind legs to place a paw
on each of Kristin's shoulders, then looked past her at the
stranger. Jamie was not certain whether it was just panting or
baring its teeth. Kristin was staggering and he thought she
might fall over, but she managed to push the animal away,
whereupon he dropped to all fours before rearing again at
Jamie.

'Lucifer!' Kristin snapped, and he sat down, now definitely
panting, then followed the pair of them into the house. 'Lucia!'
Kristin called. 'There will be two of us for lunch.'

Lucia appeared at an inner doorway. 'Yes, milady.' She
looked Jamie up and down, but made no comment. He had
to wonder if her mistress made a habit of bringing strange
men home to a meal.

'Up here,' Kristin said, and led him up the stairs into her
private sitting room. He found himself again staring at her
legs. 'Sweet or dry?'

'Sweet or dry what?'

'Sherry, my darling boy.'

'Well, whatever you're having.'

'Don't you drink sherry?'

'I never have.'

'I see I have a lot to do. I would say, sweet.' She poured two glasses of Harvey's Bristol Cream. 'Try this.'

He sipped. 'This is delicious.'

'It's my favourite. Now, come and sit beside me.'

'Milady—'

'Jamie, next week you are going to join Duncan's ship and go to war. You could well be killed. Do you really want to die without having lived? That would seem to be a very unfortunate state of affairs. Didn't you enjoy that ride into Portsmouth?'

Jamie sat beside her, drank some more sherry. 'Of course I did, milady.'

'I know you did. You were as hard as a rock.'

'Milady . . .' He could feel his cheeks burning.

'We should have done it there and then. But somehow, the front seat of a car is not ideal. It is very restricting, for a start, not to mention uncomfortable. You are liable to get the gear stick up your ass. Believe me. When you come into me, I want it to be in a bed, with clean sheets and a soft mattress. It's just through there. Would you like to come in there?'

He spoke without thinking. 'Yes, milady. But you . . . well . . . you are a toff. I mean . . .'

'I know what you mean.'

'And then, you're Mr Morant's mother . . .'

'Every woman is, or should be, somebody's mother.'

'He's my skipper.'

'But he's not here, is he? As for my being a toff, toffs are there by accidents of birth or circumstances. They are no better, and in fact are often a good deal worse, than non-toffs, if there is such a word. But they all share the same characteristics. The men all have dicks and hands. The women all have breasts and buttocks and vaginas. And they all want—' She stood up and held out her hand. 'You were going to spank my bottom, remember?'

Explosive Moments

'Well?' Duncan asked. 'What do you think of it?' In the confines of the engine room he was stooped.

Jamie tried to concentrate. This was the first time the pair had been alone since the crew had reassembled after Christmas, and the boat had finally been put into the water. For that period he had been the outsider. The other seamen had had no doubt at all that his presence had been specially requested by their skipper, who had apparently wanted him so badly he had managed to get him out of training school a month early. No one had made any overt comment on that; nor had there been any hazing: the MTB was so small that anything said or done in the crew's quarters forward was liable to be known to the skipper, aft. But they were all clearly waiting for this utter tyro, in their eyes, to prove his worth.

Jamie was perfectly willing to do that, when given the opportunity. But crouching shoulder to shoulder with this large, friendly and, as far as he was concerned, utterly admirable man, after that afternoon with Kristin . . . He could, and did, tell himself that he would have had to be either a eunuch or a saint to resist so compulsive a woman, even if he had known what he was doing when he did it. Just as she had known exactly what she wanted. So, was she utterly wanton, or just a lonely, sex-starved old woman?

Well, for a start, the word 'old' did not come into it at all. In terms of her birth certificate she might just qualify, at least when compared with himself. But he had never encountered a girl with her energy, or her velvet flesh. He could still feel the firm softness of her breast, the caress of her nipple across his palm, the curve of her buttocks. As for what lay between . . .

But then, he had never imagined that any woman would want to be touched there, would reveal such unbelievable pleasure at being touched. She had said almost nothing, had made very little sound at all, save for the occasional sigh of ecstasy. She let her hands, her lips and her tongue do the talking, left him dreaming of her every night, wondering, could it ever happen again?

The evidence of her divorce trial suggested that it could . . . but not necessarily with him, if he wasn't present when the mood overtook her. Then she was – utterly wanton. Did that matter? Only in the unbearable thought that she might even at that moment be achieving a similar ecstasy with another man. Or worse, another boy!

'Well?' Duncan asked.

'I have never seen anything so beautiful, sir.'

'Have you ever seen anything this big?'

'Ah . . . no, sir. I haven't.'

'But you can cope with it.'

'I think so, sir. If the parts are bigger than anything I have ever worked with, they're the same parts.'

'Absolutely. Well, let's take her out and make sure everything is working.' Duncan turned his head as Petty Officer Harris appeared in the doorway. 'Problems?'

'I hope not, sir. Lieutenant Leeming is here.'

'Carry on, Goring.' Duncan went on deck. 'Good morning, sir.'

'Good morning, Lieutenant. Is she ready for sea?'

'Yes, sir. I'm about to give her a run. Would you like to come along?'

'You'll have your run, but it won't be a trial.'

'You mean I am returning to the flotilla, sir?'

'Yes, you are.' It was difficult to be certain whether or not he was pleased about that. 'Are you fully fuelled?'

'Not yet, sir. I was about to do that also.'

'Do it now. We leave in an hour.'

'Leave for where, sir?'

'I haven't been told that, yet. I gather we'll find out when we are at sea. But I also gather it will be a long assignment.'

'Ah . . . yes, sir. Are we allowed . . .?'

'You are not allowed to contact anyone on shore at this time. Things may become more relaxed later on. One hour.' He went to the gangway. 'Oh, by the way, you're to get the Cross – I assume for that action last month. Congratulations. You'll be our first DSC. It's an honour for the flotilla.'

He jumped on to the pontoon and strode away.

'Well, indeed congratulations, sir,' Harris said.

'Why me? You were all in it with me.'

'You took the risk, sir.'

'You mean I risked all of your lives.'

'Well, I suppose you did, sir. But more importantly, you risked your career, if that sub had managed to sink us.'

Duncan put his hand up to scratch his head, then remembered that he was wearing his cap and lowered it again. 'You heard the man, Petty Officer. Let's get to it. What'll your wife think, you just disappearing like this?'

'She's been a Navy wife for twenty-three years, sir. She'll know I am going to turn up again at some time.'

'Hm,' Duncan commented. He wondered if everyone else was going to be as broad-minded.

'Do be quiet, Lucifer,' Kristin said, descending the stairs to open the front door before Harry could get to it. 'Why, Cindy! What a pleasant surprise. Did you have a good Christmas?'

'I wish to speak to Duncan. Oh, get away, dog.'

'I wouldn't bite her, Lucifer,' Kristin advised. 'You don't know where she's been. If you want to speak to Duncan, I suggest you go to Portsmouth.'

'I've been to Portsmouth, and all they told me was that he wasn't there. They wouldn't tell me where he was. The beastly man was quite rude. I would like you to complain to that admiral friend of yours.'

Kristin allowed her into the house. 'And you thought he might be here?'

'Well, where else would he be?'

'As he is in the Navy, I can think of a hundred places.'

'In a small motorboat in the middle of winter? It's blowing a gale out there.'

'He enjoys heavy weather. Why do you need to see him so urgently. You're not pregnant, are you?'

'Oh, really, Krissy. Sometimes you can be positively obscene.'

'I'm sure you meant, by your standards, all of the time. You haven't answered my question.'

'Well . . . he was supposed to have tonight off, and take me to the dance at Woburn. I just wanted to check that he was coming. And now he's disappeared. Not even a message.'

'I think you need a drink. Come upstairs.'

'I do not *want* a drink,' Lucinda declared. 'I want to speak to Duncan. This is the last straw.'

'Promises, promises. I can't help you, Cindy. I didn't even know he had tonight off. Are you sure you're not imagining it?'

'Are you calling me a liar?'

'Would I do that? Well, if you're not going to have a drink, I am.' She went up the stairs.

Lucinda followed her. 'I demand to know where he is, what he is up to. You can find out from that admiral, can't you?'

Kristin poured two glasses of sherry, just in case the silly girl changed her mind, sat down, and draped one leg over the other. 'I have no idea. I am certainly not going to ask him.'

'You don't care what may be happening to your son. Or has happened.'

'I do know that whatever it is, it is something he has been told to do.'

'Oh . . . you are impossible.' Lucinda flounced back down the stairs, slammed the front door behind her, and a moment later there came a grating of gears, just audible above the whining of the wind.

The wind! Kristin sipped her drink and gazed out of the window at the trees swaying to and fro. Definitely a gale. And Duncan was probably out in it. With Jamie. That afternoon remained vivid in her memory. So young, so fresh, so eager . . . and so virile. She wondered if she had ruined his life, or given him something to live for. And to fight for.

She hoped he was going to come back. And Duncan, of course.

'Flotilla will reduce speed to one thousand revolutions,' Leeming said over the radio.

'Probably a good idea,' Duncan muttered, and thumbed the intercom. 'I am reducing speed to one thousand, Goring. All well down there?'

'Yes, sir. One thousand it is.'

Duncan eased the throttle back, just as another sheet of green water came hurtling over the bow, momentarily submerging the torpedo tubes before slapping against the bridge shield. So much for not being allowed to go to sea in heavy weather. This *had* to be important.

'I'm not sure there wasn't some ice in that,' Harris commented.

The two officers were alone on the bridge, as the little ship bucked and plunged its way into the seas and the howling wind. Both wore oilskins and heavy gloves, but their faces were exposed to the near freezing air, made to seem colder than perhaps it was because it was coming straight at them.

How the MTB was taking the seas was impossible for them to judge, save by feel, but they could gain some idea by looking at their sisters. In front of them *Eighteen* was plunging from wave to wave, often exposing her propellers; that *Twenty* was doing the same was obvious to both men, because they could hear the sudden high-pitched whine of their propellers as they cavitated. More dramatic was the sight of *Nineteen*, abeam of them if some distance to starboard to make up the other wing of the V formation. She was showing almost her entire hull as she leapt out of the water and came down again with a crash, while sheets of spray flew high into the air.

'Let's hope the yard did a good job of patching us up,' Harris remarked.

'Um. Perhaps you should check that out, Petty Officer.'

'Aye aye, sir. But when are you going to be relieved? You must be frozen stiff.'

'I'll take another half-hour. Check the hull, and see if Wilson can spare a cup of cocoa. Oh, and get a report on the fuel situation from Goring.'

'Aye aye, sir,' Harris agreed, and left the bridge.

Having been reminded of it, Duncan was suddenly aware of how much his shoulders and arms were aching. It was certainly no night to be at sea in a small boat. Travelling along the south coast of England had been relatively pleasant. With the wind in the north the seas had not been big, and the winter sun, if not really dispensing any warmth, had given the scene a wild grandeur, the green to their left contrasting with the blue and white of the sea.

But it had been just on dusk when they had rounded the North Foreland, and then they had been steering straight into the teeth of the gale. Duncan had taken a watch below during the afternoon, but he had felt obliged to resume the helm as conditions worsened and they were approaching the Thames estuary, where there was a lot of shipping. But Leeming had led them through the traffic with consummate skill, and now they were well out into the North Sea to avoid the shallows off the Essex coast. With a long, bleak night ahead of them. Going north. That suggested all manner of interesting possibilities.

Jamie appeared beside him, carrying a mug. 'Cocoa, sir.'

'Good man. What have we got down there?'

'A lot of banging and crashing. But she's doing well.'

'And may I presume you know these waters?'

'I have sailed them, sir. But more often on the French side.'

'Which is cleaner, right?'

'Well, yes, sir, it is. In the Channel. It gets very messy north of Calais. Although it's sandbanks rather than rocks.'

'Well, we're obviously not going there. Fuel?'

'Just over half, sir.'

'That's quite good.'

'Yes, sir. But we've only been using two-thirds power. And now we're down to half-speed.'

'That's better than tearing the guts out of her.' He finished his cocoa, 'Hello.' The radio was crackling.

'Flotilla Leader to all ships. We are going to turn through the banks and put into Harwich. This is for fuel only, but crews will have a couple of hours to stand down. No one is to go ashore.'

'And still not a word of our destination,' Jamie mused.

'I would say it's pretty obvious: Scapa Flow. Don't tell me you've sailed up there as well.'

'No, sir, I have not. Tricky, isn't it?'

'If a U-boat can do it, so can we.'

By dawn they were off the Yorkshire coast. Spirits were high. They had had a couple of hours sleep in the calm of the port and the wind had dropped; it was still fresh, and the sea remained lumpy, but conditions were a great improvement on yesterday. And while they had been in port, Leeming had confided to his two sub-lieutenants, Duncan and Beamish, that they were indeed bound for the fleet base.

'Things have been tightened up since the *Royal Oak*, but they're still agitated, with continuous alarms and false sightings. All of these have to be investigated, and it's a bit much to have destroyers charging about the place all the time. That's going to be our job.'

'Thounds like fun,' Beamish remarked. He was a red-faced young man, RNR, who spoke with a pronounced lisp.

'Any idea how long we'll be up there?' Duncan asked.

'None at all.' Leeming grinned. 'You won't be missing any yacht races, if that's what's bothering you.'

Silly clot, Duncan thought. He was wondering how his womenfolk would take his sudden disappearance. Mother did not bother him; she took all life as it came, even if she believed in living it to her own rules wherever possible. But Lucinda would be doing her nut, especially as they had been going to that party last night.

'Aircraft approaching, sir,' remarked Able Seaman Rawlings. 'Bearing green oh four oh.'

As lookout, he had been using the binoculars. Duncan turned his head, but for a moment could see nothing: the planes were coming out of the low January morning sun. 'How many?'

'Three. Flying low, not more than three thousand feet.'

'Any identification?'

'Not yet, sir.'

The radio crackled. 'On the assumption that those are hostile,' Leeming said, 'the flotilla will scatter, and adopt a zigzag pattern, but keep making north. Confirm.'

'Aye aye,' Duncan and Beamish said.

'I would say they are hostile, sir,' Rawlings said. 'Twin-engined, long body. Could be Messerschmitt 110s.'

'Not possible,' Duncan said. 'No fighter has the range to reach here from Germany and get back. They'll be Heinkels.' He spoke into the tannoy. 'We are being approached by hostile aircraft. I shall now be initiating a zigzag pattern. Machine-gunners will man their weapons, but I want all hands on deck until the emergency is over, wearing their steel helmets and life jackets.'

Harris joined him, to give him his bright-orange inflatable waistcoat and his hard hat. 'You think they'll be able to spot us?'

'Probably not the ships. But they'd have to be blind not to see our wakes.'

'Where do you reckon the RAF is?'

'They'll be around, I'm sure. But we need to remember that even a near miss from a bomb could tear us apart.' He watched the rest of his crew appear on deck, amongst them

Jamie. The boy was the only one of them who had not yet been under fire, but he looked perfectly calm.

'They're definitely approaching, sir,' Harris said.

'Very good. Stations for zigzag procedure,' he shouted.

The four machine-gunners were already in position. Jamie, Wilson the cook and Rawlings the lookout grasped stanchions, and Duncan put the helm hard down, swinging the ship to port, away from the others. Leeming had already increased speed to streak away to the north, while Beamish had fallen away to the east. Duncan counted up to ten, while keeping the rev counter at just over a thousand.

In the far distance he could make out the land, presumably the mountains of Scotland, while behind him his wake carved a broad white band across the heaving blue.

'Here comes one,' Harris said. 'They've split up.'

'Fire whenever possible,' Duncan shouted, and a moment later one of the machine guns chattered into action, followed by the others, but there was no chance of their hitting anything, as in the same instant Duncan opened the throttle, to send the MTB leaping across the waves at near to full speed.

'Missed,' Harris commented.

Duncan looked over his shoulder and saw the plume of water where the bomb had landed, a good hundred yards astern. A twist of the helm had the MTB altering course violently to starboard, to race north-east.

'Here's *Nineteen* coming back,' Harris said.

The MTB was streaking towards them, a huge white bone in its mouth.

'We don't want to run into him,' Duncan muttered, and another twist of the helm sent him more easterly, crashing across *Nineteen*'s wake. Beamish waved, and he waved back.

'Just a game, really,' Harris said.

'What are the nasties doing?'

'Circling, while they try to decide what to do next. Uh-uh, they're coming again. Machine guns.'

'Shit,' Duncan muttered. A line of bullets would be less easy to avoid than a single bomb. 'Frighten them off!' he bellowed, and swung the helm hard to port.

All of the boat's machine guns again opened fire, although again with the MTB swerving to and fro they had very little chance of a hit. However, whether disconcerted or not, the

Heinkel overshot its target, its bullets carving a line of leaping wavelets across the surface of the water.

'Going round,' Duncan shouted, swinging the helm to starboard. As he did so, he saw *Nineteen* coming round as well, perhaps a quarter of a mile away. She also was blazing away with all of her guns, but this Heinkel was sticking to her.

'Hurricanes!' Harris said. 'Well, glory be.'

Duncan cast a hasty glance up at the approaching fighters, six of them, then resumed his concentration to get his boat straight, and heard a tremendous whoompf!

Both he and Harris turned together, and gasped together. Where *Nineteen* had been a moment before was now a column of flame-tinged smoke.

'Holy shit!' Harris muttered.

The machine guns had stopped firing, the crew as shocked as their officers. The Heinkel had soared away, accompanied by her sisters, intent now on escaping the Hurricanes. Duncan spun the wheel to turn back, at the same time reducing speed.

'What the hell happened?' Leeming's voice was strained; he had also turned and was coming back.

'She stopped a bullet,' Duncan said.

'They've got one of the bastards,' Rawlings called.

Duncan looked over his shoulder, saw the bomber in flames falling towards the sea. Above it were three floating parachutes.

'I hope the buggers freeze,' Harris growled.

'I'll get that lot,' Leeming said. 'Any survivors from *Nineteen*?'

Twenty had now lost way almost completely, and was moving slowly towards the casualty. But there was nothing there, save for a smouldering, sizzling mess on the surface.

'There are no survivors, sir,' Duncan said.

'Shit!' Leeming commented. 'Resume course. Half-speed until I catch up with you.' He had also slowed right down as he manoeuvred to approach the now floating airmen.

'I can help you,' Duncan suggested.

'No, keep going. This little fracas might have attracted other attention, and one of us at least has got to get to Scapa.'

'Aye aye,' Duncan acknowledged and increased speed again as he turned to the north.

Jamie had come up to the bridge. 'At least they can't have known what hit them.'

'That'll cheer up their wives and sweethearts,' Harris observed.

And mothers, Duncan thought. 'Have the men stand down, Mr Harris.'

'In a brief action in the North Sea this afternoon,' the BBC newsreader said, 'one of the Navy's new fast motor torpedo boats was sunk by enemy air attack. However, one of the enemy aircraft, reported to be a Heinkel 111, was shot down by the RAF. The crew were picked up. Unfortunately, there were no survivors from the MTB, which apparently exploded. Next of kin are being informed.'

Kristin switched off the set. She felt at once cold and sick. 'Next of kin are being informed.' No one had informed her, yet. But it didn't have to be Duncan . . . and Jamie! The two lives she valued more than any others.

It had been her idea that they should serve together, to lend each other mutual support, to allow Duncan to draw on Jamie's knowledge of the sea and navigation, to allow Jamie, by observing Duncan, to raise his social sights and approach to life more to the level she was looking for. With what ultimately in mind? That was not a question she was prepared to answer, truthfully, even in the privacy of her own brain – because she was afraid of the answer. Easy to pretend that she had a streak of the Svengalis in her. Or, perhaps more accurately, the Henry Higginses, with Jamie playing the part of Eliza Doolittle in a sex-reversal role. Now . . .

She was being paranoid. With some twenty MTBs in service, the odds were twenty to one against the loss being Duncan's boat. Yet the way he had suddenly taken off without a word to her or to Lucinda . . . He had certainly been sent somewhere, very hurriedly and very secretly. She had to find out. She reached for the telephone, and it rang. Oh, my God! she thought. But didn't they always send a black-edged telegram? She picked up the receiver. '*Digame.*'

'Krissy?!' Lucinda's voice was shrill.

'Shit!' Kristin muttered.

'What? What did you say? I didn't hear you.'

'I said, how lovely to hear your voice. I assume you have been listening to the news.'

'He's dead! Duncan's dead! Oh, my God, he's dead!' She began to sob, noisily.

'Oh, do pull yourself together. Why should he be dead?'

'Didn't you hear? The boat blew up. There were no survivors. The man said so.'

'But he didn't say it was Duncan's boat, did he?'

'He said it was a motor torpedo boat. That's Duncan's boat, isn't it?'

Kristin sighed. 'Duncan commands an MTB, yes. But it's not the only one. Listen, go and pour yourself a double brandy and then take a pill. I'll be in touch the moment I hear something.' She hung up. She was being unreasonably hard on the girl, she knew. Lucinda was only replicating her own thoughts, even if in a somewhat hysterical manner. But she felt like having a double brandy herself.

She picked up the phone again, gave the number. 'I'm afraid Admiral Lonsdale is busy,' the woman said. 'If you have a legitimate query, I will put you through to the duty officer.'

'I assume I am speaking to Miss Williams,' Kristin said, assuming her 'let it be done, now' tone.

'Why, yes. Ah . . .'

'Lady Eversham. We have met. Kindly put me through to the admiral.'

'Ah . . .' There was a click, but Miss Williams left the key open, no doubt, Kristin thought, deliberately. 'I'm sorry to bother you, sir. I have Lady Eversham on the line, insisting – well . . . Shall I get rid of her?'

'I'll take it,' Jimmy said. 'Kristin!'

So much for her, Kristin thought. 'Jimmy! I'm sorry . . .'

'I quite understand. He's all right.'

'Oh, my God! I think I'm going to cry.'

'I didn't know you did that sort of thing.'

'But . . .'

'His boat was in the flotilla that was attacked, but was not hit. The other – well, it seems to have been rather a nasty business. Those boats really are terribly vulnerable.'

'Duncan thinks they're marvellous.'

'He's a very enthusiastic officer. Well, ah . . .'

'You mean, if he survives.'

'We must all hope to survive, Kristin. Would you . . . ah . . .?'

'No,' Kristin said. 'No more string-pulling. He's doing what he wants to do, and what he's required to do. Thanks a million, Jimmy. You have made my day.'

'And what are you going to do with the rest of the day?'

'Get quietly drunk,' Kristin told him.

'There it is!' Rawlings shouted, standing in the bows of the MTB. 'There . . . Shit! It's gone. Must have dived.'

'In eighteen feet of water?' Harris asked.

'There was something, sir.'

'Of course there was,' Duncan agreed. 'But it can't have been a submarine.'

The MTB was proceeding slowly and carefully through the shallows on the eastern side of the sea loch; in here the water was calm, and visibility was excellent. The alarm had been given by a watcher on the shore that something was moving in the water, and they had been obliged to respond, in the middle of their lunch.

All the crew were now on deck, and someone called, 'There it is again.'

Heads turned. 'That's a seal,' Jamie said.

'So it is,' Duncan agreed. 'We've probably ruined his digestion as much as he's ruined ours.' He pushed the throttle slightly forward, and the boat moved quietly through the still waters. 'Make to port captain, Petty Officer. Intruder investigated and ascertained to be seal. Never mind,' he told his crestfallen sailors: 'in another week we'll be home on leave.'

He gazed at the buoys marking the wreck of the *Royal Oak*. Like his men he was thoroughly bored. They had now been in this back of beyond for more than three months, mainly in appalling weather, and with absolutely no action beyond an occasional, and very limited, air raid, which, as the MTB pontoon was roofed with concrete, had put them at very little risk.

This had been bad for morale, he knew. The last time they had fired a shot in anger had been moments before *Nineteen* had blown up. Thus that was the last action memory any of them had, and therefore it was the memory they would all carry into combat the next time they were engaged. The problem was compounded by the fact that they did not know how it had happened. A bomb falling squarely on the tiny wooden hull would have been acceptable, because it would have had to be a freak. But suppose it had simply been a bullet penetrating the wooden skin and setting off the still half-full fuel tanks? When in action, and for all their speed and manoeuvrability, that would always be a possibility.

Now they were due for a break, and he hoped they would benefit. As for himself, of course he wanted to see Mother again, and Lucifer, and see that *Kristin* was in good shape; although Mother had in fact apparently checked the yacht out from time to time, according to her letters, he wanted to see for himself. As for the rest of it, however . . . There had also been letters from Lucinda, reams of them. As she did not know where he was, she had to write care of the Naval Post Office, and as deliveries were not very regular, her letters were liable to arrive in batches of three.

They made heavy going. The recriminations about his sudden disappearance in January had been submerged in the increasing recriminations when he had had to tell her that their March wedding was no longer a possibility. He had not yet had a reply to his note that he would be available in April, but he did not suppose she was going to be very happy about that either. This was because he had been unable to give her a firm date for his furlough. He had suggested that their best bet, if she really wanted to get married while the war was on, was a registry office, although he knew that she had set her heart on the whole hog. She and Mother wouldn't even be able to arrange a reception, with hardly more than a week's notice. Mother, of course, would be hugely amused by the whole situation. He had never known Lucinda to be hugely amused about anything.

Which brought up the real point: did *he* want to get married – to anyone right now, much less Lucinda Browning? It had seemed a good idea at first. She was an attractive, cuddly little thing, certainly on his social and intellectual level, and in the early days of their relationship had seemed very eager to please. But that had been before last summer's racing season had begun.

He had tried taking her out for a day's jolly on *Kristin* last April, just on a year ago. They had not left the Solent, and she had been violently seasick, as well as terrified every time the schooner had heeled to the wind. After that she had declined further invitations, until the day she had said, 'You are going to get rid of that boat once we're married?'

He had been appalled. 'Get rid of *Kristin*? "That boat", as you call it, is my life.'

'Up till now. But my darling Duncan, *I* am going to be your life from now on.'

His inability to confirm that statement had led to their first quarrel. He had, in fact, presumed that their engagement was at an end, without a great deal of regret. But that wasn't the case. She had obviously felt that once they were married she would be able to take control of his life. Had he been his mother, now, he would simply have told her, 'Bugger off; if you can't fit into my life style, bad luck.' But a gentleman simply didn't do that sort of thing, and much as he envied his mother's carefree and, some would say, irresponsible approach to life he was terribly aware that he was a gentleman, and the heir to a title.

The trouble was, while he would never have regarded himself as a lady's man, he did like female company, of the right sort. Before that fateful party when he had fallen under the spell of a bubbly, vivacious and, he now knew, unrepresentative little blonde, he had had a succession of girlfriends, few of whom had seriously resisted the temptations of bed. Having become engaged, however inadvertently, he had determined to turn over a new leaf and save himself only for his future wife.

This had not been difficult to do last summer: he always did eschew women every summer in favour of sailing his boat, and the end of the season had coincided with the call to arms, with all its excitement and consumption of time. But that had been eight months ago, and for the past three he had done nothing save parade around this landlocked harbour . . . and chase the occasional seal. He was definitely feeling extremely randy. But even if he didn't still also feel tied to Lucinda, there was simply no alternative available. The rather raw-boned Scottish girls they encountered ashore seemed highly suspicious of any sailor, and in any event they had been warned off by the padre soon after their arrival, officers and men, with the simple reminder that up here in the heart of Presbyterianism, anyone who got a girl in pod would be required to marry her forthwith. There were quite a few Wrens about, spick and span in their uniforms, and some of them were extremely attractive; but by the rules of the service they also were untouchable, certainly without complete mutual consent and a good deal of assistance from her barrack-mates in keeping it quiet.

So, was he planning to return to Lymington and put the rocks to Lucinda? He wondered what she'd do if he refused to accept 'Oh really, Duncan, do stop that' as an answer.

The boat coasted into her dock; he handled her now as easily as he handled his Bugatti. 'Close her down,' he said into the tannoy, 'and fall out.'

'Aye aye, sir,' came the reply from various parts of the ship.

Duncan went below, and down the after companionway. Jamie was just emerging from the engine room, wiping his hands on a rag. 'All well?'

'Just about, sir. How long have we got?'

The sunken *Nineteen* had been replaced, so they were able to operate in lengthy shifts. 'Twenty-four hours, anyway.'

'Then with your permission, sir, I'd like to run an oil change.'

'You have it. Big job?'

'No, sir. Just tedious.'

'How long?'

'A couple of hours.'

'How much assistance will you need?'

'I don't need help, sir.'

'Good man. Carry on. And then, next week, it's home. Looking forward to that?'

'Ah . . . I suppose so, sir.'

Duncan frowned. 'You don't sound very sure.'

'Well . . . right now I'm doing what I like best.'

'Messing about with an engine. You must have a girl waiting for you at home? – a good-looking fellow like you?'

'I don't actually have a girl, sir.'

'Then why are you blushing?' Duncan grinned, and slapped him on the shoulder. 'I'm not going to pry. I'm sure a week at home will do you good. Providing you keep your hands off the wrong sort of engine. Stick to the one that runs on petrol rather than alcohol.'

He went aft, into his cabin, and closed the door, leaving Jamie staring after him. If you only knew, he thought. But if he were ever to find out! As for him . . . Obviously if Duncan turned up at home for a week's furlough Kristin would realize that the whole crew would also be on leave, and then . . . His trouble was that while he was terrified of seeing her again, he desperately wanted to do so. To think of again holding so much naked *woman* in his arms almost made him feel sick with desire. But where could it end? Where could it possibly end?

Petty Officer Harris slid down the companion. 'Skipper down here?'

'He's in his cabin,' Jamie said.

Harris knocked. 'Excuse me, sir. Message from flagship. All commanding officers to report immediately.'

Duncan opened the door. 'You reckon that means me, Petty Officer?'

'Well, sir, it said all. Better to report and be turned away than not to go.'

'Good thinking. Take command.' He put on his cap, hurried along the dock to where a launch was waiting, as were Leeming and the *Fifteen* boat commander, Jeremy Orton. 'Any idea what this is all about?'

'Must be big,' Leeming commented.

They were ferried out to *Warspite*, a thirty-six-thousand-ton monster armed with eight fifteen-inch guns. She was an old ship, launched in 1913, having been one of the first oil-fired battleships in the Navy, but still represented enormous firepower; Duncan had to wonder if he would ever serve in, much less captain, such a floating city.

They were piped aboard, saluted the bridge, and were escorted by a lieutenant into the wardroom, where there was a considerable assembly already. Rear Admiral Whitfield greeted each man as he entered, with his invariable mixture of courtesy, humour and knowledge. 'Leeming! I saw you at it this morning.'

'That was Morant, sir.'

'Ah, yes. Morant.' The admiral shook hands. 'They're dragging their feet over your investiture, aren't they? I suppose they have to wait for a full roster to fill His Majesty's morning. What was the problem today?'

'I'm afraid it was a seal, sir.'

'Are you partial to seal meat?'

'I don't know, sir. I let it go.'

'Sporting of you.'

He turned his head as his aide-de-camp stood beside him. 'I think everyone is here, sir.'

'Very good.' Whitfield walked to the end of the room, and every officer came to attention. 'At ease. I am sure you will all be pleased to know that we are going into action at last. At least, there is a prospect of it. As you know, the Norwegians have been somewhat partial in preserving their neutrality: they forbid us to enter their territorial waters, while permitting Jerry full use of them. Just remember *Altmark* and *Cossack*. That what was virtually a German warship – as she was tender to the *Admiral Graf Spee* – should have been allowed to take refuge in their fjords to avoid capture, although it was well known that she had on board three hundred British merchant seaman, taken from ships sunk by the pocket battleship, and bound for Nazi prison camps, was a gross breach of the laws of neutrality. That the Norwegian government should scream foul when Captain Vian took *Cossack* into the fjord, seized *Altmark* and freed our people is outrageous. Now, in addition to all that, we have learned that German vessels bearing iron ore from the north of Sweden are being permitted to use Norwegian territorial waters to regain their homeland, with their cargos of essential war-making materials. We have therefore received a signal from Mr Churchill, the First Lord of the Admiralty, that the Cabinet has agreed that we can no longer kowtow to neutral opinion, but should take action immediately. Our destroyers are being equipped now and are being sent in to lay a carpet of mines throughout those prohibited waters.'

He looked round their faces. 'The Norwegian government is being informed, as I speak, that the operation will commence tomorrow morning at dawn. Obviously we want the job completed as rapidly as possible, without bloodshed if possible. It is not anticipated that the Royal Norwegian Navy will attempt to interfere. As you probably know, that navy is a very small force, and its heaviest units are a couple of old and outdated coastal battleships, displacing only a few thousand tons each, and with limited firepower. However, it is our intention to provide our ships with all the protection they may need, and so the entire fleet it putting to sea at dawn as well. Let me emphasize that as far as any Norwegian ships are concerned, this is not to be an aggressive operation. Wherever possible, any Norwegian ship appearing to be preparing to fire on our people, or actually doing so, should be warned of the consequences. If, after receiving such a warning they continue to fire, then you are empowered to return fire, but again, wherever possible, your aim should be to dissuade or deter your opponents from further action.'

Another pause, another look around the now sombre faces. Duncan had no quarrel with the necessity for the operation, but he could not help but feel – as he knew his fellow officers would be feeling – that what was going to happen was a brutal bullying act, only justified by the interests of national survival.

'However,' Whitfield said. 'There is another aspect of the situation which may, at the end of the day, be of the more importance. By the rules of civilized warfare, we are also obliged to inform the German government of our intention so that they can, if they have any sense, cease this illicit traffic before there is serious loss of life. On the other hand, they may attempt to do something about it. Thus the heavy units of the fleet will be in close support of the destroyers. I shall be in personal command in *Warspite*. Thank you, gentlemen. Each of the mine-laying skippers will receive precise instructions as to the area for which he is responsible. Our aim is to have the operation completed and be back home in forty-eight hours. Good fortune.' His gaze swept the faces for a last time. 'I would like the three MTB commanders to join me in my day cabin.'

The three lieutenants exchanged glances, while the rest of the officers filed from the wardroom, each trying to work out why they had been singled out for special attention. A flag lieutenant was waiting to escort them to the admiral's quarters, where Whitfield was waiting for them.

'Sit down, gentlemen,' he invited. 'You may smoke.'

'We do not, sir,' Leeming said. 'It does not go with our ships.'

Whitfield raised his eyebrows.

'Petrol engines,' Leeming explained.

'Oh, quite. Your boats are somewhat vulnerable.'

'Well, sir, I suppose any boat is vulnerable when it is being shot at.'

'Point taken. However, some are more vulnerable than others. I have a task for which your boats could have been specially made, and for which they are the only possible ships, given the time span available. But I must require you to volunteer, if you think it can be done. If you do not, then I wish

you to say so, and it will not adversely affect either your repu-
tations or your records. Understood?'

'Yes, sir,' the three lieutenants said together.

'Very good. I am informed that you are equipped to carry
depth charges.'

'We do carry depth charges, sir,' Leeming said.

Whitfield glanced at one of the sheets of paper on his desk.
'Four, is it? I am also informed that if these charges were to
be removed, they could be replaced by mines – as many as
twelve per boat.'

'I should think that would be feasible, sir.'

'Very good. Andrews.'

The flag lieutenant unfolded the chart on the table.

'The fleet,' Whitfield said, 'is putting to sea tomorrow
morning to cover the destroyer flotillas which will do the actual
mine-laying. Now, we know that the Norwegians do not maintain adequate patrols in the Norwegian Sea, so it is unlikely
that they will become aware of what we are doing until they
are informed of our plans. Then there will almost certainly be
protests, and a diplomatic incident, and that sort of thing. But
hopefully the job will have been completed before these get
very far and there will have been no loss of blood. However,
we also need to mine the waters of the Kattegat, to discourage
any trade which may have come through Norway by train, to
be shipped down the outside of Denmark to the Elbe. Now,
there is no possibility of a flotilla of destroyers penetrating
those waters undetected, certainly if they are supported by any
heavy units. The Norwegians certainly maintain patrols there,
if only to protect themselves from any possible German moves,
and our submarines tell us that the Germans also maintain a
presence in these waters. Of course we have submarines capable
of laying mines, but as I have said, in the context of this operation that would simply take too long.

'The dilemma therefore is how to lay the mines tomorrow
night without being forced to engage any Norwegian force,
which in this instance may possibly be supported, rather
grotesquely, by Germany.' He straightened to regard the three
young officers.

'Point taken, sir,' Leeming said. 'In, drop our mines, and
out, before anyone realizes we are there. May I measure the
distance?'

'It is just over three hundred and fifty nautical miles,' Andrews said. 'And your range is . . .?'

'One thousand. Piece of cake, sir.'

'It is liable to be anything but that if you are detected,' Whitfield pointed out. 'That is why I am asking you to volunteer.'

Leeming glanced at Duncan and Orton, and received brief nods. 'We volunteer, sir.'

'Very good. Timing?'

'To be on the right side of any mishaps, fourteen hours in, fourteen hours back, one hour allowed for dropping the mines. Those are maximum figures.'

'You'll want to be off the Norwegian coast in darkness. Fortunately, there is still a lot of it about. So let us allow a time span of nine hours of darkness. That will be from eight at night to five the next morning. That means leaving Scapa at ten tomorrow morning. That is eight hours after the fleet itself sails. It will involve ten hours of daylight across the North Sea, and a further ten hours of daylight on the return journey.' Another look at their faces. 'There won't be any air cover until you are nearly home.'

'I think *Nineteen* was unlucky, sir.'

'Let us hope so. Well, gentlemen, thank you. You will commence the mine-loading immediately. I will wish you good fortune. There will be leave for you and your crews when this job is completed. Carry on.'

'Thank you, sir.' They saluted and left the cabin.

'There's going to be some gnashing of the teeth in Lymington when I don't turn up,' Duncan remarked.

'Ah, you'll only be a couple of days late,' Orton pointed out, 'if the man keeps his word about leave when we come back.'

Leeming grunted.

'What, don't you believe him? He's an admiral,' Orton protested.

'Oh, I believe him,' Leeming said. 'But I wouldn't start looking forward to it until we see *if* we come back.'

Death and Glory

As ordered, work began immediately on the three MTBs, dockyard hands taking them over to remove the depth charges and replace them with rows of mines, watched with interest by the crew. Duncan found it disturbing that in virtually being commanded to volunteer, which he would have done anyway, he had also been volunteering the lives of his men, entirely without their knowledge or concurrence.

They certainly had to be put in the picture, at least partially. 'As you may be gathering,' he told them, 'we are going to mine the Norwegian coastal waters to stop the German trade in iron ore. This is a fleet operation, and we have been allotted a very small section of it, but it is one for which we are uniquely equipped because of our speed. We leave at ten tomorrow, and we will be back for lunch on Tuesday. Any questions?'

'Does this mean our leave has been cancelled, sir?' AB Grimes asked.

'By no means. It may be delayed by one day. We were due to go on the tenth, now it may be the eleventh.' He grinned at them. 'As they don't know precisely when we're coming, our loved ones won't know we're late. A word, Goring.'

Jamie waited on the bridge.

'Did you complete your oil change?'

'I was going to do it after lunch, sir.'

'And I told you that you had twenty-four hours at least. There is no possibility of a hitch? If there is, the change will have to be postponed.'

'I don't anticipate a hitch, sir. Is it a long trip?'

'Something over seven hundred miles.'

'All at fairly close to full speed?'

'That is correct.'

'Then I would say the oil change is very necessary, sir. We

certainly don't want a hitch while we're under way. I should also say that the tanks are only just over half-full.'

Duncan nodded. 'The moment you have completed your change, we shall fuel up to the brim.'

'Yes, sir. Big job, is it?'

'A very big job, Jamie. And I won't pretend it won't be dangerous.'

Jamie grinned. 'But judging by what happened to *Nineteen*, if we get hit, we won't know a thing about it.'

Duncan regarded him for some seconds, then he nodded. 'You're probably right.' If that really is a comfort, he thought.

Even if no one save himself knew where they were actually going, he could feel the tension building. They had a lot to do that afternoon, preparing the ship and, as soon as Jamie was ready, motoring across to the fuel barge; the other two boats had already topped up. But once that was completed, there was nothing to do but wait.

Leeming came over at dusk to have a gin and see for himself that all was ready. 'It's a good forecast: south-westerly Three to Four, so it'll be a quarter sea. If it doesn't change, there'll be a bit of a chop coming back, but I shouldn't think we'll care by then. The bad news is that visibility is going to be good throughout. So we'll just keep our fingers crossed that everyone on the other side is feeling dozy. Your people all right?'

'Like me, and you, they want to be at it.'

Leeming nodded, finished his drink, and stood up. 'There will, of course, be absolute radio silence until we're back here. If anything goes wrong – anything at all – you cannot call for help except by lamp.' He grinned. 'On the other hand, if the forecast is the least accurate, we'll be in visual contact all the way, there and back.' He shook hands. 'There'll be champagne for lunch on Tuesday.'

The very long night was ended abruptly by the bugle calls and the sound of immense engines beginning to rumble, and huge anchor chains being weighed. Duncan dressed and went on deck to watch the fleet put to sea. His crew joined him. 'Will they see action, sir?' Harris asked.

'They don't mean to, if it can be avoided,' Duncan said.

'Cor blimey, ain't it empty,' Rawlings remarked, as the last ship passed through the narrows. 'Just us chickens.'

There didn't seem much point in attempting to go back to bed, even if he knew that it was going to be a long twenty-four hours once the operation started. The moment it was light Duncan went ashore and walked up the shallow hill that overlooked the sea; inside the landlocked harbour it was impossible to gauge the conditions outside. But as Leeming had foretold, they looked good enough, with a fresh south-westerly breeze pushing up the occasional whitecap, while in the distance he could still make out the larger fleet units beneath the plumes of smoke.

He turned back to look at the harbour, which, however suddenly bereft of warships, was the usual hive of activity. Apart from the various shore offices, work was still going on to make the anchorage utterly safe from any enemy. There were several entrances to the Flow itself, but because of the strong tidal currents, often setting right across the gaps, no effort had previously been made to seal these, as it had been felt that no submarine would dare attempt them submerged, or even on the surface, which would necessarily have to be at night.

U-47 had proved that theory to be false, so now all the subsidiary channels were being blocked by rubble which were to become causeways; there were even plans to lay a road along the top of each. This left only the main channel open, and this was constantly guarded as well as patrolled by the MTBs. It was going to have to do without them, for the next twenty-four hours, but anyone who did get in would find nothing to shoot at anyhow.

'It's a grand sight, isn't it?'

Duncan turned, sharply. He had been so wrapped in his thoughts he had not heard the young woman approach, although she was wearing Wren uniform, which necessarily entailed heavy shoes. Her shoulder straps indicated that she was a second officer, which approximated his own rank, and although he knew that there were very few women who did not look attractive in uniform, this young woman was excep-tionally so, if only because she presented such a strong contrast to either of the two women who were currently dominating his life. Of medium height, she was slim, with ankles good enough to suggest that the legs above would match. Her hair was black, worn in the regulation tight bun on the back of her head beneath her cap, but again there appeared to be enough of it to be worth releasing – while her face, with its clipped features and lively green eyes, was intensely attractive. As was her low voice. 'I startled you. Alison Brunel. We have met.'

'Indeed.' They had encountered each other at various fleet receptions over the past couple of months, but had never got close enough to hold a conversation. 'You know, there is something I have wanted to ask you. Brunel?'

'Sorry,' she said. 'No famous relatives. Not even remotely. Whereas you . . .'

'The fact that my grandfather, for some totally obscure reason, was given an hereditary peerage, is no claim to fame.'

'But you have some. Sinking a U-boat, single-handed.'

'It was actually nine-handed. But as you seem to know so much about me, may I not know something about you?'

She assumed a quizzical expression. 'Do you think you'd be interested?'

'I know I'd be interested.'

'Mm. I suspect I may have made a mistake in breaking in on your reverie. I only wanted to wish you good fortune.'

He frowned. 'That is top secret.'

'Indeed. I command the cipher section.'

'Ah!'

'And I should not be talking to you at all. But you looked so pensive. Now I must be getting back.'

'Hold on. You haven't answered my question.'

'Ask me again, when you come back. Tomorrow. Listen, come back and I'll buy you a bottle of champagne.'

'Then I will come back. But at least tell me what you were doing up here.'

'I was taking the air.' She smiled. 'And following you.'

Now what the devil had she meant by that? He had been tempted to follow her, but time was passing and she could well be a distraction from what lay ahead. On the other hand, she had suggested she wouldn't mind running into him again, when he got back from his mission. Supposing he did.

Then what of Lucinda? What indeed?

'What's it like out there, sir?' Harris asked, as they had breakfast.

'Couldn't be better.'

'Signal from Leader, sir,' Clarke said, reading the Morse flashes. 'Prepare for departure.'

'Stand to,' Duncan said. 'All correct below, Goring? Bilges clean?'

'Aye aye, sir.'

'Very good.' Duncan put on his greatcoat – even if it was mid-morning and mid-April he knew it would be cold out on the water – and climbed on to the bridge, followed by Harris. Leeming's engine was already purring, and when the lieutenant turned round to survey the rest of his flotilla, he saluted. Leeming returned the salute, and the Leader moved quietly away from its berth.

Duncan switched on the engine, listened to the reassuring growl from beneath him. 'Cast off forward, cast off aft,' he called.

The warps were taken in, followed by the fenders. 'Keep your eye on the Leader, Mr Harris,' Duncan said, concentrating in following *Eighteen* into the narrow passage.

'Aye aye, sir.'

Duncan glanced astern, to see *Fifteen* following; then they were in the open sea.

'Signal from Leader, sir,' Harris said. 'Maintain fifteen hundred.'

'Acknowledge,' Duncan said, and eased the throttle forward. At just over twenty knots the MTB took the light chop easily, while they were hardly conscious of the breeze, coming in over the starboard quarter. Ahead of them lay nothing but open water; there was no sign of the rest of the fleet, disappeared over the northern horizon, and there was no other shipping to be seen. 'Very good, Mr Harris,' Duncan said. 'Watch below can stand down. And for the afternoon.'

'Aye aye, sir.' Harris gave the order and left the bridge. Duncan's instructions meant that he and the rest of the watch below would have nearly six hours off; the forenoon watch, which at sea lasted from 0800 to 1200, was only half completed, and the skipper was volunteering to take the afternoon watch, 1200 to 1600, as well. That would be followed by the two short, or dog, watches of two hours each. This system was necessary, because if each day was merely divided into six four-hour watches, the same men would be on the same watch every day throughout each voyage; this would include the least popular middle watch, from 2400 to 0400. Using the dog-watch system enabled each watch to change their hours on duty every day. This did not actually apply to the captain, who did not officially take a watch, but Harris knew that he enjoyed helming and was perfectly content with that.

The watch system did not apply to the engineer or the cook at all. Wilson had to be available to serve hot meals or drinks whenever required, and Jamie had to be on call at all times. By the same token, however, as long as everything was running smoothly his time was his own, and he now came up on to the bridge to join Duncan, who had already been joined by Rawlings, to sweep both the horizon and the sky with binoculars. 'Nice ride, sir,' he ventured.

'Let's hope it stays this way,' Duncan agreed.

'Aircraft bearing green three zero, sir,' Rawlings said.

'Identify.'

'He's pretty high.'

'Think he'll spot us?' Jamie asked.

'If he's looking, he'll have to see the wakes,' Duncan said.

'He's not approaching, sir,' Rawlings said.

'Then he has other things on his mind. Keep an eye on him.'

A few minutes later the unidentified aircraft had disappeared. Leeming had undoubtedly seen it too, but he made no signal, and the flotilla continued to the east, the sun now dropping behind them. Now that they were well out to sea, Duncan handed over the helm to Rawlings, but remained on deck until 1600, then retired to his bunk for a couple of hours. When he returned to the bridge the sun was setting, and cloud was gathering.

'Leader signalling, sir,' Harris said. 'Increase speed to two thousand.'

'Very good, Mr Harris. Acknowledge and carry on.'

The MTB surged ahead, now approximating thirty knots: Leeming obviously felt that with the approach of darkness they were less likely to be spotted by any patrolling aircraft, but in fact they had seen nothing since that solitary plane soon after leaving Scapa, and as nothing had devolved from that he obviously had not seen them.

Duncan used his glasses to peer into the gloom, but could see nothing. They were still over a hundred miles from the Norwegian coast. But now they would be closing rapidly. No one felt like taking a watch below; the tension was almost tangible. Wilson served dinner at eight, by which time it was pitch dark. At ten, the Leader began signalling.

'Course one one oh,' Harris said.

'Acknowledge.'

'How does he know where we are, sir?' Jamie asked.

'He doesn't, for certain. He's operating on dead reckoning,' Duncan told him, and went below to mark the alteration and assumed position on the chart. Dead reckoning, known to some as inertia navigation, in the proper hands was remarkably accurate, and was more likely to be accurate for the MTBs than any other craft. It consisted of relating the speed and course of the vessel to all the other factors that might be involved and available, such as windage, obtained by studying the wake in relation to the course being steered, or tidal movement, obtained from the various tidal charts that were available, illustrating the direction and speed for every hour. Low in the water, the motorboats were not susceptible to sideways movement except in exceptional conditions, and the wind had been light throughout the voyage, while with their speed they were not very susceptible to tidal movement either. He worked out his own position, and made it seventy miles to the Norwegian coast and, on the course they had been steering since leaving Scapa, some forty miles north of where they wanted to be. Hence the alteration.

The three boats were now streaking south of east. 'Leader signalling, sir,' Rawlings said. 'Stand by.'

'Acknowledge. You'll take aft, Mr Harris.'

'Aye aye, sir. We are going to reduce speed before dropping these things?'

'I should bloody well hope so.'

Harris made his way aft, followed by the four sailors who would handle the dropping of the mines.

'Leader signalling, sir. Land in sight. Reduce speed one thousand. Course one six oh.'

'Acknowledge.' Duncan himself was on the helm now, and

he brought the speed down, glancing astern to make sure *Fifteen* was conforming; a collision while each boat was carrying twelve mines could be the end for all of them. *Twenty* was now caught in her own wake, and bobbed like a cork for several minutes.

'Lights, sir,' Jamie said.

Duncan peered into the darkness and saw the winking light. 'Farsund Head. We're bang on. Stand by, Mr Harris,' he called.

'Aye aye, sir.'

'I see a ship, sir,' Jamie said.

'Eh? Where away?'

'Green twenty.'

'Where are her lights?'

'She's not showing lights, sir. And she's big. Holy smoke, there's another. And another.'

'Take the helm,' Duncan snapped. 'Give me those glasses.' He braced himself and levelled the binoculars in the required direction. Still invisible to the naked eye, he could now make out the dark shapes of several large vessels, steaming north. And showing no lights!

'Rawlings! Make to Leader. Look one eight oh.'

'Leader is signalling, sir. Drop mines and run.'

'You heard the man, Mr Harris.'

'Aye aye, sir.'

'Radio signalling, sir,' Clarke said.

'What?' Leeming had said that under no circumstances should they use their radios. 'Tell me.'

'*MTB Eighteen* to Flagship. Have encountered large German force steaming north, position fifty-seven degrees ten minutes north latitude, seven degrees twenty minutes east longitude, forty-five miles south-west Norwegian coast. I repeat—' A searchlight beam cut through the darkness to pick up the boat, and almost immediately there were several flashes of light and a huge explosion, much greater than when *Nineteen* had gone up in January.

The crew of *Twenty* stared in horror until Duncan realized that burning fragments of wood were dropping all around him and on to his wooden decks; he gunned the engine to move clear.

Harris had returned to the bridge. 'She can't have got rid of her mines,' he muttered.

'*Fifteen* signalling, sir,' Rawlings said.

Duncan looked back at the flashing light.

'What now?' Rawlings spelled out.

'Searchlights, sir,' Jamie said.

Several beams were playing over the water.

'Those are big ships,' Clarke said.

Harris was using his glasses. 'That's a heavy cruiser.'

'Does Jerry have anything like that?' Rawlings asked.

'*Hipper*, for a start,' Duncan said. 'Make to *Fifteen*. Run.'

'I don't think they know how many of us there are, sir,' Jamie said.

The searchlights were still playing over the surface of the sea, but had not yet picked up either of the other two boats.

'If we could sneak in and get that cruiser . . .' Harris said.

Twenty had been moving slowly away from the casualty.

'Or lure her into that minefield,' Jamie said.

Duncan looked from one to the other. 'You realize we'd be committing suicide.'

'*Fifteen* is coming back,' Rawlings said.

All their heads turned. They couldn't see the boat in the darkness, but her white bow wave was clearly visible.

'Shit!' Duncan muttered. 'Well, here we go. Torpedo crew to foredeck.'

The men scrambled forward as he brought the boat round in a sharp turn and opened the throttle. As he did so they were rocked by *Fifteen*'s wake as she roared by at full speed. Orton seemed to have entirely lost his head. But then, Duncan reflected, haven't we all?

The night was now criss-crossed with searchlights and turned into a cacophony of whistles and bells. Both the lights and the noise indicated that there were at least twenty warships out there, and more vessels beyond. Such a sizeable force, closing the Norwegian coast, could only mean an invasion, and no doubt Leeming had felt it his duty to break radio silence and inform the admiral what was happening, but Duncan couldn't see it would do a lot of good: this fleet would be ashore long before the Norwegians could be warned or take action – supposing they had the wherewithal *to* take action.

So Leeming had sacrificed himself and his crew to no real purpose. As for where that left them . . . For the moment all the German attention was taken by *Fifteen*, screaming through the darkness. The jangle of alarm bells seemed to grow louder as the white streaks of the torpedoes were spotted and the big cruiser violently altered course. But she was still using her secondary armament of five-inch guns, and a moment later *Fifteen* exploded.

To that moment Duncan had been unable to fire for fear of hitting his sister ship. But now he reckoned he was both within range and had a clear shot. 'Fire one!' he bawled. 'Fire two! And let's get the hell out of here,' he muttered as the torpedoes hissed away, swinging the helm hard over and opening the throttle to maximum. There was nothing he could do about *Fifteen*'s crew, even in the unlikely event that anyone had survived the explosion. But now there was another explosion and a cheer from his men. He looked back to see flames and hear more sirens.

'What did we get?' he asked.

'I don't know,' Harris said, 'but it was something.'

The searchlights were back scouring the water, but some distance behind them. Guns were still firing as well, but obviously without any clear idea of a target.

'They still don't know how many of us there are,' Jamie remarked.

'Well, maybe we accomplished something,' Duncan said, and thought, Let's hope it'll be worth the lives of eighteen good men.

'I think we did, sir,' Harris said. 'Look there?'

Duncan looked over his shoulder, just in time to catch the red glow before it faded. With the engine roaring and at this distance it was impossible to hear the explosion, but that there had been one could not be doubted.

'One of them's hit a mine,' Jamie said.

The crew cheered.

'Come in, Lieutenant,' invited Captain Lawrence, who as port captain commanded the base in the absence of the admiral.

The Wren secretary held the door for Duncan, and he saluted.

'At ease,' Lawrence said. 'Sit down.'

Duncan sank into the chair before the desk.

'You've had quite a night,' the captain observed.

'It seemed to go on a long time.'

'Well, let me say right away that you did a great job. Pity about the other two boats, but getting off that warning, despite the situation in which you found yourself, was both courageous and vital. The admiral wants to see you, whenever he gets back. There'll be a gong in it, I shouldn't wonder. Could be the big one.'

Duncan stared at him. The Victoria Cross? But . . . I didn't send the warning, sir.'

Lawrence raised his eyebrows. 'Say again?'

'The warning was sent by the flotilla leader, Lieutenant Leeming. Sending it revealed his position and he was sunk a few minutes later.'

'You're sure of this?'

Was that an invitation to go gong-hunting? 'Yes, sir, I am sure. We had been ordered, by Lieutenant Leeming, to observe strict radio silence. It was his decision to break that silence in the interests of the fleet as a whole.'

'And of Norway,' Lawrence remarked. 'And you say he was right under the guns of the German squadron?'

'Yes, sir. They were totally blacked out and we never saw them until we were within a few hundred yards.'

'Then it was indeed an heroic action. But you attacked them, with two small wooden boats, after seeing your leader destroyed.'

He seems determined that I should have a medal, Duncan thought. 'Sub-Lieutenant Orton attacked them, sir. I followed.'

'And Lieutenant Orton also bought it. Tragic. Did you get a shot off?'

'I fired both our torpedoes, sir.'

'And got a hit?'

'I can't swear to that, sir. There was an explosion, but I can't say what it was. There were quite a few ships close together, and frankly, we were in a hurry to get out of there.'

'Quite. The Germans have issued a communiqué. It actually covers their occupation of Norway – it also covers their takeover of Denmark – in which they claim the action was necessary to prevent British forces from invading. Well, obviously, they would make some such claim. They also say, in passing, that their fleet was attacked by a large number of unidentified torpedo boats. The implication here is that these boats were Norwegian and therefore they fired the first shots.

That of course won't wash and we are countering it with a communiqué of our own which will also rubbish their claim of a 'large number' of MTBs. The important thing is that they admit that one of their ships was hit by a torpedo, and that another struck a mine. They do not concede that either one might have sunk, but then we would not expect them to. So, all in all, Lieutenant Morant, but for the loss of life involved, for which you can in no way be held responsible, it was a highly successful action. I congratulate you and your crew. Now I am sure you feel like a good night's sleep.'

'Yes, sir. And thank you.' Duncan stood up. 'May I ask what the situation is now?'

Lawrence shrugged. 'I suppose "confused" would be the best word to sum it up. The Norwegian government, and their army, were obviously taken completely by surprise, and this German invasion force seems to have been a massive affair. We're not just talking about the fleet you ran into; they seem to be putting down paratroops way further north, and there is naval support up there as well. Our units have already been engaged. Anyway, Oslo seems to have fallen, and the king and his government, and the better part of the army, have retreated north and are preparing to fight. Their navy, such as it is, or was, appears to have been wiped out.'

'So are they protesting about our mine-laying?'

Lawrence grinned. 'I don't think so. I believe the PM is going to make a speech tonight, and I'm pretty damned sure he will offer the Norwegians all the help in our power.'

'Have we any help to give them, sir?'

'We have a pretty major fleet up there. I imagine the plan will be to seize a port so that we can land troops. The question is: can all this be done before the Germans take over the entire country?'

'So what are my orders, sir?'

'Your orders?'

'Well, sir, I command a perfectly serviceable ship, even if she is only the last one we have up here.'

'That, Lieutenant Morant, sums up the situation admirably. You command our only remaining MTB in these waters. I don't know what the admiral may have in mind for you, but right now I have no doubt at all that what you need is a spell of R and R. You, and your crew, are relieved of duty until further notice. I don't mean that you can abandon your boat. You will maintain her, ready for sea at a moment's notice, and within a day or two you will be required to resume your patrols around the Flow; but until the admiral returns, or new craft are received from the south, you do not leave the harbour. Understood?'

'Yes, sir,' Duncan said, reluctantly. But he felt obliged to point out, if only for the sake of his crew, 'We're actually due for leave.'

'I know that. But in these present circumstances it will have to wait until the situation becomes clearer, and certainly until the admiral gets back. Go and have a few stiff drinks, and tell your men to do the same. Dismissed.'

Duncan had reached the outer door of the long, low building when a voice said, 'Who's been trying his damnedest to get killed, then?'

He turned to watch her coming along the hall; she looked even more attractive than he remembered, partly because she was not wearing her hat. 'It wasn't intentional. I suppose you know all about it?'

'I handled the messages to the flagship, yes. And their replies. You're quite the flavour of the month.'

'As I have just explained to the captain, it's a case of mistaken identity. I was just following my leader.'

'But you survived. Always remember Napoleon's maxim: that a lucky general is more valuable than a good one.'

'Brrr.'

'Oh, quite. I imagine they were friends of yours.'

'Comrades.'

'Ah. So what about that bottle?'

'Say again?'

'I was going to buy you a bottle you champagne, if you came back. So . . .'

'Miss Brunel,' he said, seriously, 'if I share a bottle of champagne with you, right this minute, I am liable to want to get into your knickers.'

'This evening,' she said. 'Seven o'clock at the pub. I'll be wearing them.'

'Are you sure you want to do this?' he asked, sitting beside her at a corner table. She was wearing a frock instead of uniform, and he had never seen a sight he liked more, mainly because she had loosed her hair, which settled in dark profusion on her shoulders.

He had, in fact, not wrestled as hard with his conscience as he should have. This was partly due to the fact that he had had a lot to do, bringing the crew up to date with their situation – that their leave was again being postponed – and warning them not to do anything with their time off that they might regret, which in view of his present situation was a piece of prize hypocrisy. He had also been very tired, had tumbled into his bunk after lunch and been out to the world for four hours. Now he was fully refreshed, but for that reason the more aware, not only of what had happened last night but of his overall predicament.

There had been an open bottle of champagne on the table when he had arrived, with two glasses, and she poured. 'If I wasn't, I wouldn't be here.' She raised her glass. 'Here's to us. But you have obviously accumulated some doubts.'

He brushed his glass against hers, drank. 'Oh, I want to be here. It's just that . . .'

She picked up his left hand to look at it. 'No ring. Don't tell me: you're engaged.'

'Well, I suppose that's part of the problem.'

'Intriguing.'

'Well, you see, because I'm engaged, I haven't – well . . . it's been just on a year.'

She regarded him for several seconds. 'You realize that is the sort of challenge no red-blooded girl could possibly resist – even if you're making me feel it may be highly dangerous to be alone with you. But before . . .?'

'Oh, good Lord! I'm not a virgin, or anything like that. Once upon a time . . . but the fact is . . .'

'You are the son and heir of a lord, and she is no doubt the daughter of an earl, and there is a code of conduct that has to be observed. Is that true? I always thought the aristocracy were as randy as hell.'

'You could be right. But . . . ah . . . not as regards their wives. Or future wives.'

'Sounds a bit backward to me.'

'As you say, it's a sort of code. But you . . .'

'Oh, I'm raring to go. Not because I'm engaged to a stiff or anything like that . . . Oh, I do beg your pardon.'

'Feel free.'

'You mean she *is* a bit of a stiff?'

'Um.'

She topped up his glass. 'Your call, Lieutenant. The way I look at it is: by the law of averages, you shouldn't be sitting there at all. I don't know how many narrow scrapes you have had in the past, but taking on an entire German battle fleet in a little wooden motorboat, and surviving, has got to be up there with the narrowest.'

'But you wanted to get together before I ever went on that mission.'

She sipped her champagne. 'I think it's a mistake to attempt to analyse sexual desire, just as it's a mistake to try to analyse love. But if that's the way you want it . . . I decided some months ago, after our first meeting, in fact, that there was a gorgeous hunk of man with whom I'd like to get together. But I wasn't going to rush it. I kind of hoped you'd come on to me, given time. It wasn't until yesterday morning, when I realized you had been given virtually a suicide mission, that I understood I didn't have all the time I thought. I wanted to do something about it, so I did. And kept my fingers crossed for twenty-four hours.'

'And you always do what you want to do. Regardless.'

'Is that a crime?'

'Certainly not. You remind me of someone, who is very dear to me.'

Alison raised her eyebrows. 'You must tell me about her, some time. She sounds like the woman you really should marry. I suppose some people would say that I am, and she is, amoral. But then, war is an amoral business. We are brought up to believe that killing people is morally wrong – and then we are suddenly told that it is our bounden duty to kill as many people as possible, simply because we don't agree with their point of view.'

'Simplistic.'

'The truth usually is. So have you gone right off me? Or worse, off the boil?'

'I am on the boil, Alison. And it's for you. But—'

She held up her finger. 'No tomorrows, until we get there.

But in the short term . . .' She opened her handbag and took out a packet of condoms. 'Only three. But I think that should be enough.'

'If they had women admirals, you would get my vote. But . . .' He looked around the crowded bar.

'I share a room in my barracks with a very trustworthy friend. She will be waiting for us at nine o'clock, both to make sure that you get in without being seen, and to get you out again when you are ready to leave. That gives us just time to have a quick bite to eat. But we can finish this bottle first.'

Duncan realized that he was completely out of his depth. It was not that he had never met a woman who so knew what she wanted and was prepared to go out and get it, it was simply that she was so utterly a carbon copy, at least character-wise, of Kristin, and while he admired his mother immensely, he had always been quite sure that any man who got too close to her was on a hiding to nothing, whatever transient moments of pure bliss might be coming his way. His trouble was that he had a tendency to fall in love with women who gave their all, and one of the few really attractive things about Lucinda was that he knew she had never given her all to anyone else. And therefore . . . He reached across the table to hold Alison's slender fingers. 'I seem to be entirely in your hands.'

'Not entirely,' she said. 'There is something I should tell you.'

'Not that you are actually married . . . to an admiral.'

'It's far worse than that. I *am* a virgin.'

Part Three
Rescue

'A second Adam to the fight,
And to the rescue came.'

John Henry, Cardinal Newman

Domestic Matters

'Duncan! Oh, my darling boy!' Kristin embraced her son, as best she could, as Lucifer was attempting to do the same thing. 'You didn't let me know you were coming! Of course you couldn't.' She kissed him. 'Lucia!' she shouted. 'Champagne! Do behave, Lucifer. Come upstairs.' She held Duncan's arm to escort him. 'It's been in all the papers. They're saying that Leeming is to get a posthumous Victoria Cross. Are you going to get one too?'

'Of course not, Mother. He led. We just followed.'

'You all could have been killed as well,' she grumbled. 'It's very unfair.'

Lucia arrived with the champagne, and Kristin poured. 'Still, you're here. That's what matters.'

He brushed his glass against hers. 'I'm also getting another stripe. That's what really matters.'

'Are you?' She kissed him again. 'That should make Lucinda happy. Does she know you're back?'

'Ah . . . no.'

'She was so upset when you didn't arrive last week. I thought she was going to have a nervous breakdown. We must let her know immediately, so we can make plans. How long are you home for?'

'I have a week's leave. But I think I am going to be stationed in Portsmouth for a bit longer than that, while the boat is overhauled.'

'That's tremendous. Well . . .' She reached for the telephone.

'Mother!'

Kristin replaced the receiver, and turned to face him. '*Digame.*'

Duncan drank some champagne, while he tried to get his thoughts in order. He had in fact been trying to do this for the past week, with no very great success. The point was, as regards Mother, not that she would dream of criticizing him for shagging another woman while officially engaged, but that she would be quite unable to understand that he might have fallen in love with anyone after so brief an acquaintance. Or perhaps at all.

The problem was that he didn't know if it was possible either. He was sufficiently capable of introspection to understand that after the trauma of the action – of seeing his two sister ships blown to bits – he had been on an emotional and sexual high, akin to what he had read about soldiers after storming a well-defended town in the old days. But he did know that all of his desires, and too many of his thoughts, were centred on that diminutive body, on the image of her undressing while facing him, slipping her knickers past her thighs and down her slender legs, face composed but with pink spots in her cheeks, of understanding the treasure she was about to place in his keeping.

Alison had not raised that point. No tomorrows. She seemed for some time to have been coming to the conclusion that in the situation in which she had found herself, a situation that embraced everyone at Scapa Flow, everyone in the entire armed services, one should decide what one wanted from life, and go and get it as rapidly as possible, before it, or you, disappeared. She had decided she wanted sex before she was blown up by a bomb, and she had further decided, after looking the entire base over, that he was the man she wanted it with. So . . . it's been great. See you around.

They had only been able to see each other twice again before his orders to take his boat south – a replacement flotilla had arrived – for refitting and reassignment. But on the second occasion, as she had seen the orders, she had again arranged with her friend that the bedroom should be available – together with a fresh packet of condoms.

Then he had insisted they talk. 'I would like to see you again,' he had said.

He had been lying on her at the time, and she had gazed up at him with those unpredictable eyes. 'I would like that too. Maybe you'll be re-assigned to Scapa.'

'I meant, again and again and again. Always and always and always.'

As she had started having trouble with her breathing, he had rolled off her, and after a moment she had risen on her elbow the better to look at him. 'Pillow talk,' she had said, 'should never be taken seriously.'

'I have never been more serious in my life.'

'Because five days ago you realized that life might not be there too much longer.'

'Because five days ago I did not believe heaven existed.'

She had regarded him for several seconds. 'You're engaged to be married.'

'One of the more serious mistakes in a mistake-laden life. I intend to correct that.'

'Won't that involve you in being blackballed from your club, or whatever?'

'Their problem, not mine.'

'And will you do this whether I want it or not?'

'I must, now. I love you.'

She made a moue.

'You don't think that's possible? Don't you feel anything for me?'

'I could feel a great deal for you, I think. But I am just an itinerant young woman feeling her way through life. I also have a job to do, which I regard as responsible and very necessary. I have never allowed myself to consider vagaries like love. I . . .' She bit her lip.

'Say it?'

She shrugged. 'I also have red blood in my veins. I can feel lust. I have always regarded that with a pinch of salt. Is it really possible, or acceptable, for a well-brought-up young woman to look at a man and think, I would like to lie naked in his arms, I would like to have him inside me . . .?'

'I hope you're not disappointed.'

'I'm entranced. I would like to lie here for ever. But . . .'

'Why think of buts? I'm not suggesting you give up your job. I just want to know that you will be coming to me, eventually. And that until then, we'll see each other whenever possible.'

'And nobody else?'

'I'd like to think that. If you like, I'll send you a ring.'

'No rings. Not right now. I think we're both on cloud nine, and we can't stay there. Write to me, until we can get together again.'

'And until then?'

'Some famous politician once said, "A law which cannot

be enforced is a bad law." So, a promise that it may not be possible to keep is a bad promise.'

'I love you.'

'And I think I am falling in love with you. Let's put our faith in those.'

Kristin was studying him while she sipped champagne. 'It seems to me that you really must have a problem, if you can't put it into words.'

Duncan took a deep breath. 'I'm in love.'

'That's a problem? I've been in love all my life.' While he had been brooding, she had been thinking: If Duncan is here, then Jamie has got to be here too, only three miles away. Was she suggesting, even to herself, that she could possibly be in love with an eighteen-year-old boy? 'Not that I approve of your misfortune,' she said. 'And it seems to have taken you a hell of a long time to be sure of that. Do you reckon she's in love with you? If so, she has a very odd way of showing it.'

'I am not referring to Lucinda,' Duncan said, speaking very slowly and carefully.

Kristin refilled both their glasses, then leaned back in her chair. 'I really think that you need to elaborate.'

'She is a Wren, Second Officer Alison Brunel.'

'Brunel?'

'Forget it. She is not remotely related to any Brunel you may ever have heard of.'

'I'm glad of that. And of course she is stationed at Scapa and you have been having nookie for the past four months. I think that is a very healthy state of affairs. But I think you need to reflect a bit. Have you worked out what happens with Lucinda?'

'Well . . . I'll have to break it off.'

'Absolutely. But you will remember that as your engagement was a big item in *The Times*, the *Telegraph*, and the *Guardian*, not to mention *The Tatler*, the breaking of it will hardly get less attention. I imagine Lucinda will make certain of that.'

'I thought you'd be pleased.'

'Oh, I am. I just want you to know what you're doing. And why. If you're breaking your engagement to marry a girl you have been happily shagging for the past four months, isn't that rather like buying a cow you have been allowed to milk, free of charge.'

'Mother!'

'So I'm a vulgar bitch. Everyone knows that. Except perhaps your little Wren. What about her people?'

'I have no idea.'

'You haven't met. I suppose that's reasonable. But she must have told you about them, in between bouts of unbridled passion. I mean, you have to draw breath at some time, and smoke a cigarette – I forgot, you don't smoke. But four months . . . You can't just have spent that time saying hello, and so to bed.'

'Mother!!'

Kristin raised her eyebrows.

'You have, as usual, got hold of entirely the wrong end of the stick. I have not known Alison for four months. Well . . . we actually did meet a couple of months ago, but there was nothing in it. We only got together a week ago, the night I got back from that Norwegian thing. We have actually only spent three nights together.'

Kristin put down her glass. 'Do you realise that you are mad? Mad nice, perhaps, instead of mad vicious, but still stark raving. You know absolutely nothing about this girl apart from the fact that you enjoy lying between her legs. But I'll bet she knows all about you.'

'Well . . . did you know anything about Dad when you allowed him into your bunk?'

'Of course I did. It was his boat.'

'And you fell in love with him, at first – well . . .'

'Of course I did not fall in love with him. I never did that. I fell in love with his dick and with what he was doing with it.'

'Oh, Mother! You are impossible.'

'I always tell the truth – at least to myself. Just as you should admit that you have fallen in love with an ass and a pair of tits, almost certainly because they have been in such short supply over the past year.'

He glared at her. 'Are you telling me you are going to oppose my marrying Alison?'

They both knew that he was thinking of her allowance, which kept him in the style to which he was accustomed.

Kristin stretched out her hand to stroke his cheek. 'I will never oppose you, Duncan, in anything you really wish to do. I just do not wish to see you hurt. Or made a fool of. You must admit there has to be a chance that this girl sees herself more as the future Lady Eversham than simply as your wife.'

Duncan held her hand. 'Will you reserve judgement until you meet her?'

'Certainly. When will that be?'

'Well . . . this goddamned war . . .'

'It is annoying, isn't it? But look on the bright side. But for the war you would never have met this girl. And but for this war, you would already have been married to Lucinda, and doomed to a lifetime of misery.' She cocked her head as Lucifer began to bark and she heard the car engine. 'I think she's learned that you're back. Well . . .' She stood up. 'I have to go out.'

'Mother! You are deserting me.'

'There are some things a man has got to do for himself. Don't forget that Lucia is standing by to serve some more champagne, that Lucifer will bite her if necessary, and that Harry is available to protect you both. I will see you later. I hope.' She went down the stairs, as the front door opened. 'Why, Cindy. How lovely to see you.'

'Duncan is here, isn't he? Why hasn't he called me?'

'I think he was just about to do that. I know he can't wait to see you. He's upstairs. *Hasta la vista.*'

'Fill her up,' Kristin told Probert.

'Yes, milady. But . . . you filled her up the day before yesterday.'

'Well, top her up, then. Here are the coupons.' She went into the office. 'Hello, Mrs Goring. I just stopped by to congratulate you on Jamie's triumph. You saw the photograph?'

'Oh yes, milady. It was a bit difficult to work out which one was him.'

'Well, what do you expect from a newspaper? Still, he, they, all are famous. MTB torpedoes battleship. *Magnifico.*'

'Jamie says that's not true.'

'He's being modest.'

'But he says it wasn't a battleship, it was a cruiser. And he says they didn't sink it. In fact, he feels that they didn't even hit it. He says it's more likely she struck one of the mines they had just laid.'

'Same thing. Is he around?'

'Well, no, milady. He's gone into Lymington. To look at the yacht. He says he promised Mr Duncan to do that as soon as he had a moment.' She looked surprised that Kristin hadn't known that.

'Ah,' Kristin said. 'Of course. I hadn't expected him to do it so quickly.'

'Oh, he's devoted to Mr Duncan.'

'I know that. Well, congratulate him for me when he gets home.' She returned to the Bentley. 'All correct, Mr Probert?'

'Full to the very brim, milady.'

'*Bien.*' She got behind the wheel and was in Lymington ten minutes later.

'Milady,' said the yard foreman. 'How nice to see you.'

'I've come to see the boat.'

'Of course.' He led her across the somewhat soggy yard, between the forest of yachts awaiting attention. There was no one around, as most of his staff had joined up. 'This place gets more dismal every day.'

They entered the large shed. The two masts had been taken out and lay on the ground; the sails had been stored. The schooner sat on several legs, towering above them; a ladder rested against the hull, leading up to the deck. Against the wall there was propped a bicycle. *The* bicycle! The sight of it gave Kristin goose pimples.

'Is the keel repaired?'

'Well, no, milady.'

'Why not?'

The foreman grimaced. 'I can't repair her until I get some lead.'

'Well, I suppose she is not going anywhere for a while.'

'Someone down there?' Jamie called, from the deck.

'Yes,' Kristin said. 'I'm coming up.'

'Ah,' the foreman remarked. She was wearing a skirt.

Kristin smiled at him. 'You don't have to look, if you don't want to. I'll just take off my shoes.' She stood on one leg and then the other to remove her courts. 'Would you object if I took off my stockings as well? I'm wearing garters, not a suspender belt,' she added, reassuringly, as she raised her skirt.

'I think that's my telephone ringing,' the foreman said, and hurried off.

Kristin rolled down her stockings – they would have been too slippery to risk the ladder – then climbed. Jamie waited to hold her hand and help her over the rail. 'Why are Englishmen so afraid of sex?' she asked, and smiled at him. 'Some Englishmen.'

'I think it has something to do with being brought up to believe that women are soft, fragile creatures who need to be protected at all times from the seamy side of life. If you take the opportunity to look up a woman's skirt you are considered a cad and a bounder.'

'And if you don't you are also a twit.' She smoothed her skirt. 'Who's my great big hero then?'

'Me?'

Kristin slid down the companionway into the saloon. 'Duncan says you all are.' She turned to face him as he joined her, surrounded by the unique smell of a ship out of commission. 'Were you scared, when those other boats went up?'

'There wasn't actually time to be scared.'

'How I wish I could have been there with you.'

'Then I would have been scared.'

She put her arms round his neck and kissed him on the mouth. It took him a few seconds to respond, then his arms went round her in turn, his hands slipping tentatively down her back to caress her buttocks.

'I didn't believe that first time happened,' he said when he got his breath back. 'I thought it had to have been a dream.'

'Why wake up?' Still in his arms, she looked right and left. 'Where are all the mattresses?'

'Stowed.'

'Shit! Ah, well, we'll each take a turn underneath.'

'What happens if the foreman comes back?'

'Then,' Kristin said, 'he'll be either a twit or a cad.'

'Ah, Morant,' Fitzsimmons said. 'Welcome back.'

'Thank you, sir.' Duncan had taken the opportunity to have a second stripe added to the sleeves of his tunic and felt much more confident than the last time he had been in this office.

'I see that you are in all the newspapers again – for all the wrong reasons.'

'That was not my idea, sir.'

'I didn't think it was. The young lady seems to have taken considerable umbrage.'

'It is her nature, sir.'

'It is my impression that most women take umbrage when their engagement is terminated. You did do the terminating?'

'I'm afraid so, sir.'

'Well, Lieutenant, I am not going to pry into your personal problems, although I am sure I speak for all your brother officers when I say that I feel that you are well out of a woman who, the moment her engagement is broken, for whatever reason, summons every gossip columnist she can lay hands on and gives a press conference on how badly she has been treated.'

'Thank you, sir. I appreciate that.'

'From the point of view of the Navy, there are more urgent matters. I understand that you have been offered a change of scenery, but that you wish to remain with MTBs.'

'Well, sir, I feel I understand them, and how they should be used. Tactically.' he added, tactfully. 'I also know that I have a very good crew, which I would like to keep together.'

'Hm.' Fitzsimmons got up and went to the window. 'What do you think of her?'

Duncan stood at his shoulder. 'That is a big boat.'

'Seventy-two feet overall, thirty-five tons standard. You'll see she has the two twenty-one inch tubes forward, eight depth charges aft and four machine guns.'

'Performance?'

'She has a three-shaft Isotta–Fraschini engine which delivers three thousand four hundred and fifty brake horsepower and has produced forty-five knots on trials.'

Duncan whistled.

'She also has nineteen-hundred-gallon tanks. So you will appreciate that she is quite a ship.'

Duncan was still trying to assimilate the idea of a seventy-foot, thirty-five-ton boat being shifted at forty-five knots.

'She requires a crew of ten,' Fitzsimmons went on. 'You are welcome to invite your present crew to transfer with you. But they are also, of course, being offered other berths, so it must lie between you and them.'

'You mean I am to command that ship, sir?'

'You will command a flotilla of three of them, Lieutenant.

But *Seventy-Two* is yours, yes.' He raised his eyebrows at the expression on Duncan's face. 'Don't you like that idea? I would have thought, if you intend to stay in MTBs, that you would want to have the newest and best, so far.'

'I think the idea is bloody marvellous, sir. I'm just trying to get used to it.'

'Well, I would like you to take command immediately, and assemble your crew. Your other commanders will be along in a day or two, and you'll have a further couple of days to shake down.'

'And then, back to Scapa, sir?' Duncan could not keep the eagerness from his voice.

Fitzsimmons returned behind his desk and sat down 'Why on earth would you want to do that?'

'It's where the action is, sir.'

'Not for motorboats. It's all big stuff now. And frankly, you're well out of it. It's a bloody awful mess. A shambles of contradictory orders and futile ideas. Now there's even talk that those troops we have got ashore are going to have to be pulled out because we cannot sustain them. This after losing a whole clutch of destroyers and some major units.' He sounded genuinely distressed.

'I hadn't realized it was that bad,' Duncan said. What a fuck-up, he thought, with Alison waiting for him. 'So what will be my duties?'

'Anti-submarine patrols. Hence the extra depth charges. You have proved that with your speed and manoeuvrability you can take the beggars on, and with your range your can cover the Western Approaches as well as the Channel and the Irish Sea.'

'Yes, sir. With you permission, I'd like to go down and have a look at the ship.'

'Of course. Yes, Miss Brodie?'

The Wren was hovering in the doorway, looking agitated. 'A signal has just come in, sir.'

'Well?'

'At dawn this morning German units crossed the borders of Holland, Belgium . . . and France.'

'Well,' Kristin said. 'Maybe at last we'll get this thing sorted out.'

'Maybe,' Duncan said. 'At least it'll remove Lucinda from the gossip columns.'

'Silly little bitch,' Kristin growled. 'So where are you off to now, with your new wonder boat?'

'I have absolutely no idea. As you can imagine, there is a monumental flap. All I have been told to do is get used to her. I had hoped to be sent back up to Scapa, but . . . there it is.'

'You could try telephoning,' Kristin suggested.

'Not quite the same thing. But I suppose it'll have to do.'

'Before you start that,' Kristin said, 'tell me about your crew.'

'I'm hoping they'll all transfer to the new boat.'

'Excellent.'

'They'll have to volunteer, of course. They're being offered transfers out of MTBs. I suppose their lordships feel one can take just so much of it.'

'They'll volunteer,' Kristin said. One of them will, anyway, she thought. I'll see to that.

'Hello!' Duncan shouted. 'Hello! Can you hear me?'

'Yes,' Alison said. 'Just. I've been reading the newspapers. You didn't have to do that.'

'I told you I would.'

'I know. But I didn't expect you to be so brutal about it. I feel awful.'

'Because you've been reading her version of events. Your name wasn't mentioned, you know.'

'It might have been better if it had.'

'Definitely not. I can't imagine what she might have called you. Listen, any chance of you getting leave?'

'While this thing is going on in France?'

'It doesn't involve us – the Navy. If you could get leave at the end of this month . . . There's to be an investiture on the thirtieth. I'd love you to be there.'

'Well, I'd love to be there too. But . . .'

'You could meet my mother.'

'You mother? Gosh!'

'And my father. But only Mother matters.'

'Will she want to meet me? According to that article – well . . .'

'She was mainly responsible for ending the engagement.

Well, perhaps that was the part of the article that was the least accurate. Yes, she can hardly wait to meet you.'

'What? You mean she knows about me?'

'Of course. I have no secrets from Mother.' As there was no comment, he went on, 'Can you come down? You must be due for leave about now. As I said, the investiture is set for Thursday the thirtieth. If you could come down a day or two before, and maybe spend a week . . . We could even get married. Mother would be delighted.'

'And I would be marrying you, and not her?'

'Eh?'

'Just joking. I'll see what I can do.'

'Well, listen, I'm going to be out on this new boat I've been given quite a lot of the time over the next couple of weeks. So when you get your dates sorted out, telephone this number. Write it down.'

She did so. 'And this is . . .?'

'My home.'

'You said you might not be there.'

'My mother will be.'

'Ah.'

'That all right?'

'If you say so, Duncan. I'll be seeing you. I hope.'

'Petty Officer! Welcome aboard.' Duncan shook hands, and looked past Harris at the sailors on the pontoon. 'All here?'

'Not Clarke, sir. He opted for a destroyer. And there are two new men. This is some boat.'

'Let's hope she proves as good as old *Twenty*.' He went down to greet the crew, welcoming each one. Jamie was at the end. 'Well, Goring, not tempted by a destroyer?'

'Never, sir.' As if I would dare, Jamie thought, if it might upset Kristin. She seemed to have taken over his entire life. The possibility of not seeing her again was the only aspect of the future that frightened him.

'Well, everyone on board,' Duncan said. He showed them over the ship, and then went down to the engine room. There was much more space here than on *Twenty*, and even full head room. Jamie was standing with his hands on his hips as he looked around him. 'What do you think?'

'Tremendous.'

'Forty-five knots, so they say.'

Jamie whistled. 'When can we give it a go, sir?'

'Just as soon as the whole flotilla is got together.'

The other two skippers arrived that afternoon, both RNR. Colley was a lanky young man who rather pointedly looked at Duncan's insignia. Harmon was short and stocky, with bristly dark hair. 'It' a pleasure to serve with you, sir,' he said.

'Repeat that when you've done it,' Duncan suggested. 'Do you know MTBs?'

They looked at each other. 'I'm from a destroyer,' Colley said.

'Cruiser,' Harmon muttered.

'Ah. But you have experience of small boats? Yachts, maybe?'

'I've sailed dinghies,' Harmon volunteered.

'I've crewed on a J,' Colley said proudly.

'Have you now. What races?'

'Well, I didn't actually crew in a race. They were trying us out.'

'And you didn't make selection.'

Colley flushed. 'No, sir. I didn't make selection.'

Duncan grinned. 'Well, don't worry about it. You've made selection here. As soon as your crews are on board we'll take them out. One at a time,' he added, as he would obviously have to accompany each one.

'I'm afraid, sir,' he told Fitzsimmons, a week later, 'that my flotilla won't be ready for active service for at least another month. That is, not without endangering themselves and any other boat that comes within a mile of them.'

'I've seen them trying to moor,' Fitzsimmons agreed. 'But you may not have that much time. You've seen the news coming out of France?'

'Some if it, sir. I know it's not going very well.'

Fitzsimmons snorted. 'There's an understatement. It's a bloody shambles. It's extremely likely that Jerry is going to get through to the coast, and perhaps nab a seaport or two. If he can start bringing his ships into the Channel, we are going to have to take him on with everything we have.'

'But if he can reach the Channel . . .'

'Yes, Lieutenant, that will mean he has burst right through our lines. Now, this is confidential. We are of course committed to staying on the Continent and fighting alongside our French and Belgian allies for as long as possible. But there may come a time . . . The fact is, the BEF is the only army we happen to have. If it were to be absolutely destroyed in some last-ditch battle – well, we'd have nothing left to defend these islands, except the Navy. I repeat, this is absolutely confidential, and is not to be repeated even to your commanders, but plans are being laid to bring them off if necessary.'

'Bring an entire army off?'

'Three hundred and fifty thousand men.'

'Where would this evacuation take place, sir?'

'There are several seaports along that coast – Ostend, Zeebrugge, Gravelines, and on the French side, Dunkirk and Calais. The trouble is, as I'm sure you know, being a yachtsman, that those coasts also have shallows, mainly sandbanks, extending a good way offshore. That rules out the use of any large troopships except via the access channels to one of those ports, and obviously, if an evacuation does become necessary, Jerry is going to target those channels as well as the ports. Boats like yours, with virtually no draft, may be invaluable.'

'To lift off three hundred and fifty thousand men, sir? I have accommodation for ten crew.'

'But you have the speed to come and go.'

This man is stark, raving mad, Duncan thought.

Even Fitzsimmons seemed to understand that some kind of an explanation was necessary. 'I know the concept sounds ridiculous, Duncan. But plans must be laid, if only for the sake of morale.'

'Of course, sir,' Duncan agreed, reflecting that things must be bad: Fitzsimmons had never used his Christian name before.

'So, get your men ready for sea, and await further orders. What you must do immediately is unload all of your depth charges and torpedoes.'

'Sir?'

'If you are required to take part in an evacuation, you will not be chasing submarines or firing at enemy craft, but you will need to save every pound of weight and you will need every inch of space, above and below decks. You will retain your four machine guns for defence against air attacks. I know people, including your own crew, are going to ask questions, but you will answer none of them. You have been given an order, and you are carrying out that order, even if you have no idea of the reason behind it. Understood?'

'Yes, sir.'

'Very good. As of now, all leave is cancelled.'

'Yes, sir. Ah . . . Thursday . . .'

'Oh, yes, of course. Your investiture. I'm afraid that is on hold until this is over.'

'Yes, sir,' Duncan said grimly.

Shit, shit, shit, he thought as he went down the stairs. But as it did not appear as if anything was going to happen for the next couple of hours, at least, he drove over to Lymington.

'Duncan!' Kristin cried. 'Oh, dear. You just missed her.'

'What?'

'Your friend, Alison. I've just been talking with her on the telephone. She sounds rather a nice girl. Very positive.'

'Yes, Mother. She is – very positive. What did she say?' He was actually hoping that she had been unable to get leave, as that would avoid a kerfuffle.

'She'll be here on Wednesday night. She's coming by train, and she has a week. She sounds quite excited.' She peered at her son. 'Isn't this what you wanted to happen?'

'It's a complete fuck-up,' Duncan said. 'There's all kinds of a flap on, because of what's happening in France. All leave has been cancelled, and I, and my crew, are required to remain on board and on stand-by for the foreseeable future.'

'Ah . . .' Kristin frowned. 'I know I'm not very up on military matters, but how can what is happening in France have anything to do with a flotilla of motorboats in Portsmouth?'

'Sorry. That is top secret. Listen, you'll have to meet the train.'

'I have no idea what she looks like.'

'I have told you what she looks like: petite, black-haired, very pretty. And wearing a Wren uniform with two bars.'

'What am I supposed to do with her?'

'You're putting her up, Mother. Remember? Get to know her.'

'And where will you be?'

'I have absolutely no idea.'

'But you won't be with us.'

'I will if I can.'

Kristin considered. 'She is coming to see you, you know. Not me.'

'I know. But, unlike Lucinda, she appreciates that there's a war on.'

'Hm. Can I take her to bed?'

'What?'

'Well, if she's coming all the way from Scapa Flow to have sex, she's going to be pretty fed up when she discover there isn't going to be any.' Or for me, she thought, if Jamie is also confined to barracks.

'Mother, you are absolutely impossible! Listen, this is a very well-brought-up young woman, whom I intend to make my wife. I may say that she was a virgin when we got together.'

'Good God! Oh, well, I suppose we all have to start somewhere.'

'So I would not like her to get the wrong impression about us. You. Please, please behave yourself.'

'Or you'll beat me. I know.'

'*Mother!* I have to rush. Just remember that my entire future happiness is in your hands.'

'You have just told me,' Kristin pointed out, 'that my hands mustn't come into it.' She blew him a kiss. 'I'll look after your popsie. Just try to hurry back.'

'You must be Alison,' Kristin announced. Not only did the young woman fit Duncan's description, but she was the only woman on the platform wearing a Wren uniform.

'Then you are . . . Gosh!' Alison looked uncertain as to whether she should curtsey.

'I am Kristin Eversham, yes,' Kristin acknowledged. 'Does your exclamation mean that you don't like the look of me?'

'Oh, good heavens, no, milady. It's just that – well . . . Duncan's mother . . .'

'Should be gray-haired, bent and have the shakes. I entirely agree with you. Perhaps unfortunately, I gave birth to him when I was seventeen years old. Take this bag, will you?' she told a porter who had incautiously come within earshot.

'Yes, ma'am.'

'I can carry my own bag,' Alison protested.

'One of the reasons I look younger than my years,' Kristin pointed out, 'is that I have always believed in doing nothing that can conveniently be done by someone else. Come along.'

She set off along the platform, Alison hurrying at her side, the porter following with the bag.

'It's awfully good of you to meet me,' Alison said. 'Duncan . . .?'

'Is tied up. There is an almighty flap on.'

'Yes. I know. I almost didn't get here. Gosh!'

'What now?'

'Is this your car?'

'Yes, it is. Don't you like Bentleys?'

'I've never driven in one.'

'It's quite comfortable, really. Put the bag in the boot,' she told the porter, and took a pound note from her handbag. 'Thank you.'

He gazed at the note in stupefaction, then touched his cap and hurried off before she realized her mistake.

'Excuse me,' Alison said, 'that was a pound note.'

'I think it was, yes,' Kristin agreed. 'They all look alike to me.'

'But . . . for carrying one small bag?'

'I never carry change,' Kristin explained. 'It weighs so much. Do get in.' She started the engine as Alison settled herself on the soft leather upholstery and stared at the walnut panelling. 'When you said you nearly didn't get here . . .'

'When I changed trains in London I heard an announcement that all service leave had been cancelled. I suppose I should have gone back to Scapa, but as I was nearly here, and maybe had not heard the announcement . . .'

Kristin started the car. 'I think I am going to love you,' she said. 'I already do.'

'I hope you like dogs,' Kristin said, as she unlocked the front door.

'I love dogs,' Alison said. 'My parents have . . . Gosh! Ooof. Ow!'

She found herself sitting on the ground with what seemed to be a white elephant standing over her.

'Lucifer!' Kristin remonstrated. 'Do behave. You haven't been introduced. And anyway, you can't have her: she belongs to Duncan.'

'Is that his name?' Alison asked, slowly extricating herself as Lucifer subsided.

'Well, it seemed appropriate.' Kristin held her hand to help her up. 'Are you all right?'

Alison smoothed her skirt while she peered at her uniform. 'It seems all right. Damn!'

'There's a ladder. You can wear a pair of mine.'

'I have a change in my bag.'

'Of course. Still, you must let me buy you some more. Harry! Will you take Miss Brunel's bag upstairs.'

'Of course, milady. Ah . . .'

'Oh, put it in Mr Duncan's room. That's where you'll be sleeping,' she explained to the embarrassed Alison, 'unless you'd rather use one of the spare rooms.' As Alison obviously couldn't think of anything appropriate to say, she went on, 'You need a drink. Everyone who gets tumbled by Lucifer needs a drink. Up here.'

She went up the stairs, and after an anxious smile at Harry, Alison followed. 'I've never been in a house with a butler,' she confided, following Kristin into the sitting room.

'You mean Harry? He's actually Duncan's valet. But with Duncan away, he doesn't have much else to do. Cream do you?'

Alison cast a quick glance at the sideboard to ascertain what she was referring to. 'Yes, please.' She decided not to reveal to her hostess that she had never had a boyfriend who employed a valet, either. 'When do you expect Duncan?'

Kristin handed her a sherry glass. 'I don't. Happy days.'

Alison allowed the glass to brush her lips. 'Say again? Oh, I'm sorry. It's a naval expression. You took me by surprise.'

'At which I am not surprised.' Kristin sat on the settee and patted the space beside her. 'Unlike you, as Duncan was on board his boat, he had no choice but to listen to the orders. It appears all leave has been cancelled for the foreseeable future.'

'Sh – oot.'

'I would say what you originally felt,' Kristin advised. 'This war is getting beyond a joke.'

'If . . . Well, I suppose I should go back to Scapa.'

'That seems ridiculous. To come all the way down here, and then turn round and go the whole way back the next day.'

'Yes, but—'

'Duncan had three objectives in view,' Kristin said. 'One was of course to get you back between the sheets, which at this moment is all he can think about.'

Alison stared at her with her mouth open.

'The second was to marry you while he had you around.'

Alison closed her mouth.

'And the third was that you and I should get to know each other, as obviously, if number two works out, we shall be seeing a lot of each other. So, as we have to put numbers one and two on hold, the best thing we can do is start on number three. Or doesn't that appeal to you?'

'Of course it appeals to me, milady—'

'In that case you need to start calling me Kristin.'

'Kristin.'

'Don't you like it? It was my mother's name. She was Swedish.'

'Oh.'

'Didn't Duncan tell you he has Swedish blood? My other half is Spanish. I'm not sure Papa ever knew quite what to do with Mama. I mean, she was a beautiful woman, and he liked owning beautiful things. But as I'm an only child, he seems to have run out of ideas pretty quickly.'

'Please, I didn't mean to upset you. I think Kristin is a beautiful name – as you are a beautiful woman.'

'I could go for Alison, too. Do you know, I have a feeling you and I are going to get on terribly well. I never got on with Lucinda terribly well. In fact, I hated her guts. But then, I think she hated mine. Did Duncan tell you about Lucinda?'

'Only her name,' Alison said cautiously. 'Are your mother and father still together?'

'As a matter of fact, they are. In the same vault, I mean. But not in the same coffin. Mama wouldn't have liked that, and she went first.'

'I'm terribly sorry.'

'Don't be. If they weren't both dead, I wouldn't be living here now. Duncan wouldn't have his Bugatti or the yacht.'

'Oh. I thought . . .'

'Everyone makes that mistake. Duncan's father has a big title, and not much else. Mind you, once upon a time . . . Let me get you another drink.'

'I'd rather see Duncan. Having come all this way.'

'I thought I'd explained to you that he isn't here.'

'You did. But you know where he is.'

'Of course I do. But we can't get to him.'

'Trust me,' Alison said.

The Beach

'I am sorry, ma'am,' said the shore patrol. 'You must have a pass.'

'I am Second Officer Alison Brunel,' Alison told him. 'And I am carrying an urgent message from Rear Admiral Lonsdale to Lieutenant Morant.'

'Well, ma'am . . .' He looked at Kristin.

'It is to do with this lady. Are you suggesting that I should return to the admiral's office and tell him I have been refused permission to carry out his order?'

The seaman opened the gate. 'I think you need to hurry, ma'am.'

Kristin squeezed Alison's arm as they went towards the dock. 'I adore you. You remind me of myself.'

'Just remember you promised to save my neck when this comes out.'

'Oh, I shall,' Kristin promised. 'Jimmy Lonsdale is one of my closest friends. I shall take full responsibility. But if you are cashiered – well, you'll be able to stay with me and marry Duncan anyway.'

'We might have to wait until we come out of gaol. Um. I think, when the man said we needed to hurry, he was stating the exact truth.'

They had reached the dock and were surrounded by the noise and bustle of ships preparing for sea. Fortunately, everyone was so busy no one had the time to look at the two women.

'That one.' Kristin pointed. Duncan had shown her a photograph of his new boat.

It was definitely preparing to cast off, as were the other two boats on the pontoon, even if all three looked rather odd. The women hurried down the gangway, shoes slipping. 'Duncan!' Kristin shouted.

He was not to be seen, but Harris was on the bridge. 'Ma'am?' he inquired.

'We wish to speak with Lieutenant Morant.'

'He's not on board, ma'am.'

'Oh, good Lord!'

'But you are expecting him back?' Alison asked.

'Yes, ma'am. At any moment.'

'We'll wait for him,' Kristin decided. 'Permission to come on board.'

'Well, ma'am, I don't really think—'

'I'm his mother,' Kristin explained, and opened the gangway. 'Don't worry, we won't get in your way. We'll wait below. But . . . Where are your depth charges?'

'Unloaded, ma'am.'

'And your torpedoes?'

'Yes, ma'am.'

'But you're preparing to go to sea.'

'Yes, ma'am.'

Kristin regarded him for several seconds, but as he was obviously not going to elaborate, she said, 'As I said, we'll get out of your way.'

Alison had joined her, and they pulled open the door to the mess and disappeared. Harris scratched his head, uncertain how to handle the situation, and gave a sigh of relief as he saw Duncan hurrying along the dock. 'We're off,' Duncan shouted. 'Now.'

'Where?' Colley asked.

'Follow me. You'll get your orders at sea.'

He vaulted the rail and arrived on the bridge, in the same instant switching on the ignition. 'Cast off aft, cast off forward.'

The warps were brought in, and he eased the throttle forward; *Seventy-Two* slipped away from the dock, followed immediately by her two sisters.

'Oh, my God!' Harris remarked.

'Petty Officer?' Duncan was concentrating on negotiating his way through other boats and pontoons.

'There is something you should know, sir.'

'For God's sake, don't tell me someone's ashore. My orders were that no one was to leave the ship.'

'Yes, sir. No one has left the ship. We have a full comple-ment. Plus two.'

'What?' They were through the various obstacles and he

eased the throttle forward at the same time thumbing his mike.
'One thousand until we are past the Nab; then prepare for full
speed. Course oh nine oh. Now, what are you talking about,
Petty Officer?'

'Why, Duncan.' Kristin stood in the hatch, 'Are you taking
us for a ride?'

Duncan turned his head. 'What the . . . Holy Shit! Mother?'
He peered at Alison. 'My God! Alison? What the hell are you
doing here?'

'I have come eight hundred miles to see you,' Alison
pointed out. 'I think you should at least say you are pleased
to see me.'

'Of course I'm pleased to see you,' Duncan said. 'But don't
you realize that I've been ordered out.'

'I'll come with you.'

'What? And . . .' He turned to look at Kristin.

'I could not possibly permit Miss Brunel to put to sea with
ten great hairy men and no duenna,' Kristin pointed out.

'Nab tower dead ahead, sir,' Harris said, realizing that his
skipper had lost concentration.

'Why there it is,' Kristin said. 'And you are . . .?'

'Petty Officer Harris, ma'am.'

'Mr Harris. I can see you're busy. Show me where I should
go. I don't want to be in the way.'

Harris looked at his commander.

'Oh, for God's sake get her out of sight,' Duncan said – though
he suspected what had happened had been seen by everyone in
the harbour. 'You too, Alison. You can come up later.'

She blew him a kiss and followed Kristin and the petty
officer into the mess. Duncan grabbed the mike. 'Leader to
flotilla. Increase to two thousand.'

'Aye aye,' came the reply from his subordinates; he couldn't
tell whether they were laughing or not.

Harris joined him.

'All well below?'

'At the moment, sir. Your mother seems to wish to explore
the ship.'

'Well, it'll keep her out of mischief.'

'Yes, sir.'

His tone was doubtful. 'What the hell was I to do?' Duncan
asked. 'Throw them overboard?'

'Well, no, sir,' Harris agreed. 'You couldn't do that. The other young lady . . .'

'Is my fiancée.'

'Ah.' This time the petty officer managed to get a great deal of meaning into his tone. 'May I ask where we are going, sir?'

'Dunkirk.'

'Dunkirk,' Harris remarked. 'Isn't that very close to a war zone, sir?'

'It is a war zone, Petty Officer. It appears that the BEF has been utterly defeated. Belgium has surrendered and our people are trapped. Our orders are to get as close inshore as we can, pick up as many men as we can, and take them to Dover. We'll put the ladies ashore then.'

'Yes, sir. They're still liable to be exposed to enemy fire on the first trip.'

'I know that too, Mr Harris. We must make sure we're not hit.'

'Yes, sir,' Harris agreed, less convinced than ever.

Duncan looked over his shoulder to make sure the other two boats were still behind him, and saw to his relief that they were. He thumbed the mike. 'This is the flotilla leader,' he said. 'I can now tell you that we may be going into action for the first time. Our orders are to proceed to the harbour of Dunkirk, manoeuvre as close to the beaches north of the port as we can, and take off as many members of the BEF as we can. They are waiting for us. I don't need to tell you that this very serious situation has arisen because of the total defeat of the Allied forces in Flanders, which has been compounded now by the unconditional surrender of the Belgian Army, which has left the BEF's left flank exposed. Now, gentlemen, we cannot do anything about that situation, but I wish you to remember that every soldier we can bring back to England will fight again, for England. Every man who doesn't get back will not fight again in this war.

'Now, our principal problem will be air attack; as far as we know there are no German surface units in the vicinity. So keep a lookout overhead and keep your machine guns manned. In these circumstances there is no value in us acting as a flotilla. You will load your boats to the maximum number that can safely be accommodated, take them to Dover, disembark them, and return, as often as is required until you receive other orders.

Refuelling will be available as and when needed. You should pay no attention to what may be happening to the rest of the flotilla; concentrate on getting there and back. I look forward to seeing you all again when this is done. Until then, good luck and Godspeed!'

He closed the mike and took the helm back from Harris.

'Stirring stuff,' Alison commented, having come up to the bridge. Like him she had strapped her cap under her chin.

'There are greatcoats below if you aren't warm enough,' he told her.

'I'm warm at the moment. Are you very angry with me?'

Duncan eased the throttle forward, and the MTB gained speed. To his relief it was a perfect spring day, with only a light breeze and a flat-calm sea; *Seventy-Two* creamed across it as if she was the Bugatti. But by the same token, there was a complete absence of cloud cover to protect them from prying aircraft. 'We'll discuss that when this is over,' he shouted. 'Where is Mother?'

'I don't know. Somewhere below.'

'Let's hope she doesn't touch any switches.'

'She's quite a woman, your mother.'

'She makes her own rules. One day she may come a cropper.'

Seventy-Two was now up to full speed. 'This is some ship,' Alison shouted. 'How long to Dunkirk?'

'Two and a half hours, barring accidents. Say half past twelve. But it's less than an hour back to Dover. Lunch will only be a little late.' He grinned at her. 'Sorry you came?'

'I wouldn't have missed this for the world. Are you sorry I'm here?'

'If I didn't have to keep both hands on the wheel I'd kiss you.'

Harris studied the horizon, and the looming coast of France as the Channel narrowed.

'There you are,' Kristin shouted.

Jamie had been studying various dials; now he turned so violently he all but lost hold of the stanchion he was grasping. 'Milady?!! But . . .'

Kristin was hanging on to the stanchion by the engine-room door: the sea might be flat calm, but down here the vibration was tremendous. 'Do you spend all your time in this racket?'

'Most of it. But what are you doing here? Does the skipper know you're aboard?'

'Well, of course he does.' Kristin shifted her grip to another stanchion and came further into the confined space.

'And he's happy with that?'

'I don't think he is, no. But there's not a lot he can do about it now. Aren't you going to kiss me?'

Jamie looked at his hands.

'I'm not asking you to feel me up,' Kristin pointed out. 'Not right now, anyway. Just kiss me.'

Jamie obliged, his body bumping against hers, but carefully keeping his hands away. 'You shouldn't be here.'

'Don't you start. Why shouldn't I share in the fun?'

'Fun? Milady, you do realize that if these boats get hit they are liable to explode?'

'Are you scared?'

'Well . . .'

'It'll be a hell of a way to go. But I have to go up top. I don't see how you can stand this noise and this heat. Will you be coming up?'

'Maybe when we get there.'

'Be sure you do.' She kissed him again.

'Whee!' Kristin cried, as the wind whistled about her ears and scattered her hair. 'Where is that?'

'Boulogne to starboard, milady,' Harris explained. 'Folkestone to port. We're nearly there.'

Kristin nudged her son. 'Aren't you speaking to me?'

'Later,' he said.

Kristin arched her eyebrows as she looked at Alison.

'He's concentrating,' Alison explained.

'He's miffed, you mean. Listen,' she shouted. 'These men you are picking up. Some of them may well be wounded. You'll need the help of two beautiful nurses.'

What he might have replied was lost in a shout from Rawlings, who was sweeping the sky with his binoculars. 'Aircraft!'

'Confirm, Petty Officer,' Duncan said.

Harris levelled his glasses. 'Ours, sir.'

'Let's hope it stays that way.'

The sea had suddenly become very crowded. The two other boats of the flotilla were still on station behind them, and now they had been joined by other MTBs, destroyers, tugs, all heading in the same direction.

'Look there,' Alison said.

They were abeam of Calais now, still outside the sandbanks, although close enough to see the shells bursting over the town; but that had not been what she was commenting on. In front of them were the flames rising from Dunkirk, and they could see other explosions as well, while the sea was a mass of ships, weaving and turning. Most of them were too big to get closed inshore, but they had put down all the boats they had, and these were crawling across the surface of the sea like a mass of caterpillars, making for the beaches, which were crowded with men, some actually standing waist deep in the water to enable the boats to reach them the more easily.

'Aircraft, bearing green twenty,' Rawlings said.

England was behind them, certainly not on the starboard bow. Harris and Duncan looked at each other.

'We came here to do a job, Petty Officer,' Duncan said. 'I want every man on deck, wearing his life jacket and his steel helmet. And I want the machine guns manned.'

'Aye aye, sir.' Harris hurried off.

'Mother, Alison, kindly go below.'

'Why?' Kristin asked.

'Because we are extremely likely to come under fire.'

'But is it not true that if we are hit we will explode anyway?'

'It's possible.'

'Then I'd feel safer up here.'

'Me too,' Alison agreed. 'We can't do much good to anyone hiding below.'

Duncan glared at them, then turned to see Jamie emerging from the hatch. 'Jamie! Find something for these women to wear. A tin hat each, and a life jacket.'

'Aye aye, sir.' Jamie disappeared again.

'Now you listen,' Duncan said. 'There is some point in your staying up. But if you do, you keep out of the way and you keep your mouths shut. That is an order. Understood?'

'Aye aye, *sir*,' Kristin said.

Alison saluted.

Duncan glared at them again, then turned back to concentrate. He had been reducing speed while speaking, and the boat was now gliding almost silently through the water, which of course made her the more difficult to handle, especially in such a crowded piece of sea. They passed perilously close to a packed destroyer whaler, which gave them a cheer, probably, Duncan thought, because the soldiers had spotted the two women on the bridge.

The water was now green, and the beach was still some fifty yards away. 'Mr Harris, get someone up on the bow with a boathook to check the depths.'

'Aye aye, sir.'

Harris went forward himself with the long pole, which he used to prod over the rail. 'No bottom.'

That meant at least six feet, but the beach was shelving. The nearest group of men had stopped about thirty yards away, up to their thighs. That meant he'd be on the ground, there. 'Speaking trumpet,' he snapped.

Jamie, who had returned on deck with the women's gear, handed him the loud hailer.

'We need you a little further out,' Duncan bellowed. 'You won't drown.'

Seventy-Two was now stopped, and starting to drift sideways, and still the waiting men hadn't moved.

'I have bottom,' Harris called.

'Here they come,' Rawlings shouted.

The approaching aircraft were dropping from the sky.

'Messerschmitts,' Jamie muttered.

'Shit!' Duncan commented.

It went against his every instinct to just sit still and wait to be blown out of the water, but to abandon those men . . . If only they'd make a move.

'Crikey!' Jamie commented.

Duncan looked from the sky to the foredeck, and saw his mother making her way to stand beside Harris. 'Come along now,' she called. 'We haven't got all day.'

Alison had also gone forward. Whether it was the sight of the women or the noise from behind them, the men now surged forward. Jamie and Rawlings joined the two women and together with Harris were hauling men over the side.

'Wounded below,' Kristin commanded. 'We'll get to you in a moment. Fit men aft. Lie down, but right up against each other.'

She had, as was her custom, taken command. Duncan looked at the beach, on which the aircraft were concentrating. The noise was appalling: the roar of the engines, the shouts of the men as they sought shelter, the screams of those who were hit, seemed to be increased by the visual effect of the strafing, the clouds of sand being thrown skywards, the sprawling bodies of the dead and wounded . . . and the remarkable calmness of those who were surviving – some, onshore, vainly firing their rifles at their tormentors, the majority continuing in their lines, which now stretched well into the sea in every direction.

Duncan saw *Seventy-Four* only a short distance away from *Seventy-Two*, also loading men. He could not make out *Seventy-Three*, but so far as he could tell none of the ships had been hit in this raid.

On the foredeck men were still being helped on board. The after deck was now entirely covered with bodies, and more were being taken below. 'Sixty is our limit,' he called.

The women ignored him. Kristin was hauling a clearly badly wounded man over the rail, assisted by Jamie. Her skirt and blouse were stained with blood, but the man was smiling at her. 'I'm dead,' he said, 'and you're an angel.'

'Thousands would argue that point,' Kristin said. 'Let's get you below.'

She looked at Jamie across the stricken man; they both knew he was dying. Then she jerked her head, and between them they got him to his feet, to be half-dragged, half-carried to the hatch.

Harris had been counting. 'Sorry, chaps,' he said. 'That's sixty. We'll be back as soon as we can.'

The soldier who had already pulled himself halfway up the rail and was staring at Alison, waiting to receive him, hesitated for a moment, then obediently dropped back into the sea.

'They're coming this way,' Rawlings shouted.

Duncan looked up and saw two Messerschmitts wheeling away from the beach towards the ships. 'Open fire!' he bellowed. 'Stand clear! Stand clear!'

He put the engine astern and the boat slid backwards into deeper water, but when he turned the helm he was surprised by her sluggishness.

'Everyone hold on,' he called, and thrust the throttle forward. *Seventy-Two* increased speed, but clearly, with more than seventy people on board she was not going to make anything like forty knots.

There was a roaring zoom, and one of the fighters passed

low overhead, but whether it had been distracted by the machine-gun fire or by his sudden increase in speed, it did not appear to have hit anything, and Duncan, now making something like twenty-five knots, was through the various waiting ships and heading west.

Harris joined him. 'Think we'll make it, sir?'

'What was the Irishman heard to say as he passed the sixty-seventh floor after falling off the top of the Empire State Building?'

Harris grinned. 'So far so good.'

'Absolutely. What's it like below?'

'Pretty grim. But those two ladies are doing wonders. Your mother is a real ball of fire. There's a strong resemblance.'

'I'll take that as a compliment. Now, I think you should tell Wilson to break out everything he has: tea, coffee, cocoa, brandy – whatever. Every man should get something to drink. And the ladies.'

'Aye aye, sir. And you?'

'A cup of coffee would be very acceptable, Petty Officer. But only after everyone else.'

Even at twenty-five knots, Dover was under two hours away, and if the sea had been crowded, the harbour was seething.

Alison joined him as they approached the breakwaters. She had removed her tunic and her hat, and her shirt was soaked with sweat and blood. 'Where's your life jacket?' he demanded.

'It got in the way. Listen, I just wanted to say, I think you're tremendous.'

'Snap. But I'm being paid.'

'Again, snap. It's your mother who's bloody marvellous.'

'I imagine she's having the time of her life.'

'Did you know that two of the men have died?'

'Shit! I didn't know that. I'll talk to her when we get in.' He took one hand off the wheel to squeeze her arm. 'Right now ...'

'Of course.' She disappeared and he turned up the radio.

'You'll be met, *Seventy-Two*,' the harbour office said. 'Speed dead slow.'

'Um,' Duncan said, but he saw the reason as he passed between the pier heads; while he was coming in a whole host of boats was coming out, and within was a kaleidoscope.

As promised, a harbour launch was waiting for them. 'Follow me!' the coxswain shouted through his loud hailer.

Harris joined him. 'How's the fuel situation?' Duncan asked.

'Two-thirds in hand, sir.'

'Then we won't be fuelling right now. Tell the passengers to be patient.'

The soldiers on deck were starting to get up, making the ship unstable. Harris went aft to tell them to settle down, while the machine-gunners left their posts to handle the mooring warps. A moment later they were alongside. 'We need medics,' Duncan shouted at the men waiting for them.

'Wilco.' People bustled.

'All right, chaps,' Duncan called, 'time to go.'

The men got up and began shuffling towards the gangway. A sergeant left the line and came up to the bridge. 'I'd like to thank you, sir, on behalf of my people.'

'I'm glad to have got you here, Sergeant. You know that not everyone made it.'

'I know that, sir. But I would like to thank the ladies personally.'

'You get ashore. I'll thank them for you.' He winked. 'They're not supposed to be here.'

'Oh. Right. Will you go be going back again, sir?'

'In about ten minutes.'

'God Almighty! Well, sir, may I wish you every success.'

Duncan shook his hand, then returned his salute. The medics were on board now, and a few minutes later they emerged carrying five bodies on stretchers. 'They're not all dead?' he asked.

'No, sir. Only two. Your nurses did a good job.'

'Ahoy, *Seventy-Two*,' came a call from the dock. A lieutenant-commander stood above him. 'Are you ready to return to sea?'

'Yes, sir,' Duncan said.

'Do you need anything?'

Duncan glanced at Harris.

'Nothing at the moment, sir.'

'Next time around, sir,' Duncan said.

'Very good. Carry on.' The lieutenant-commander walked away.

'You heard the man,' Duncan said. 'We leave in ten minutes. Tell Wilson to get some hot soup going. We'll have a proper meal when we return this evening.'

He swung himself into the mess. The table was stained with blood, and the place stank. 'I'll get this cleaned up now, sir,' Jamie said.

'Good man.' Duncan stood above the two women, who sat together on one of the settee berths. 'You have been magnificent. I am so very proud of you. But I'm afraid you'll have to hurry. We're off again in a few minutes.'

'Hurry where?' Kristin asked.

'Off the ship, Mother. I assume you have money for train fares?'

'I have not got any money for train fares. I have not got any money at all.'

Duncan looked at Alison.

'Gosh,' she said. 'My handbag is still at your house. We left in such a hurry . . .'

'All right. Don't panic. I have enough to get you home.'

'I am not going home,' Kristin announced.

'Well, I don't see how you can go anywhere else. Have you looked in a mirror recently?'

'I don't have to look in a mirror. I know that I cannot possibly make a hundred-mile train journey covered in blood. I'd be arrested.'

'So what do you propose?'

'I will stay with you until you can take me back to Portsmouth and my car.

'That may be several days.'

'So?'

'You intend to spend several days looking like Dracula after a hearty meal. Not to mention in danger of your life.'

'If I'm in danger, then we all are. As for my appearance . . .' She looked past him at Jamie, who had just returned, equipped with a bucket and brush. 'Jamie will lend me a shirt. Won't you, Jamie?'

'Oh. Ah . . .' Jamie cast an embarrassed glance at his skipper. 'If you wish me to, milady.'

'Oh, for God's sake. And you . . .' Duncan turned to Alison.

'I have come eight hundred miles to spend a week with you,' Alison reminded him. 'That is what I am doing.'

'Excuse me, sir,' Harris said from the hatch. 'The harbour control is asking if we're ready to depart.'

'Shit! Just keep out of sight,' he told the women, and went on deck.

'Is he always this bad-tempered?' Alison asked.

'He likes to do things by the book,' Kristin explained. 'Now, Jamie, you promised me a shirt.'

The breeze remained light, the sea remained calm, and they were back at Dunkirk in a matter of minutes, Wilson and the women only just having time to serve a hasty meal to the crew, who remained at their posts. They found that the situation had deteriorated; the sky was packed with enemy aircraft, the town was blazing more fiercely than before, and even as they approached they saw a vast explosion and one of the destroyers seemed to break in two.

'What's our priority, sir?' Harris asked.

'Charity begins at home,' Duncan said, and spun the wheel, at the same time reducing speed.

The sea was filled with people, many of them soldiers who had only recently been brought out to the supposed safety of the ship.

'Must be damned near a thousand of them,' Harris said.

But other boats were clustering, ignoring the bombs which were being scattered over them.

'If we get through this it'll be a bloody miracle,' Wilson muttered, peering through the galley port.

'So why worry about it?' Kristin asked him. She had replaced her dress with the shirt, which came to just above her knees and resembled a nightshirt.

'You're not leaving too much to the imagination,' Alison had pointed out. 'Don't you have a bra?'

'I never wear the things.'

'Well, at least do the buttons up.'

This she had done, but Wilson obviously found the close presence of so much clearly delineated breast and exposed leg a distraction.

Now she said, 'We should go up to help.'

'I will,' Alison decided. 'I think you should stay here, milady; otherwise we won't be able to keep the numbers down. We'll bring the wounded to you.'

'I wonder how many spare shirts Jamie has,' Kristin commented.

* * *

They filled the ship and were back in Dover by five o'clock, still miraculously without being hit.

'What the shit?' Duncan asked as they approached the pier heads.

Issuing from the harbour was a vast armada of boats, most of them quite small, chugging into the evening, manned by two or three men each.

'Where they hell is that lot going?'

'I would say, Dunkirk, sir,' Harris suggested.

'They'll be committing suicide.'

'As you say, sir.' Harris's tone indicated that he considered they were merely joining the club.

Duncan continued to study the yachts and motorboats, while he reduced speed still further; there was no way he could get into the harbour until they were all out, as they were observing no sort of order, or even steering very straight. Now he remarked, 'Good God!'

'Sir?'

'Hand me those binoculars, Petty Officer.' Harris did so, and he levelled them, then handed them back. 'What do you see over there?'

Harris studied the mass of boats in turn. 'You mean that yellow and red motorboat? Bit of a lark, that. He's liable to attract Jerry's attention more than anyone else.'

'That monstrosity, Petty Officer, belongs to my father.'

'Oh. I do apologize, sir.'

'Don't. As I said, it is a monstrosity. And, believe it or not, it is named *Pumpkin*. But it has some power. And I suppose he feels he has to do his bit. Mother!' he called down the hatch. 'Can you come up?'

Kristin pushed her head through the hatch. 'I thought I wasn't allowed on deck?'

Duncan turned his head to look at her. 'Good God! Under no circumstances are you allowed on deck. Stay right there. But there is something I would like you to look at. Pass her the glasses, would you, Mr Harris?'

Harris obeyed, carefully attempting not to look at her.

'Green sixty,' Duncan recommended.

Kristin adjusted the focus. 'Good Lord!'

'Aren't you proud of him?'

'Don't you think he needs his head examined?'

'Absolutely. But don't they all? And it is rather splendid. Makes you proud to be British. I must give him a call when this is over.'

'Well, I might just join you.'

'Harbour control is signalling that it is clear to come in, sir,' Harris said.

'Down you go, Mother.'

'Back to the salt mines,' she grumbled, but she obediently disappeared.

By dusk they had completed another delivery, and when they came alongside, the lieutenant-commander peered down at them as the soldiers filed ashore. 'Your fuel situation?'

'We have enough, sir. The less fuel we have the faster we can go.' And, Duncan thought, the less chance there is of us going up if struck by a bullet. Or even two.

'Well, just remember you're no use to God nor man if you run out. Very good. Take four hours off.'

'Sir? There are still a couple of hundred thousand men over there.'

'I know that, Lieutenant, but you and your men are also no use to anybody if you fall asleep on the job. One watch below and then you're on duty again. You'll be back over there by midnight.'

Duncan returned his salute, and then switched off the ignition. 'You heard the man, Mr Harris. Everyone to eat and a kip.'

'Sir.'

Harris reached the hatch and encountered Jamie coming up. 'Is there a problem, sir?'

'We're giving your engine a rest, Jamie. And you. And . . . Oh, my God!' He went below. 'Come aft,' he told the women.

'What's going to happen to us now?' Kristin inquired.

'We are required to take a watch off before going back. Are you still determined to stay on board?'

'Yes, we are,' they replied together.

'Very good. I'll have some dinner sent in to you here.'

'Don't be ridiculous,' Kristin said. 'I want to eat with the crew.'

'Mother!'

'If you don't agree, I'll take this shirt off and go on deck.'

'Oh, for God's sake. But as soon as the meal is over you and Alison will retire here.'

'You're the one who needs the good night's sleep.'

'I will get it forward. I'm sorry, but you will have to share the one bunk.'

'But of course,' Kristin said. 'Isn't that what I always wanted?'

He gazed at her, and then left the cabin.

'Just what did you mean by that?' Alison asked.

Kristin smiled. 'Simply that I want to get to know you, so much better.'

They had completed another crossing by 0300. Still the weather held, although the night was dark, and the only hazard was running into some other boat; no one was showing any lights. Now, as he approached the beach yet again, Duncan could see the first light creeping over the dunes, and realized that this could be an even longer day; the numbers of men emerging from various gullies and hastily dug foxholes did not seem to have diminished.

He pressed the engine-room intercom.

'Sir?' Jamie asked.

'Fuel?'

'We're down to a quarter on both tanks, sir.'

'Right. This time we'll fuel as soon as we get back.'

Alison emerged with steaming cups of coffee for Harris and himself. 'Good morning, Captain.' He squeezed her fingers as he took the mug, and she responded. 'What a gorgeous morning.'

'Too gorgeous. I suspect we are going to have company before too long. Mr Harris?'

'Aye aye, sir.' Harris gulped his coffee, handed the mug back to Alison, and hurried forward with his boathook. On the beach the men were already lining up and entering the water.

'Kristin tells me your dad is somewhere about,' Alison remarked.

'He was last night. As a matter of fact . . .' He levelled the binoculars. 'What the devil is the idiot doing?'

'That's no way to speak of your father,' Alison protested.

'He's gone aground. Shit!'

Alison took the glasses. 'Actually, I'd say he's anchored. Although it looks to me as if the tide is falling. And there's no one on deck.'

'The tide *is* falling.' He picked up the loud hailer.

'Does he know that?'

'He should. He's done a hell of a lot of yachting in his time. That's how he met my mother.'

'Ah,' she said enigmatically.

There were quite a few soldiers gathered round the motor-boat, but none of them was making any effort to get on board, and as he watched, a head appeared out of the hatch. 'Ahoy!' he bellowed. 'Do you need a hand?'

The head jerked and turned. 'Duncan! Thank God! My engine's gone.'

'Hang on.' Duncan pressed the intercom. 'Jamie! Get up here.'

'Aye aye, sir.'

Jamie appeared a moment later, followed by Kristin.

'You just stay there,' Duncan told his mother. 'Jamie, he seems to have a problem. Can you nip across and see if you can sort it out? Be as quick as you can.'

'Aye aye, sir.' Jamie went on deck and dropped over the side into chest-deep water.

'Where are you sending him?' Kristin demanded.

'To give Dad a hand.'

She looked in the indicated direction. 'Oh, the clot! He's on the ground. What's Jamie supposed to do – push him off?'

'His engine has broken down. If Jamie can get it going he should be able to kedge himself off; he has an anchor out. Look out.'

Kristin looked down. She was halfway up the companion from the cabin, which was filled with men, all of them preoccupied with the view. But Duncan was looking up, and when she did the same she could see the black dots dropping from the sky.

'Come on, come on, come on,' Duncan muttered. 'How many, Mr Harris?'

'That's our lot, sir.'

'Well, get them aft.'

'Aye aye, sir. Sorry, you chaps,' he told the waiting men 'We'll be back in an hour.'

They looked longingly at him, and then at Alison, standing beside him – she had lost or taken off her steel helmet and her hair was blowing in the wind – before stepping back.

'Scatter!' an officer on the beach bellowed, as machine guns began to chatter.

'Machine-gunners!' Duncan bawled. 'Alison, get below! Jamie, where the hell are you?'

As if in reply, the engine of the motor launch spluttered into life. 'Brilliant!' Lord Eversham shouted.

'Get him back here!' Duncan bellowed. Not a hundred yards away the beach was being torn up, and he was surrounded by the chatter of his own machine guns. Instinctively he put the engine slow astern to move into deeper water.

Jamie appeared on the deck of the launch and jumped over the side, wading out and then swimming towards them.

'Dad!' Duncan shouted. 'Get out of there.'

But both Eversham and his two crew were on the foredeck helping soldiers on board, while Kristin had abandoned both modesty and discretion and was hanging over the side of the MTB to reach for Jamie's hand, as was Alison, eagerly assisted by four of the soldiers.

'Shit!' Duncan muttered, but as he did so his crew burst into cheers; one of the Messerschmitts had swung too low, and received a stream of bullets into its belly. Smoke and flames issuing behind it, it soared past them and plunged into the sea.

'Good shooting!' Duncan yelled.

'Another one!' Harris called.

This one was coming from the other side, out to avenge its downed comrade. But Jamie was on board.

'Get below!' Duncan shouted, spinning the helm and gunning the motor.

He was too late. A stream of bullets tore up his deck, to the accompaniment of screams of agony, and splashes as several people went over the side. Duncan found he was holding his breath even as he instinctively brought the engine back to neutral, waiting for the bang that would be the last thing he, or anyone on board, would ever hear.

But there was none; even if the deck had been penetrated, his tanks were nearly empty. And he was still surrounded by anguished sound. He looked down at the side decking, and his heart constricted as he saw Alison lying there, motionless, surrounded by a pool of blood, while Kristin crouched beside her.

Harris had seen her too. 'I'll take her, sir,' he said.

'Circle and pick up those fellows overboard,' Duncan said and slid down the ladder.

'Aye aye, sir.' Harris spun the helm, at the same time thumbing the intercom. 'Wilson! Tell me if we're making water.'

Duncan stooped beside his mother. 'Is she . . .?'

'I'm all right,' Alison said. 'I'm all right.' Her face twisted with pain.

'I'll take her below,' Duncan said. 'See what you can do about these others.' There were several wounded men on deck, and he could tell that one at least was dead. He scooped Alison from the deck, carried her inside, and down the companion to his cabin.

'You must get up there,' she gasped. 'You've a ship to command.'

'You're losing blood,' he protested.

'I'll survive. Save the ship.'

He hesitated, but he knew she was right. He squeezed her hand, then went up the companion. Kristin was kneeling beside a wounded soldier. 'Alison,' he said.

'I'll get to her in a minute,' Kristin said. 'You get on deck.'

Duncan went up. Harris had brought the boat round and stopped her, while the crew, including Jamie, were on the foredeck helping the men up over the side. 'How is your lady, sir?' the Petty Officer asked.

'I don't know yet. Are we intact?'

'Not quite, sir. Some of those bullets went in pretty low. But the pumps can cope. And most of the damage is forward. If we can get up some speed, and lift the bow, we should get home all right.'

'Then let's do that.' He took the helm. 'All aboard? Then hold on!'

'They're back!' Rawlings shouted.

'Oh, shit!' Harris commented, uncharacteristically.

Duncan looked up, saw the bullets carving into the sand, fifty yards away, and heading straight for . . . 'Oh, my God!' he muttered

The Messerschmitt had soared over *Pumpkin*, sending a another stream of bullets into the red and yellow hull. As the watchers on the MTB gasped, the launch exploded.

The Missing

'Captain Lawrence? Lonsdale, Portsmouth, here.'

'Yes, sir.' Lawrence had been warned who was on the line by his secretary.

'I understand that you have on your staff a Wren officer who used to be known as Alison Brunel.'

'Ah . . . I'm not sure I'm quite with you, sir. I do have an officer on my staff named Alison Brunel, but she has been posted AWOL, and there is a warrant out for her arrest. Am I to understand that you know where she can be found?'

'Lady Eversham is in hospital.'

'Ah . . . I think we are talking at cross purposes, sir. I was referring to Second Officer Brunel.'

'So am I. As of ten o'clock this morning she became Lady Eversham.'

'But you say she is in hospital.'

'That is where the wedding took place, yes. She was married from her hospital bed. I attended the ceremony myself.'

'I see, sir.' Though from his tone he clearly did not see at all. So he stuck to first principles. 'But if I understand you correctly, we are still talking about the officer who is absent without leave.'

'I would like to explain that, Captain. Second Officer Brunel, as she then was, arrived in Portsmouth last Wednesday morning, unaware that all leave had been cancelled.' He stared across the desk at Kristin, to leave her in no doubt that he knew he was lying, at her request. 'She had come down to visit her fiancé, Lord Eversham. You will know him as Lieutenant Duncan Morant.'

'Good God!' Lawrence commented.

'He was actually still Lieutenant Morant when she arrived, and she was on board his MTB when he received orders to proceed immediately with his flotilla to Dunkirk. There was no time to put her ashore, so she went with him' – he continued to stare at Kristin – 'and I may say, played a most gallant part in the rescue of several hundred soldiers from the beaches. However, when the MTB was strafed on Thursday morning, she was one of the casualties. Her shoulder was broken by a bullet. Oddly, this happened at almost the same time that she ceased being Alison Brunel and fell into line as the future Alison, Lady Eversham. Lord Eversham was killed just about then, you see.'

There was a brief silence while Lawrence digested this. Kristin supposed he might be scratching his head. He now began to clutch at straws. 'I thought there was already a Lady Eversham, sir? Or was she blown up as well.'

'Well, of course she wasn't, my dear fellow.' Lonsdale now smiled at Kristin. 'But she is now the Dowager Lady Eversham.'

'Of course. Silly of me not to have realized that. And you say Miss . . . ah . . . Lady Eversham is in hospital. May I ask for how long?'

'I'm afraid it may be another fortnight. And then she will need to recuperate.'

'I see. So I shall have to find a replacement cipher officer for . . . a month?'

'A replacement is on her way to you now. In all the circumstances, I have decided to transfer Lady Eversham to my staff here in Portsmouth – as soon as she is fit for duty again, of course.'

'Of course, sir.' Lawrence's tone suggested that he was relieved at this turn of events. 'Would you congratulate the young lady for me, sir?'

'What, on being hit in the shoulder?'

'On being so suddenly elevated to the peerage, sir.'

'Ah. Yes. I shall do that, Captain Lawrence. I am assuming that the charges against her ladyship will be withdrawn.'

'I think that would be appropriate, sir.'

'Thank you. It has been a pleasure talking with you. Good morning.' He hung up and looked at Kristin. 'What does it feel like to be a dowager?'

'In one sense it is quite romantic. As long as it is not taken to mean old and grey.'

'I can't imagine you ever being old and grey, Kristin. But

'. . . No regrets for poor old Donald? He died a hero's death, you know.'

'So did quite a few other people. Of course I didn't wish him to be killed. But we were all in the firing line.'

'I want to talk to you about that. You had no business being there, you know.'

'Every other member of my family was there.'

'It was their business to be. Even Alison, although she also shouldn't have been there, was at least a serving member of the Navy.'

'Donald was not a serving member of the Royal Navy. Nor were all the other yachtsmen and boat owners who were there.'

'They were men.'

'Oh, really Jimmy, that is most offensive. However, I will forgive you because you have sorted out Alison's problem. Now tell me, what is going to happen in France?'

'I'm afraid it's beginning to look very nasty. The fact is that, with the evacuation of the BEF, we have only the Highland Division left on the Continent.'

'But don't the French have the best army in the world?'

'I'm afraid that was a piece of pre-war propaganda that went straight down the drain when the shooting started. I can tell you that there are strong suspicions that they may be thinking of calling it a day.'

'You mean surrendering to Germany? You can't be serious.'

'They may reckon it's their only chance of saving something from the wreck.'

'And where will that leave us?'

'With a lot to do. I am talking about the Navy. If Jerry gets hold of the Atlantic seaboard of France, with all those ports – Calais, Boulogne, Dieppe, Le Havre, St Malo, Brest, Bordeaux, perhaps even the Channel Islands – as U-boat bases . . .'

'What did you say? Can he take the Channel Islands?'

'If France were to surrender, I don't see what's to stop him.'

'But they're British territory. We'd *have* to stop him.'

'What with? We may have rescued the better part of the BEF, but we certainly didn't bring back any of their equipment. They have to be got into trim to resist an invasion, if it comes.'

'The Navy is intact.'

'I have just explained that the Navy is going to have rather a lot to do, Kristin. Certainly we have not got the ships, or the men, to spare trying to defend a few small islands of no strategic value and with a population less than that of the average English town. Anyway, I shouldn't think the islanders would be very happy if we started fighting over them, with the total destruction that would ensue. No, if that worst-possible scenario does crop up, as we can't possibly protect them, our, and their, best course would be to declare them open, and thus undefended, territory. That is a well-known international convention, and should be respected, even by Jerry.'

'But that won't necessarily stop him occupying them.'

'I'm afraid it probably won't. But he'd have to do it in a civilized manner.'

'Shit!'

Lonsdale raised his eyebrows. 'You are making me think there is something personal in this.'

'There is. I have a house in Guernsey.'

'I never knew that.'

'Well . . . it was Donald's house, actually. When we split up he changed all the locks, so I couldn't use it. But it's mine, now. I have got the keys.'

'Isn't it actually Duncan's?'

'What is Duncan's is mine.'

'Message understood. But I'm afraid you may have to write it off for the duration.'

'Which may take months. Or even years. By the end of which it will have been thoroughly looted.'

'I'm afraid that is a possibility. Occupying armies, even of the most civilized variety, do tend to regard unoccupied houses as fair game. But Kristin, don't you have half a dozen houses scattered about the place? Surely you're not going to lose sleep over letting one of them go?'

'You don't understand,' Kristin said. 'When we were newly married, and madly, sexually, in love with each other, Donald had me painted.'

'Ah.'

'In the nud.'

'Ah.'

'In a very provocative pose.'

'Is it a good painting? – a good likeness?'

'It is a magnificent work of art. None of your modern impressionist drivel. And it is a perfect likeness. It could have been a photograph.'

'Imagination boggles. And this painting is in the Guernsey house.'

'That is correct.'

'Well . . . if everything one reads about Goering, and his tendency to snaffle any old masters, or even young masters, he can lay hands on is true, I suspect that he is going to be a very happy man. But there it is.'

'Jimmy Lonsdale, I hate you.' She got up. 'But if you really feel that I have been a naughty girl, you may come to dinner tonight, and I will let you spank me. *Hasta la vista.*'

'Lieutenant Eversham,' the King said, pinning the ribbon of the Distinguished Service Cross on Duncan's breast, 'I was so terribly sorry to hear of your father's death. I hope it is some comfort to you to know that he died like the hero he was.'

'Yes, sir. Thank you.'

'Is your mother bearing up?'

'Yes, sir. Very well. She's here today.'

'Of course. I must have a word with her. Ah . . .' He had clearly just remembered that the senior Evershams had been divorced.

Duncan saw no reason to let him off the hook. 'I know she would appreciate that, sir.'

'And now you're married yourself. Is your wife here as well?'

'My wife is in hospital, sir.'

'Oh, I'm sorry to hear that. Not serious, is it?'

'A broken shoulder, sir.'

'Oh.' He was now clearly at a loss as to what to say next, and Duncan was touched on the shoulder by the waiting aide-de-camp. He stepped back, saluted, and joined his mother, who was seated beside Leeming's mother; she had just received the posthumous VC earned by her son.

'That was a long chat,' Kristin remarked.

'It was mainly about you,' Duncan said enigmatically.

* * *

'I wish I could have been there,' Alison said. She sat up in bed with her left arm and shoulder bandaged and in an elaborate sling which was suspended from a bar above her and prevented her from moving, 'instead of sitting here getting bed sores. Do you know, I have to call a nurse even to scratch?'

'Tell me where. Scratching you is about the nearest I am going to get to consummating the marriage for the foreseeable future.'

'I am told I should be out of here in another ten days. And then I have a fortnight's R and R. We should be able to get something done. When you think I travelled eight hundred miles to be with you . . .' She had been studying his expression. 'Don't tell me. You're going somewhere.'

'I'm told the boat will be ready for sea in ten days, yes. But as far as I know I'll be operating out of Portsmouth.'

'Well, then . . .'

'It seems likely to be a little fraught. Have you heard the news?'

'We don't get a lot of news in here.'

'France has surrendered.'

'Oh, the buggers! What does that mean for you?'

'Nobody knows, for sure. But almost certainly it means increased German activity in the Channel, by both surface craft and U-boats. We haven't any details yet about the actual terms, but it seems obvious they'll demand the right to occupy, and use, all the Channel ports.'

'And you have to stop them.'

'We will have to take them on, yes.'

Her right hand sought his fingers. 'You're not going to go and get yourself blown up, are you? I mean – well, I'm just beginning to get used to being addressed as milady.'

'Whatever happens to me, my dearest girl, from now on you will always be addressed as milady, even if you have to attach a "dowager" to it.'

'Brrr.'

'Have you heard from your folks?'

'They can't believe it yet. They're going to try to get down to see me. And you.'

'I'll look forward to that. They'll stay with us, of course.'

'Will Kristin be happy with that?'

'Yes,' Duncan said definitely. 'Now, listen, I have to go

back up to London for a few days – some kind of sympo-sium on naval tactics. I suppose they can't bear the thought of my hanging around here with nothing to do. I'll be back on Sunday. When did you say your folk would be down?'

'Monday, I think.'

'That's fine, I'll be here. Can you manage without me for five days? Mother will be in, every day.'

'Just come back,' Alison said, and turned her face up for a kiss.

'God,' Kristin remarked, looking up at the hull. 'What a mess.'

'She took a beating, yes, milady,' Hawkins said. He wasn't sure what this glamorous woman was doing in the yard anyway, but she had shown him a pass signed by Rear Admiral Lonsdale. 'Those hits below the waterline . . . She was lucky to get back.'

'I know,' Kristin said. 'I was on board.'

'Milady?'

'Up to my ankles in water when we reached Portsmouth,' she explained. 'But that was in the engine room.'

Hawkins preferred not to comment.

'So how long will she be up here?'

'She'll be in the water in another week.'

'Um. I don't see any of the crew around.'

'Well, there's nothing for them to do here, right this minute, milady. They've been given shore leave. They're due back on Monday. As you can imagine, there's lots of work to be done to get her ready for sea.'

'Monday,' Kristin said thoughtfully. 'Hum.'

'Milady?'

'Just thinking. Thank you, Mr Hawkins.'

She returned to her car and drove away from the yard. Damn, she thought. Damn, damn, damn. But it had only been a stupid pipe dream anyway.

And in the meantime, if he was on holiday . . . She stopped at Goring's Garage. 'Good afternoon, Mr Probert. Mr Jamie about?'

'Well, no, milady. He went into town.'

'On his bicycle?'

'Yes, milady. I think he was going to look at the yacht. Shall I tell him you asked after him?'

'Why, thank you, Mr Probert. That would be very nice.'

She drove to the yard. Thursday was early closing, and the little yachting port was somnolent, although the Yarmouth ferry was operating. The yard was deserted – even the foreman was absent – the various yachts looking as forlornly abandoned as always, the more so because in such perfect summer weather they should all have been out on the Solent, at the very least. But the bicycle leaned against the wall of the big shed.

Kristin parked, went inside, regarded the schooner, which seemed to grow more derelict every time she saw her. But she hadn't come here to look at the yacht. 'You up there, Jamie?' she called.

His head appeared at the rail. 'Milady?'

Kristin climbed the ladder. 'What do you do here, all by yourself? – have a private moment?'

He helped her over the rail, but now he knew what she meant. 'Think, I suppose. And remember.'

'About women? I hope the woman is me.'

'When I think about women, I think about you.'

'But you don't think about me all the time.' She took him in her arms.

'Not out here, milady,' he protested.

'There is no one else around. We could go out there and fuck in the centre of the yard.'

'Milady!'

'I know.' She released him and went down the companion. 'Bare boards. Brrr. Do you know, I had an idea that we might go away for the weekend.'

'Milady?'

'Wouldn't you like that?'

'Well, yes, milady, but . . .'

Kristin sat on one of the bunks, kicked off her shoes, and pulled up her skirt to roll down her stockings.

'Why do always you do that?' he asked.

'I don't like having sex with my stockings on. I like to be naked when having sex. Haven't you noticed?'

'And you only want to be with me to have sex.'

'Now, Jamie . . . you have been philosophizing. I have nothing against philosophy, but you should never let it interfere with the important things in life.' She lifted her jumper over her head, but left her pearls in place, resting on her breasts. I would love to have a weekend with you, just the two of us, all alone, in a huge bed, with clean sheets, and no risk of interruptions . . . Do you like that idea?'

He could not stop himself caressing the soft flesh, feeling the nipples harden into his palm. 'I should love that, milady. But—'

'I know. You have to report for duty on Monday.'

'Today is Thursday, milady.'

'I know. But I am leaving tomorrow. Ow!'

He had inadvertently squeezed too hard. 'Leaving?'

'I am going away for the weekend. That's why I had thought you might be able to come with me. But I can't promise to be back by Monday. I wouldn't want you to be posted AWOL.'

He kissed her.

'But once the boat is back in the water,' she said, 'I don't suppose there'll be much leave.'

'I don't know what's going to happen,' he confessed. 'I don't even think the brass have any idea. One thing is pretty certain, though: once the Germans get hold of the Channel ports, there's going to be a lot more activity in the Channel. That's our patch.'

'And they seem to be gobbling them up at a rate of knots since the French dropped out,' Kristin said. 'So this may be our last get-together for a while.' She hugged him, almost fiercely. 'Fuck me, Jamie. Oh, fuck me.'

'You are looking great.' Duncan leaned over the bed to kiss his wife.

'I'm feeling great. See?' Her arm was out of the overhead sling, although still secured against her breast.

'No pain?'

'Well, the odd twinge.'

'When are your mum and dad arriving?'

'After lunch.'

'Right. I'll get Mother to meet them and bring them here, and then take them to the house.'

'Won't you be here?'

'I'm afraid not. I'm just dashing home for one or two things, then I have to get back to the boat. She goes into the water this morning, and we have to be ready for sea in three days' time. The big boys are anticipating that the Channel is going to be filled with German ships within the week. So . . .'

'But, Mum and Dad . . .'

'Relax. I told you, I'm stopping by the house now, to put Mother in the picture. She'll take care of them. And you'll be home in another couple of days, you say.'

'But you . . .'

He grimaced. 'I'll be back as soon as I can.' He kissed her again, and she held his arm with her good hand.

'This flap has nothing to do with the news about the Channel Islands, has it?'

'That Jerry may have occupied them? That hasn't been confirmed yet. Although we do know the buggers bombed St Peter Port yesterday. Killed a few people too. That after the islands had been declared open. But, sadly, I suppose, what happens there means nothing in the overall picture. If Jerry does take them over, he'll thump his chest and claim to have conquered part of the United Kingdom. As everyone who knows anything about geography knows that they are not part of the United Kingdom, he'll just be making a fool of himself. Strategically, they are of not the slightest importance to anyone. Now I must rush.'

'Do come back.'

Duncan had left the Bugatti at the station while in London. Now he parked before the house, and opened the front door.

'Woof!' Lucifer was in his arms.

'Hold on, old chap,' he protested. 'I'm in uniform.' He set the dog down and went up the stairs. 'Mother?' Both cars were in the garage.

'Oh, Mr Duncan,' Harry said from below. 'I didn't hear you come.'

Duncan looked down at him. 'Mother out the back, is she?'

'Well, no, sir.'

'So?'

'She's not here, sir. She went away. For the weekend.'

'Went away – where?' Probably with Lonsdale, he reflected. But could the admiral risk the possible scandal?

'Ah . . .' Harry was looking highly embarrassed. 'She went to Guernsey, sir. On Friday's ferry.'

Duncan slowly descended the stairs. 'She did *what*? Why?'

'She said something about picking up something from the house there, sir. I know she took the keys.'

Duncan snapped his fingers. 'That bloody painting. Of all the crazy, mixed-up women . . .'

'Sir? She said she'd be back today.'

'Today? The Germans occupied Guernsey yesterday.'

'Sir?'

'Hadn't you heard? What a fucking awful mess.'

'She could have got out in time, sir.'

'Then why isn't she here?'

'Well, I suppose the ferry hasn't docked yet.'

'Harry, if the Germans occupied Guernsey yesterday, there isn't going to be a ferry today. Or tomorrow. Or any time in the foreseeable future.'

'Oh, dear. You mean . . .'

'Yes. But—' Again he snapped his fingers. 'Did she take all her passports with her?'

'I don't know, sir. She had an overnight bag.'

'Right. Well . . . I have to go to Portsmouth now, and I don't know when I will be back. I want you to use the Bentley and meet the two o'clock from London. On board will be a Mr and Mrs Brunel. I'm afraid I don't have a description, but you must find them.'

'Yes, sir.' Harry's tone was doubtful.

'Don't let me down on this, Harry. You will take them to the hospital to see Lady Eversham, who happens to be their daughter. You'll wait for them, and then bring them here. They will be staying for a while.'

'But . . . you say you won't be here, sir?'

'That is why I am putting you in charge. Tell Lucia to make up one of the spare rooms, and give them everything they wish. It won't be for very long. I mean, you won't be on your own for very long. If my mother doesn't manage to get back in a day or two, my wife will be out of hospital at the end of the week. She'll take over.'

'Yes, sir,' Harry said, more doubtfully yet. 'Her ladyship hasn't actually been here, before.'

'Of course she has. Her bag is in my room.'

'Yes, sir. I placed it there myself. But she didn't stay. She and her ladyship – I mean, her dowager ladyship – left immediately.'

'Well, they had to go to Dunkirk, don't you know.'

'Yes, sir.' Harry had clearly abandoned any idea of making sense of the conversation, and decided to stick to facts. 'What I was meaning was – well, she won't know any of the usual arrangements . . . your mother's arrangements . . .'

'So you will guide her, where necessary. However, should she wish to make any arrangements of her own, you are to go along with her. As of this moment, she is the mistress of the house. Right?'

'Ah, right. And the dog?'

'What about the dog?' Duncan ruffled Lucifer's head.

'On the occasion of her previous visit, sir, Lucifer knocked her over.'

'Good God! Did he? But I'm sure it was a mistake. She loves dogs,' he added, optimistically. 'Now, Harry, I know I'm dumping a lot on your plate, but there happens to be a war on, and I know you can cope. *Hasta la vista!*'

'Ah, Duncan.' Rear Admiral Lonsdale smiled at the son of his favourite woman. 'I see your boat is back in the water. No problems, I hope?'

'I haven't checked her out yet, sir. Ah . . .'

'Well, be a good lad and check her out immediately. And check *Seventy-Three* and *Seventy-Four* as well. I want you ready for sea by tomorrow.'

'Yes, sir. May I ask if there is any news from Guernsey?'

Lonsdale raised his eyebrows. 'Guernsey? We have no units there, thank God.'

'My mother is there, sir.'

'*What?*'

'She seems to have gone across on Friday, while I was in London. My father had a house on Guernsey, you see. I think her idea was to pick something up that—'

It was Lonsdale's turn to snap his fingers. 'That painting!'

'Sir? You know of that?'

'Ah . . . yes. Your mother told me of it. I haven't seen it, of course,' he hastily added. 'Although I know she did not wish it to fall into the hands of the Germans. But to take the risk of going over there to get it . . .'

'You know what Mother is like, sir.' Well, you jolly well should, Duncan thought. 'And I don't think she had any idea how fast the Germans would move.'

'And you're sure she's not on her way back?'

'I think we can assume, sir, that if she is not back now, she isn't on her way.'

'Damn, damn, damn. But . . . your mother has more than one passport, has she not?'

'She has triple nationality, sir.'

'Triple?'

'My grandmother had her christened in Sweden, and she kept up that passport. She also has a Spanish passport and, as a naturalized Englishwoman, she has a British passport as well.'

'Hm. And you think she would have all three with her?'

'I would say that is probable.'

'The sticking point is liable to be that naturalized British bit. On the other hand, if she doesn't show that passport at all, she can simply pass herself off as a Spanish citizen, and get out through France and into Spain. In which case we should be hearing from her any day.'

'And if she can't get out, sir?'

Lonsdale frowned. 'Well . . . she can't come to any harm, can she? I mean, she's a very wealthy woman. Isn't she?'

'Yes, sir, she is. But, I suppose because of that, she never really gives a thought to her personal finances. She is just as likely to have gone across with only a few pounds in her purse.'

Lonsdale stroked his chin. 'All right, Duncan. Leave it with me. I will see if contact can be established. I'm sure there must be a Spanish consul or something in Guernsey whom we can utilize.'

'Thank you, sir. It's just that I feel we must do something, as quickly as possible.'

Lonsdale frowned. 'You don't suppose she's in any danger, do you?'

'Well, sir . . .' Duncan hesitated. 'My great-grandmother – that is, my mother's grandmother – was Jewish.'

'Good God! But you mother went to a convent, didn't she?'

'We have a confused background, sir. My great-grandfather was a Roman Catholic, and by the terms of the marriage agreement, any children of the union were to be brought up in that faith. In any event, my great-grandmother converted.'

'So from then on the family has been Roman Catholic. I never knew you were a Catholic, Duncan.'

'I'm not.'

Lonsdale scratched his head.

'As I said, it is a little convoluted, sir. My father was a rather strict Anglican, and he would not consider bringing up his children – or in my case, as I was an only child, me – in any other faith.'

'I thought no Catholic family would permit a marriage in those circumstances?'

'Normally they would not. But circumstances were a little fraught. Mother had already been expelled from her convent, and the scandal had become known. So . . . well . . .'

'They felt obliged to bite the bullet. Yes. I see. But Kristin is definitely a Roman Catholic.'

'I wouldn't go so far as to say that, sir.'

'Eh?'

'I have never heard my mother express any kind of religious belief, sir – save in the old Greek gods.'

'You're joking.'

'Actually, sir, if she worships anyone, it is Eurynome.'

'You have lost me.'

'Eurynome was the Pelaegian great goddess, the fount of all things, the Creator. She emerged from the Chaos, tall, long-haired, beautiful of face and body, and naked, and sought only to dance her way across and around the universe. That has been my mother's philosophy all her life.'

'Good heavens!'

Duncan realized that his boss was recalling the number of times he had 'danced' around the universe with her.

'But you say she was the fount of all things.'

'Inadvertently, sir. In the course of her passage through space she naturally created a wind, Boreas, who – I quote the legend – lusted after her. He couldn't do much about it as a wind, so he turned himself into a giant snake, named Iphion, and Iphion – again I quote – wrapped himself around her thighs. She does not appear to have objected to this. From their union, as I said, sprang all things: the earth and the sea and the sky, and everything in them.'

'And I suppose they lived happily ever after.'

'Well, no, they didn't actually. They lived happily, on Mount Olympus, for a few eternities, and then Iphion made a mistake. He looked down on the seas and the forests, the pastures and the flocks, the animals and the fishes and, of course, the men and the women, and he said, proudly, 'To think that I created all this.' This offended Eurynome, who felt, I would say with some justification, that *she* had created all this. So she hit him. In fact, she beat him up, broke various parts of his body and knocked out all of his teeth. Then she condemned him to crawl in the dust for the rest of time.'

'Sort of encapsulated history of human relationships,' Lonsdale remarked. 'However, we seem to be getting away from the point. Whether Kristin regards herself as a re-incarnation of Eurynome or not, she is right now beyond our reach. I have promised to see what I can do through our Madrid embassy, but success will depend entirely on the Spaniards' willingness to co-operate, and as their govern-ment supports the Nazis, that co-operation may be difficult to obtain, But it is all we can hope for. Your business, as of now and until you receive further orders, is ASW. You have one submarine to your credit already. See if you can add to that. But you are absolutely forbidden to take your boat anywhere near Guernsey. I wish that clearly under-stood.'

Duncan stood up and to attention. 'Aye aye, sir.'

'Very good.' The admiral allowed himself a smile. 'I have never doubted – and what you have just told me confirms it – that your mother can survive anything that she wishes to. We'll get her back.'

Kristin sat before the desk, uninvited, and crossed her knees. '*Este es ridiculo*,' she announced.

The handsome, immaculately dressed young officer who sat on the other side of the desk, looked at his waiting sergeant – who shrugged. 'You must speak English,' the officer explained, in that language. 'My French is not very good.'

'I happen to have been speaking Spanish,' Kristin pointed out.

'Why were you doing that?'

'Because I am Spanish.' With difficulty she restrained herself from adding, 'Cretin.'

The officer gazed at her for several seconds. He obviously liked what he was looking at, but then, so had everyone else in this building the Germans had requisitioned as an admin-istrative headquarters. Then he picked up the passport, and the accompanying piece of paper on his desk and studied them, and then compared them with an entry in the copy of *Who's Who* that also waited on the desk. 'It says here that your name is Kristin, Lady Eversham, and that your address is Eversham House, Castle, Guernsey.'

'No, no,' Kristin said. 'Not Castle. It is pronounced Catel. No "s", you see.'

'It says "Castle" on this paper.'

'I don't think that paper was written by a Guernseyman.'

'But there is a castle.'

'Well, the remains of one. If you are keen on castles, there are several better ones on the island.'

'And this castle is where you live?'

'Good God, no. I live in Eversham House. That is when I am here.'

'But you are here.'

'At this moment, yes. But I wish to leave.'

He studied the passport again. 'Lady Eversham,' he mused. 'How shall I address you?'

'Milady will do.'

'Milady. You are the wife of Lord Eversham?'

'The widow.'

'Your husband is dead?'

'Well, that would seem to be obvious. He is dead, because you blew him up.'

'What?'

'Oh, I don't mean you personally. He was in his boat, and one of your airplanes dropped a bomb on him.'

'That is very sad.'

'Don't cry over it. We were divorced.'

He looked about to scratch his head, then took refuge in facts. 'Your husband is an officer in the Royal Navy. Was.'

'No, no. That is my son. My husband was a layabout.'

'And now you wish to return to England, to be with your son.'

'My son is hardly ever there. I wish to return to England because that is where I live.'

'You do realize that you are an enemy alien?'

'How can I be an enemy alien on English territory?'

'This island is now German territory.'

'It's a point of view. But if you will look at that other

passport, you will see that I am a Spanish national. Spain is not at war with Germany.'

The officer opened the second passport. 'Why do you have two passports?'

'Because I have dual nationality.'

The sergeant made a remark, in German, and the officer opened the third passport. 'My God! You have *three* passports.'

'I happen to have Swedish nationality as well.'

'I do not believe you. I think you are a spy.'

Kristin regarded him from beneath arched eyebrows. 'How terribly romantic. Unfortunately, I have no idea what you are talking about.'

'I should lock you up to await trial.'

'Ah. If you are going to do that, you must allow me to make a telephone call. That is the law.'

'Bah! Who do you wish to telephone?'

'General Franco.'

'What?'

'General Franco,' Kristin explained, 'is a friend of my father. He dandled me on his knee when I was a baby. I know he will wish to be informed that I am being held illegally and against my will.'

The officer stared at her, and she stared back. 'You will return to your house and remain there, under guard,' he decided, 'while I investigate this matter.'

'For how long am I supposed to remain there?'

'Until I have completed my investigation.'

'How *long*?'

He shrugged. 'It my take a few weeks.'

'A few weeks? Listen, I came over here for the weekend. I have two changes of clothing, and very little money. How am I supposed to live, for two weeks or more?'

'You say you have no money? It says here that you are a very wealthy woman.'

'I am a wealthy woman. But my money is all in England. And Spain,' she added for good measure.

'But you have a bank account.'

'Not in Guernsey.'

'All the banks in Guernsey are branches of English banks. Which one do you deal with, in England?'

'I really have no idea. I think I deal with all of them.'

He sighed and considered for a few moments, then nodded. 'Very well.' He spoke to the sergeant, and then turned back to her. 'The sergeant will escort you to a bank here in Guernsey and you will receive overdraft facilities.'

'Why should they do that?'

'Because you are a wealthy woman, because you will offer your Guernsey house as security, and because I say so.'

'And I may go shopping?'

'Yes. Accompanied by one of my men.'

'I see. You mean that I am under arrest.'

'I am placing you under a restriction order until I am able to confirm your claims.'

'And then you will permit me to return to England?'

'Then I may permit you to leave Guernsey and travel to Spain.'

Kristin glared at him for several seconds, then decided to smile. 'That seems quite civilized. May I ask your name?'

'It is Joachim Jurgen.'

'How quaint. So, I will go shopping now. And then, Captain Jurgen, perhaps you would care to have dinner with me tonight.'

Leopards

'I see him!' Colley shouted into the radio. 'Red forty.'

'Spread out,' Duncan commanded.

The three MTBs fanned away from each other. It was a brilliant August morning and up-Channel, they knew, there was a great deal of activity. But that was in the air. Down here, forty miles south-west of the Scillies, the only action was in the sea. The convoy they had been sent to protect, and which had reported that it was under attack from a U-boat, was still close at hand, although steaming as fast as it could for the safety of Plymouth. So far it had not suffered a casualty. But the U-boat was still about, even if it had ceased its attack on the approach of the three fast motorboats. And now, peering through his glasses while Harris took the helm, Duncan could see the movement just under the surface – but disappearing fast.

'She's yours, *Seventy-Three*,' he said. Colley was closest.

'Aye aye,' Colley replied, and zoomed towards the disturbance.

'Stand by, *Seventy-Four*,' Duncan said. If Colley were to score a hit, or even a near miss, the U-boat might well surface, and its gun could still prove lethal for a torpedo boat.

'Aye aye,' Harmo replied.

'I'll take her, Mr Harris,' Duncan said. 'Prepare our own charges.'

'Aye aye, sir.' Harris summoned his ratings and made his way aft, hanging on with every step, as *Seventy-Two* raced to the assistance of her sister.

'There she goes!' Rawlings shouted exuberantly.

Ahead of them, and astern of *Seventy-Three*, pillars of white water rose out of the sea.

Jamie had come up on the bridge. 'Think we got him, sir?'

'We'll soon find out.' Duncan glanced at the boy. They had grown closer together over the past month, because Jamie was clearly worried about the fact that Mother was in German hands – very nearly as much as himself; sometimes, he thought, even more. He could understand that. The boy had clearly been impressed by Kristin's spirit on that crossing from St Malo, and probably even more by her courage and determination during the Dunkirk operation. Even if those were the only two occasions they had ever met, he could appreciate an impressionable young fellow being over-whelmed. Well, he was pretty proud of her himself, even if he felt like wringing her neck for such an act of crass stupidity – or crass arrogance.

But that would have to wait until she came back. If she was going to come back. It was now five weeks, and the only word that had come – not out of Guernsey but from the Madrid embassy – was that the Dowager Lady Eversham was under house arrest in Guernsey while she was being investigated. For five weeks?

He really felt like bagging a U-boat.

'What do you see?' he called to Rawlings.

'Nothing, sir.'

Colley came on the radio, his tone crestfallen. 'I've lost the bugger. I'm positive he was there.'

'He was there,' Duncan agreed. 'He's gone deep. Therefore he can't have gone far. Box pattern.'

The three MTBs spread out and began performing a regular exercise, dropping their depth charges in pairs over a half-mile area. But an hour later they had seen nothing, and were down to their last pair each, while the convoy was out of sight and had to be within touching distance of Plymouth.

'Call it off,' Duncan commanded. 'Flotilla will return to base.'

'Shit!' Colley commented. 'I know he's down there.'

'I'm sure you're right,' Duncan agreed. 'But he's sitting it out, and we can't hurt him once all our charges are gone. We may just need them before we get home. Fifteen hundred.' The boats lined up and roared to the east. 'We'll be back by dark,' Duncan said.

'You really think he's still down there, sir?' Jamie asked.

'Yes.'

'He could be sunk.'

'I doubt it. If we'd got through his skin something would

have come to the surface. But there hasn't even been any oil. He's a veteran, and he has guts. Mind you' – he grinned – 'if we got at all close, he won't be very happy.'

They entered the Solent at five, and an hour later were alongside their pontoon in Portsmouth, to find a lieutenant waiting for them. 'Lieutenant Eversham?'

'That's me.' Duncan switched off the ignition; the fenders were out and the warps secured.

'Compliments from the admiral. He wants to see you.'

'Now?'

'He said as soon as you were docked.'

Duncan's heart leapt; this could only be news of Mother. But then he remembered that it didn't have to be good news. 'Bed her down, Mr Harris,' he said. 'And then the crew may stand down and have liberty. But I wish everyone back on board by ten, just in case.'

'Aye aye, sir.'

Duncan checked his uniform – his tunic was flecked with spray, but the old boy would have to put up with that – and stepped ashore; Jamie was in the engine room shutting down, and was not to be seen.

'Any joy this afternoon?' the lieutenant asked, as they went ashore and to the command building.

'Not a thing, The blighter was there, but somehow he managed to disappear.'

'Well, you can't win them all.' He led the way up the stairs.

'Any idea what this is about?' Duncan asked.

'No, I haven't. But I gather it's top secret.'

Duncan digested this, and a few minutes later Miss Williams was showing him into the admiral's office.

'Ah, Duncan,' Lonsdale said. 'Good man. Is the colonel still about, Miss Williams?'

'I think he went to the mess, sir. I know he's still on the base.'

'He'd better be. Get him back, will you, please?'

'Aye aye, sir.' Miss Williams departed.

'Sit down, Duncan,' Lonsdale invited. 'Any luck?'

'No, sir.'

'Still, I understand the convoy got in safely. Prevention is better than cure. I have some rather disturbing news.'

Duncan waited.

'As you know, the Spanish consul in Guernsey, who is actually a Guernseyman, has been keeping an eye on your mother's situation.'

'Yes, sir.'

'All his efforts to obtain her permission to leave the island and return to her homeland, in this case Spain, have so far come to nought. They seem to be viewing her with considerable suspicion, and I can't help feeling that she may have contributed to her situation by flashing her three passports, and – well, by treating anyone who does not appreciate her point of view as an idiot. I hope you do not mind my saying this.'

'It's the truth,' Duncan conceded.

'Yes. But now we have learned from Madrid that things may have taken a turn for the worse. It seems that your mother claimed a personal acquaintance with General Franco, which is one reason she has been kept in honourable confinement in her own house. However, it turns out that this claim has finally got back to the general, who, while he does not deny knowing Kristin, has said he does not care what happens to her and, more seriously, has revealed the truth about her Jewish grandmother. The Guernsey consul is doing all he can, but he very much fears that she may shortly be deported to Germany.'

'But . . . My God! If that happens, she could wind up in a concentration camp.'

'Exactly.' There was a knock on the door. 'Come?'

Miss Williams entered. 'Colonel Gubbins is here, sir.'

'Oh, fine. Come in, Colonel. I would like you to meet Lieutenant Lord Eversham.'

Duncan stood up to shake hands; as he was not wearing his cap, he could not salute.

'My pleasure, Lieutenant.' Gubbins was a stocky man with a little moustache and receding hair. 'I understand we are to work together.'

Duncan looked at the admiral; his brain was still spinning at the news that his mother's life might actually be in danger.

'I have not yet put Lieutenant Eversham in the picture,' Lonsdale said. 'Do sit down. I assume I am right, Lieutenant, when I tell the colonel that you know the waters around Guernsey like the back of your hand?'

'I wouldn't say that, sir. But' – he hurried on as the admiral frowned – 'a member of my crew does.'

'Ah. Excellent. This man knows the waters well enough to navigate them in the dark?'

'Within reason, sir. It's a rock-bound coast.'

'I take your point. Colonel Gubbins?'

The colonel cleared his throat. 'As I am sure you are aware, Lieutenant, we have taken a bit of a licking over the past few months. We have been driven from the Continent . . .'

'Lieutenant Eversham took part in the evacuation from Dunkirk,' Lonsdale put in.

'Then you'll know what I am talking about. Now there can be no doubt that the enemy are preparing an invasion of England. Whether they can succeed or not must depend largely on whether the RAF can keep the Luftwaffe from blanket-bombing our cities, our factories and our military dispositions. This, as I am sure you know, has been the pattern of all their military successes this far: paralyse the enemy, and perhaps more importantly, his civilian population, with terror from the air, and then move the ground forces in. Well, as I have said, preventing that from happening in England is the province of the RAF. However, the Prime Minister is of the opinion, with which I concur, that just to sit and wait to be hit is a mistake, both as regards the country's morale and, no less important, neutral opinion as to whether we can survive, and thus whether we are worth helping.

'I may say that he formed this opinion back in June, immediately after Dunkirk, and I was selected to create an elite body of troops who would be able to strike at the enemy, hard and viciously, and then withdraw to strike again – where, he would not know. This, it is felt, would not only keep him in a constant state of nervous apprehension, but let the world see that we are still an active fighting force. I set to immediately to create such a force. We call ourselves the Leopards.'

He paused to look from face to face, as if anticipating some reaction to the somewhat schoolboyish appellation, but there was none. 'Now, I will tell you frankly, gentlemen, that my Leopards are a long way from where I would like them to be, both as regards training and numbers. I envisage a force of divisional strength, with all the ancillary units, such as artillery, reconnaissance and medical back-up of the normal division, strong enough to seize enemy territory and hold it for a few days, inflicting maximum damage, before withdrawing.' His eyes gleamed; his ambition was clear.

'Unfortunately,' he went on, 'creating such a force takes time, the more so as we are subjected to a great deal of inter-unit jealousy over our special status and unorthodox training methods. However, that is not the point, which is that the PM has become impatient, with an invasion looming. He wants us to start striking at the enemy now, with what we have.'

'The idea,' Lonsdale said, 'is to send in a small force of Leopards, carried by a small, fast ship, to carry out a raid on enemy territory. And the territory chosen is Guernsey. That being so, I thought immediately of you, with your local knowledge.' He paused to stare at Duncan, to leave him in no doubt as to the unspoken message he wished to convey. 'Of course, this is a dangerous mission, Lieutenant, as you will be penetrating enemy-held waters, and thus you will be required to volunteer.'

'Yes, sir,' Duncan said absently, still assimilating what he had just been told. 'And my crew?'

'Well, of course. But you can tell them nothing more than that it is a dangerous mission. It must be top secret.'

'Yes, sir. May I ask exactly what is involved?'

'Colonel Gubbins?'

'We would like you to transport as large a troop of my men as you consider feasible, to a landing spot on Guernsey chosen by you, put them ashore for a couple of hours, and then pick them up again and bring them home.'

Just like that, Duncan thought. But . . . 'Did you say "troop", sir?'

Gubbins smiled. 'Don't panic, Lieutenant; they're not cavalry. In the Leopards we are divided into troops rather than companies. How many men can you safely accommodate?'

'That depends on what you mean by the word "accommodate", sir. If you mean sleeping accommodation, none. If your people would wish to be below decks during the voyage, perhaps twelve.'

'You brought sixty men at a time off the beach at Dunkirk,' Lonsdale reminded him.

'Yes, sir. But my speed was virtually halved, and I was also virtually unarmed. I hope you will not send my people into enemy waters naked.'

'There won't be any use for your depth charges; you are not to carry out any ASW activity.'

'Aye aye, sir. But I would like to have my two torpedo tubes loaded – just in case we have to shoot our way out.'

'Point taken. So, how many men are you prepared to take?'

'We can manage twenty-five, if they are prepared to stay on deck.'

Lonsdale looked at Gubbins. 'How long will the voyage take?' the Colonel asked.

'Approximately three hours there, and three hours back,' Duncan said.

'That should not be a problem, in August. How soon can you go?'

'I will have to check that out, sir.'

'What? Isn't you boat ready for sea?'

'My boat can be ready for sea in an hour, sir. But I need to check the tides.'

'What have the tides got to do with it? I'm told you can make forty-five knots.'

'Providing conditions are at the least reasonable, that is correct, sir, although not with an additional twenty-five crew. But I am not concerned with tidal speeds; it is the range that matters. In the Channel Islands, the range averages thirty feet.'

'Thirty feet? You mean . . .' Gubbins looked at Lonsdale as if he was responsible.

'Yes, sir,' Duncan said. 'That is the height of this building. And that sort of range can cover a considerable area, as the average beach has a gradual slope. That means that if I were to drop your people ashore at low water, they could have a walk of as much as a mile, over very uncertain ground, to reach dry land. On the other hand, if I were to drop them at high water, they could be faced with a return journey over that distance, when presumably they may have the entire German garrison behind them. So you see, it is a matter of choosing our time, and our place, with absolute accuracy.'

'They only wish to be ashore for two or three hours,' Lonsdale remarked, quietly.

'Still half a tide, sir.'

'You mean fifteen feet,' Gubbins said, lugubriously.

'Not necessarily, sir. Tidal movement follows an unchanging rule, which we call the Rule of Twelfths. That is to say, following low water, it rises by one twelfth of the range in the first hour, two twelfths in the second hour, and three twelfths – that is to say, by a quarter – in the third. In the fourth hour it again rises by a quarter, in the fifth by two twelfths, and in the final hour by one twelfth. Then it falls again at the same rate. These hours are of course approximate, as each tide is about ten minutes shorter than the previous one, but it is close enough for our purpose.'

'I'm beginning to get your point,' Gubbins said. 'You mean, if you were to set my people ashore within two hours of high water, if they returned four hours later, even on a thirty-foot range, the water level would be about the same as when they landed. Well, then, isn't that simple enough?'

'Provided we got our timing right, sir. This raid would have to be carried out at night, so, ideally, you wish a tide that will peak at midnight, so that you could get ashore at twenty-two hundred and be back on board at oh two hundred.'

Lonsdale pressed his intercom. 'Miss Williams, bring in the tide tables for the Bay of St Malo, will you?'

'Aye aye, sir.'

'It also has to be tied in with the moon,' Duncan said. 'We need it to be full.'

'Wouldn't it be better on a moonless night?' Gubbins asked.

'With respect, sir, I don't think even my navigator could get us through all those rocks in pitch darkness. Ideally, we want moonrise about nine.'

'Well, my word,' Gubbins commented. 'I had no idea planning an amphibious operation was so complicated. To get it right we could wait for weeks.'

Miss Williams appeared with the requisite tide tables, and the admiral studied them. 'Nothing in this life is ever perfect,' he remarked. 'The tides would be right either side of a week today, but it's only a half-moon, rising at midnight.' He looked up. 'Will you risk that, Lieutenant? There won't be another suitable tide for the next fortnight. Frankly, I don't think we can afford to wait that long. Can you do it?'

'I would have to check with my navigator, sir.'

'When can you do that?'

'As soon as I leave here.'

'Very good. I don't think we need detain you any longer, Colonel Gubbins. I'll be in touch first thing tomorrow morning.'

Gubbins looked slightly disconcerted, but he understood that he had been dismissed. He stood up. 'Very good, sir. I look forward to working with you, Lieutenant Eversham.' He saluted the admiral, and left the room.

Lonsdale waited for the door to close. 'What do you think?'

'I am wondering . . . Well, sir, what exactly is the purpose of this mission.'

'Officially, to show the enemy that he is safe nowhere, and to make him wonder, if we can do this with twenty-five men, what might happen when we can do it with twenty-five hundred, or perhaps even twenty-five thousand. And of course, to have something positive to put in the newspapers: British Leopards raid Channel Islands, etc., etc.'

'I can see that, sir. But to achieve either of those objectives, we must make the Germans aware of our presence in the island.'

'Well, of course. That is the object of the exercise.'

'How are we proposing to do that, sir?'

'By shooting up a few German installations, I imagine. Militarily it will be quite irrelevant. But the propaganda value could be enormous.'

'Yes, sir. But what about the Guernsey people?'

'Oh, no one is going to shoot them. Or damage their property.'

'But the Germans will almost certainly resent being shot up. Aren't they likely to take it out on the locals after we have left again?'

Lonsdale frowned at him.

'These people are British citizens, sir,' Duncan added.

'For the Germans to take reprisals against the locals because of a British raid would be against every tenet of the Geneva Convention.'

'Yes, sir.' Duncan's tone was doubtful.

'But if they did – well, we are fighting a war. Right now our civilians are being bombed by the Luftwaffe, and quite a few of them are dying. They aren't complaining; they know this is a price that has to be paid for eventual victory. All we can do is exact retribution when we have won. That goes for British citizens, everywhere. Now look here, I am giving you the opportunity to rescue your mother from a quite horrible fate. Once she is taken to Germany the odds on us ever seeing her again are not worth considering. Don't you want to get her back?'

'Of course I do, sir. I would just like to be reassured that this raid is not being undertaken just for that purpose. I mean, she got herself into this mess. Have we any justification for causing what may be quite a few deaths, amongst our own people, to get her out?'

Lonsdale regarded him for several seconds, then he leaned across the desk. 'Now, you listen to me, young man. The idea of a raid, somewhere in Europe, but of the maximum propaganda value, came from the very top. As I was required to provide the transport, I was approached, again from the very top, and requested to offer feasible objectives. I could have chosen a French port, or Jersey, but as the raid was going to take place anyway, with the consequent possible misfortune to the civilian population, I determined that it might as well be put to some more practical use than mere propaganda. Now, that has to be our secret, Duncan, just as getting your mother out has to be our secret. I cannot authorize you to rescue her, just as, if anything goes wrong, I will have to deny that this conversation ever took place. But she is your mother, and she is a very gallant lady. If anyone can pull this off, you are that man.'

His gaze was intense, and Duncan saluted. 'Aye aye, *sir*.'

'We are going on what could turn out to be a dangerous mission,' he told his crew. 'It is top secret, and I cannot tell you our destination or our task until we are under way. But I have to ask you to volunteer. I know that some of you are married. Thus if any man, for whatever reason, feels he cannot take part, let him say so now. You may stand down, and rejoin us when we return with no disfavour on anyone's part.'

He waited, but no one moved. 'Very good, and thank you. There are three days' leave, starting now. You will report for duty on Tuesday morning. Dismissed. Goring.'

Jamie waited, while the other men collected their gear.

'I'll give you a lift home,' Duncan said.

'That's very kind of you, sir.' He got into the Bugatti. 'Any word on her ladyship?'

Duncan drove out of the yard. 'Yes, and it's not good. I won't bother you with the murky details, but the Germans have got hold of the idea that she may be a spy.'

'Her ladyship?'

'Yes. I know it's absurd, but they are inclined to be paranoid about people who do not behave as orthodoxly as they like. There is a suggestion that she may be sent to Germany to stand trial.'

'But . . . good Lord, sir. That could mean . . .'

'That she stands a chance of being executed.'

'Can't something be done about it?'

'Not officially. At least, with any hope of success. However . . . What I am going to tell you is absolutely top secret.'

'Yes, sir.'

'I want you to tell me that it can be done.' He outlined the gist of the conversation in Lonsdale's office. 'Well? High water on Tuesday night is 2445, moonrise, such as it is, 2410.'

'There are several bays on the south coast of the island that are reasonably clean. A lot will depend on how much time we have.'

'If the operation is to be carried out in darkness, not more than four hours.'

'Four hours. I can get you in and out, sir. Everything will depend on where you mother's house is, and what sort of defences the Germans have.'

'They've only been there a few weeks. They can't have constructed any proper defences yet. And Mother's house is at Albecq. That overlooks Cobo Bay. The sea is only a stone's throw away.'

'Um.'

'Doesn't that make it very simple?'

'No, sir, it does not. I was thinking in terms of the south coast. As you know, sir, Cobo is on the west coast of the island, and it is not one of the bays I had in mind for navigation in the dark. In fact, again as I am sure you remember, the west coast of Guernsey is a mass of rocks, for a good way offshore.'

'But you can navigate it,' Duncan said, encouragingly.

'I think I could, sir, in daylight and good visibility. At night, with no moon, at least on the way in . . .'

'Are you saying it can't be done?'

'No, sir. I am saying that we will be exposing ourselves – everyone on board – to the greatest possible risk.'

'Are you prepared to take such a risk?'

'I am, sir. I was thinking of the overall objective of the raid. We won't accomplish anything, either physically or propaganda-wise, if we strike and sink before even getting to the island.'

Duncan pulled into the garage forecourt. 'Jamie, I cannot consider allowing my mother to be tortured by the Gestapo and then shot or hanged.'

I cannot consider that either, Jamie thought, because she is the most important woman in the world to me.

'So,' Duncan said. 'Are you with me? No matter what?'

'Aye aye, sir. No matter what.'

Duncan squeezed his hand.

'Easy, old boy, easy.' Duncan hugged Lucifer and then set him on the ground. 'It seems to me that they've been overfeeding you.' He looked up the stairs. 'Hi.' There was still an element of shyness every time he saw her, because he never saw her enough. But . . . 'What's this?' She was in uniform.

She came down the stairs to greet him, Harry, emerging from the back of the house, having tactfully withdrawn. 'Just trying it on.' She put her arms round his neck for a kiss.

'With what in mind?'

'I had my interview yesterday – my final interview, hopefully. I have been pronounced fit for duty. So tomorrow I report to Portsmouth, and Lonsdale's office.'

'Tomorrow.'

'Why, how long have you got?'

'Three days.'

'Shit. But I'm sure I can get home every evening. You don't mind if I drive the Sunbeam?'

'You can drive the Bentley, if you like.'

'I wouldn't dare.' They climbed the stairs hand in hand. 'Can you imagine what Kristin would say if I scratched it?'

'She would laugh. Your people get home all right?'

'Yes. Dad telephoned last night. He said to tell her that they had had a wonderful time.'

'She'll be happy about that.'

Something in his tone caught her attention. 'Tell me.'

They entered the sitting room, and he poured them each a glass of sherry, then sat beside her on the settee. She listened in silence, occasionally sipping. 'I don't suppose I can volunteer?'

'No, you can't, Alison, not this time.'

'Because you're liable to get killed.'

'Because Lonsdale wouldn't wear it. There's no point in going back after all this time and promptly being cashiered.'

She sipped the last of her sherry, got up and refilled both their glasses. 'Can you do it?'

'If we can't, nobody can. You remember Jamie Goring?'

'Of course I remember Jamie. You don't forget someone you've shared that kind of experience with.'

'True. But what you don't know about him is that he knows the waters around Guernsey as well as he knows his own back yard.'

'How well do you know your own back yard?'

'Ha ha. I'm serious. I have sailed with him over there, and if there is anyone who can get us in and get us out again, he's the man.'

'In the dark?'

'He's prepared to have a go.'

'Can he also catch bullets?'

He pulled her down to be beside him. 'We can do it. Don't you want to have Mother back?'

'Of course I do. But . . . I hope you won't be mad at me for saying this . . . I'd rather have you back more.'

He put down his glass, took hers from her hand to place beside it, then stood up, drawing her with him.

'What are you doing?' she asked.

'Taking you to bed,' he told her. 'There's time before lunch.'

The Raid

'Well, Herr Captain,' Kristin remarked, 'I hope you have something worthwhile to tell me. You have no idea how boring it is, sitting in this house day after day, with nothing to look at but the sea, nothing to read but the same dozen books that I have already read God knows how many times, and with only that idiot of a guard to speak to. He only has about three words of English.'

Captain Jurgen did not look amused. 'Yes, milady, I have something to tell you.'

'Oh, good. Have your people come to their senses at last?'

'A decision has been made regarding your case, yes. The various arguments in your favour put forward by your consul have finally been dismissed as irrelevant.'

'What?'

'And so, there are two Gestapo agents on their way here now. They will arrive tomorrow, and they will take you to the mainland and thence to Germany for trial, both as a spy and as a Jew.'

Kristin had been standing up. Now she sat down, slowly. 'A Jew? Me?'

'Can you deny that your grandmother was a Jewess?'

'Well, of course she was. But that was my grandmother.'

'It has been determined that tainted blood lasts for three generations.'

'For God's sake! Anyway, she converted to Christianity when she married my grandfather.'

'You may wish to offer that in your defence. But I must warn you that that is a fairly common defence, and is not usually recognized. In any event, the matter is now out of my hands. I am instructed to place you under close arrest until you can be formally handed over to the Gestapo. Kindly collect your things.'

Kristin found it difficult to move. It had never occurred to her that she might really be in danger. All her life she had laughed at authority, at convention, at laws where they inconvenienced her – at religion itself, sure that there would always be a hero waiting in the wings to snatch her from imminent catastrophe. In the first days of her marriage, Eversham had done that. But it had not really been his character, and he had soon not only grown tired of the role, but had told her so. Nearly all her subsequent lovers had been part of that quest for a new hero. Duncan had never let her down, but he was her son. Jamie was still an unknown quality, in the heroic sense. But whatever their potential value, they were too far away to help her now, as was even Jimmy Lonsdale, the current principal holder of the post. She was alone, and she was faced with an unthinkable future.

'I am waiting, milady.'

Kristin got up and climbed the stairs. Jurgen followed her, and into her bedroom. 'Do you mind?' she asked.

'I am not to let you out of my sight.'

She gave him a look that should have shrivelled him to a cinder, but as it didn't, took out her valise and packed the few clothes she had with her. 'I am ready.'

'What about that?' He indicated the long cardboard cylinder standing in the corner.

Kristin considered. But to take that with her would be to make her looming humiliation worse. 'It is just a worthless painting. I will have no use for it in prison.'

He shrugged. 'Then shall we go?'

She went down the stairs before him. At the foot she stopped and turned. 'What will happen to my house?'

'It would be a waste to allow it to stand empty. It will be requisitioned as quarters for some of our people.'

'Ah,' Kristin said. She supposed they might have quite a time.

'Captain Smith-Willoughby,' announced the officer from behind his moustache.

'Lieutenant Eversham.'

As their ranks were approximately equal, Duncan shook hands.

Smith-Willoughby looked past him at the waiting MTB. 'Is that our transport? A little small, isn't she?'

'She can go where a battleship can't,' Duncan pointed out, and decided against telling him she was made of wood. 'This your lot?' He eyed the twenty-four heavily armed men waiting on the pontoon.

'All present and correct,' Smith-Willoughby acknowledged.

'And would those be tommy guns?'

'Indeed. We have a couple of Brens as well, but the tommy is best suited for our line of work. We don't go in for long-range marksmanship.'

'Absolutely,' Duncan agreed. 'You wouldn't happen to have a couple of spares, would you?'

'We always travel with spare weaponry, old boy. Would you like one?'

'I think we might be able to use a couple.'

'No problem.'

'Well, then, will you board? You have been told the drill?'

'That we remain on deck, sitting or lying, and keep out of your way.'

'That seems right. We shall serve you with a hot drink halfway across. And you are welcome to stay on the bridge with me.'

'Thank you.' Smith-Willoughby turned to face his men. 'Troop will fall in and board, in single file.'

The Leopards advanced to the gangway one by one, to be received by Rawlings and Craig, gazing with some trepidation at the amount of gear carried by each man, which, in addition to the tommy gun included a wicked-looking knife, an entrenching tool, an obviously heavy haversack that Duncan guessed carried their spare magazines, a string of grenades and a canteen, as well as a tin hat; at the moment they were wearing berets. They were also carrying two Bren guns. He could only hope that no one dropped anything.

The last man in position, seated aft, shoulder to shoulder, and making a discernible difference to the trim of the boat, he gestured Smith-Willoughby to board and escorted him to the bridge, where Harris waited. 'Brass,' the petty officer muttered.

'I thought there might be,' Duncan said, and faced the pontoon. The area had been carefully cleared of any would-be spectators – even the crews of the other MTBs; but walking along the pontoon, easily identifiable even in the gathering gloom, were Rear Admiral Lonsdale and Colonel Gubbins. They looked up at the bridge. 'All correct?' Lonsdale asked.

'Yes, sir,' Duncan replied. 'ETD five minutes.'

Lonsdale looked up at the sky, where the light cloud allowed the evening to be quite bright. 'Have you had the forecast?'

'Some wind by dawn. I aim to be back by then.'

'Then I'll wish you good fortune. I wish I was coming with you.'

'So do I,' Gubbins said.

The two officers saluted, then Duncan turned the ignition switch and the engine purred. 'Cast off forward, cast off aft.'

The warps were brought in, and the boat slipped into the gloom. It was one minute to eight.

The Needles astern, Duncan handed the helm to Harris and took Smith-Willoughby into the cabin, where they were joined by Jamie. 'Engine Artificer Goring,' Duncan offered by way of introduction. 'For this trip he is also our navigator, as he knows the waters where we are going better than any of us.'

Smith-Willoughby was visibly taken aback by Jamie's youth, but he shook hands.

'We're steering two hundred,' Duncan said, 'to give the Casquets a wide berth. The Germans are certain to have a lookout manning the light tower. But visibility is good enough for us to pick up the light at twenty miles.'

'If he's still showing it,' Smith-Willoughby commented.

'He is, as far as we know; his own traffic is using that side of the Channel.'

'At just over thirty knots we should be there by ten,' Jamie said. 'And high water is midnight forty-five. Pity it's a neap, but that may be better for us getting out. Now, sir' – he bent over the chart – 'you'll see that the furthest serious obstruction is two miles out. There.'

'You think that was the one we hit last year?'

'No, sir. We were inside that one when we hit.'

'You have hit a rock off Guernsey?' Smith-Willoughby inquired.

'Not in this boat,' Duncan said, hastily. 'A deep-keel sailing yacht. *Seventy-Two* would have cleared it comfortably.'

'And it was half-tide down on a spring,' Jamie added, 'whereas we'll be coming in within two hours of high, on a neap.'

Smith-Willoughby scratched his head, obviously lost in this welter of nautical jargon.

'So when we're abeam the Platte Fougère,' Jamie went on,

'we can alter course to one nine oh. The tide will still be running north. If we're three miles off we should be clear of any obstructions, until it's time to turn in.'

'Which will be when?'

Again Jamie leaned over the chart. 'This headland is called the Hommet. It separates Vazon Bay, here to the south, from Cobo Bay in the north, and has old Napoleonic fortifications on it. If we're lucky, we should be able to identify it through those. Between it and Cobo is Albecq. It's too small to be considered a harbour, and no one uses it. But it is fairly clean up to about fifty feet of the shore. If we can find our way into there we're as well placed as we can be, both for lying unobserved and for getting back out.'

'Then that's our plan,' Duncan agreed.

'We'll need to be dead slow and have lookouts on the bow.'

Duncan nodded. 'And I want you on the bridge.'

'Aye aye, sir. I'll just help Mr Wilson serve the drinks.'

Smith-Willoughby followed Duncan back on deck. 'You must have a lot of confidence in that boy.'

'I do. He's seen me though some tight situations.'

'Hm,' Smith-Willoughby commented.

A couple of the Leopards were seasick, but they were very quiet and undemonstrative about it, and used their helmets, which were emptied over the side. The Casquets light was identified, on schedule, and a few minutes later the Platte Fougère.

'Bit different to the last time we came down here,' Duncan remarked.

'This would have been pretty impossible in fog,' Jamie agreed, having joined the officers on the bridge.

Guernsey was by no means blacked out, although the glimmering lights were sporadic. And the little ship several miles out to sea – she was not even showing her port and starboard navigation lights, much less the masthead – was clearly invisible. Jamie kept checking his watch, and at twenty to eleven said, quietly, 'I should like to reduce speed and turn in now, sir.'

Duncan immediately obeyed.

'How do you know where we are?' Smith-Willoughby asked.

'Dead reckoning,' Duncan said. 'I'll explain it on the way back.'

The captain took off his beret and put on his steel helmet, securing the strap under his chin.

'It'll be a few minutes yet, sir.' Jamie assured him.

The MTB had now slowed to an almost imperceptible glide through the water and Duncan had to work hard on the helm to keep her straight, but there remained very little wind and only the inshore swell to disturb the otherwise calm sea. Both Jamie and Harris kept their binoculars focused on the dark mass of the land and the occasional flickering lights. Then Jamie said, 'I have it, sir. Green twenty.'

'Going in, Mr Harris. I want two men on the bow. And two aft with the kedge.'

'Aye aye, sir.' Harris left the bridge.

'I'll go up, sir,' Jamie volunteered.

'I want you here,' Duncan insisted.

He was very tense, but then, he felt, so was Jamie. Unlike with *Kristin*, just to touch a rock with this thin hull would mean instant disaster, and now he remembered that he had not thought to instruct his men to wear life jackets.

'I would tell your men to stand by,' he told Smith-Willoughby. 'But make as little noise as possible.'

'We could hardly make as much noise as your engine,' the soldier objected.

'My engine is merging with the murmur of the sea. But any sharp sound could alert a watcher on the shore. Certainly a raised voice would do so.'

Smith-Willoughby made his way aft.

Slowly the MTB edged closer to the shore. Now the bulk of the headland was big to starboard. To port there was another, smaller headland, beyond which was Cobo Bay. Harris came aft. 'I have five feet.'

'I think it's time, sir,' Jamie said.

'Then go.' Duncan put the engine into neutral, and Jamie left the bridge and hurried aft. The secondary kedge anchor, a Danforth, was secured to a warp, and was now lowered over the side and dragged across the sand as the boat was still moving gently forward. After a few moments the flukes dug in and the MTB came to a halt.

As she did so, there was a scraping sound. 'My God!' Smith-Willoughby said. 'We've run aground!'

'That's the excess weight we're carrying. Anyway, there's another five feet of rise to come before full tide. She'll lift.'

Jamie had joined Harris and Rawlings in the bow. There

could be no normal dropping of the heavy steel bower, with its accompanying chain, which would rasp through the hawse pipe. But it had already been made ready, laid out on the deck, and was now lowered over the side with infinite care to enter the water with scarcely a splash, to be followed by the chain, paid out hand over hand. With the boat held by the stern and on the bottom, its purpose was merely to check any lateral movement as the tide rose.

Duncan joined them. 'I have an idea that if I ever come back here in daylight I will have a heart attack. I swear there's a rock not twenty feet away on the port side.'

'We'll manage, sir,' Harris said. 'You going ashore?'

'That is my intention. But we won't be more than fifteen minutes. You'll come with me, Jamie.'

'Aye aye, sir.'

He turned to Smith-Willoughby, who had joined them, while his men were all on their feet. 'You will have to wade.'

The captain nodded. 'Now?'

'Yes. Synchronize.' They checked their watches. '2310. Now, you know your position. St Peter Port is about four miles away, roughly due east.'

'No problem.' The captain tapped his compass.

'And you know exactly where you're going?'

'Our objectives are marked on our maps. St Peter Port isn't our only target.'

'You'll find the others are even farther away. You understand that you have to be back here not later than 0245.'

'Wilco.'

'Well . . .' He shook hands. 'Good hunting. And try not to bring the whole German army back with you.'

Smith-Willoughby grinned and signalled his men, then lowered himself over the bow and dropped into the water, which came to his waist. He waded to the shore, while his men followed one by one. Jamie found he was holding his breath as they disappeared into the gloom; if a German patrol happened to pass by at this moment . . . But there was no challenge.

'She's lifting already,' Harris said.

'That figures; those were big chaps. Now, Petty Officer, providing you monitor any sideways movement there should be no problem. The tide turns at 2345. Keep your eye on the depths, and pull her back on the kedge as required. Remember that when those people return, we'll need an extra eighteen inches of draft.'

'Aye aye, sir. But you said you'd be back in fifteen minutes.'

'That is my intention. But just in case . . . you are not to respond to any action you may hear or witness on land. In this gully you're just about invisible until daybreak. Your sole task is to await the return of the Leopards and then get them out of here, whether I am on board or not. Understood?'

Harris gulped. 'Aye aye, sir. But I would be most grateful if you'd be here.'

'So would I, Petty Officer. So would I.' He picked up one of the two tommy guns left by the Leopards. 'You ever fired one of these, Jamie?'

'No, sir.'

'Neither have I, actually. But I gather it is not a matter of marksmanship, just of spraying the opposition with bullets. On the other hand . . .' He went into his cabin and fetched his revolver. 'What about this?'

'I've never fired anything, sir – not even a shotgun.'

'Hm. Well, then . . .'

'Perhaps Goring would do better with a cosh, sir,' Harris suggested.

'Do we have a cosh?'

'We have several hammers, and a heavy-duty spanner.'

'I'll take the spanner,' Jamie decided, and went below to fetch it from the engine room.

'My God,' Duncan said. 'If you hit someone with that, you'll kill him.'

'But if I have to use the tommy gun . . .'

'I'm an idiot. Very good, Mr Harris.' He climbed over the bow and dropped into the waist-deep water, which was surprisingly cold.

Jamie followed, the spanner tucked into his belt. Rawlings handed down the two tommy guns and they waded to the shore, clambering over the rocks to gain the low wall bordering the road, which curved away to their left. 'Where, sir?' Jamie asked.

'You'll see the land rises pretty sharply. The house is up that hill.'

'Ah . . . there are a lot of houses, sir.' Some were very close to the road, in darkness.

'I know which one it is.'

'Yes, sir. But how do we get there? All of those gardens and back yards . . .'

'Oh, we don't go straight up. We follow this road round to the left, and we'll come to a lateral road leading up the hill. Our house is on that road. Come along.'

'Aye aye, sir.'

They climbed over the wall, and hurried along the road. The turn-off was only a hundred yards away. Jamie looked up at the wooded slopes immediately above him. 'I didn't know there was a wood still in Guernsey.'

'There are only a couple. That one is called Le Guet. There's an old Napoleonic-time fort on the top.'

'Do you suppose it'll be manned?'

'If it is, they obviously didn't spot the Leopards.'

'I think they went the other way, sir – round the other side of the hill. Is there a road there as well?'

'Yes, there is. You could be right. Anyway, they certainly haven't spotted us or the boat. Let's go.'

'I was just thinking that if we have to shoot anybody . . .'

'We're here to get Mother – not start a battle.'

'But isn't she under guard?'

'That's why you have the spanner. Come on.'

He advanced up the side of the road. There was not a sound to be heard above the gentle rumble of the waves on the rocks, and every house was in darkness. Not even a dog barked. But there was a light burning in the house at the crown of the shallow hill, before the road started down again.

'She's awake,' Duncan said.

'But there's no sentry,' Jamie muttered, peering into the darkness.

'Well, maybe the admiral's information was wrong.'

Or he's inside with her, Jamie thought. The thought was quite upsetting.

Duncan unslung his tommy gun and pushed the gate open, went up the shallow path and up the short flight of steps to the porch. Jamie followed, also having unslung his gun.

'It's locked,' Duncan said, trying the door, and then knocking.

This seemed just too civilized to Jamie, and he was right. The door was opened a moment later by a German soldier. Fortunately, he was too surprised to do more than goggle at the naval uniforms, and Duncan thrust the muzzle of the tommy gun into his chest. 'Back up.'

There was a noise from inside the room. Duncan thrust the gun muzzle harder, and the man fell backwards. Duncan jumped over him, and confronted another soldier, who was just rising from the table at which he had been seated; they had apparently been playing cards. 'Hands up!' Duncan commanded, gesturing with his gun.

The man got the message and raised his arms. The first soldier was trying to get up, and encountered Jamie's tommy gun in turn. He backed across the room while still sitting. Neither man had arms on his person, although there were two rifles leaning against the wall.

'I want Lady Eversham,' Duncan said.

The man spoke in German.

'English,' Duncan said.

The man goggled at him.

'He does not speak English,' said the man on the floor.

'But you do. Where is she? Lady Eversham?'

'She is in St Peter Port.'

'Doing what?'

'She is being held there overnight. She leaves for Germany tomorrow.'

'Shit!' Duncan looked at Jamie.

'We'll get her, sir.'

'In fifteen minutes?'

'Mr Harris isn't going anywhere for three hours. Where is her ladyship being held?' he asked their English-speaking captive.

'I think she was taken to our headquarters. It is on the front of the High Street. I think it was a bank.'

Jamie looked at Duncan.

'There are several banks on the High Street. But I would say that German headquarters should have a flag.'

'Then all we have to do is get her, asap. We need a car.'

They looked at each other; they had seen nothing resembling a motor vehicle since landing. Then Duncan snapped his fingers and pointed. 'What transport have you got?'

'I have no transport,' the German said.

'Jamie, shoot him in the leg.'

Jamie gulped, but levelled the tommy gun.

'There is a motorbike,' the man said.

'Can you ride a motorbike?' Duncan asked Jamie.

'Yes, sir.'

'Well, then . . .'

'I think we should take these men's tunics and helmets, sir. That'll give us more chance of getting there.'

'You're right. You heard the man. Tell your friend.'

The soldier slowly got up and took off his tunic, talking to his comrade as he did so. The two helmets were hanging by the door.

'What do we do with them, sir?' Jamie asked.

'Ah. I suppose we should shoot them.'

'Sir?'

The two soldiers insensibly moved closer together.

'I know, I know – Geneva Convention and all that.'

'I was thinking of the noise, sir.'

Duncan gazed at him for a moment, then nodded. 'Upstairs.'

They marched the two Germans upstairs, stripped the bed and made them lie on it, then tore the sheets into strips to bind and gag them.

'It won't take them more than a couple of hours to get free,' Duncan remarked.

'Well, sir,' Jamie pointed out, 'if we're not out of here in two hours, with her ladyship, we'll be done anyway.'

'Good point.' Duncan gazed at the large empty picture frame hanging above the bed. 'That's what we want.'

'Sir?'

'I mean, the picture that was in it. There's a chance it might still be here.' He hunted about the room, watched in bewilderment by both Jamie and the Germans, found what he wanted in the cupboard. 'There we go.'

'You mean to take that with us, sir?'

'Mother would like us to. Let's hurry.' He went down the stairs, Jamie behind him.

'There's just one thing, sir.'

'Yes?'

'How good is your German?'

'I don't speak any German.'

'Ah. Neither do I.'

S-Boats

They roared up the Cobo road and the Rohais. In the darkness and wearing German tunics and helmets, no one attempted to stop them; a foot patrol they passed waved at them. They swung down St Julian's Avenue to reach the Esplanade, and Jamie braked as they came into sight of the harbour. 'Do you see what I see, sir?'

Duncan, clinging on behind, his tommy gun slung, like Jamie's, but clutching the precious cylinder, peered over his shoulder. 'Shit!'

Snugly moored alongside the Albert Pier, which thrust eastward from the Esplanade, were three very large MTBs, bobbing to the almost full tide. 'Do you know anything about that class, sir?' Jamie asked.

'Yes,' Duncan said. 'Those are S-boats, the S standing for "*schnell*", or "quick". They're about a hundred feet long, displace around eighty tons. And in addition to two torpedo tubes are armed with a twenty-millimetre cannon.'

'Which is what in real terms?'

'Just under an inch. Quick-firing.'

'Wow! What kind of speed are we talking about?'

'They are powered by a three-thousand-nine-hundred-and-sixty-horsepower Daimler–Benz diesel, three-shaft, which is supposed to give them thirty-five knots.'

'A diesel?'

'They're big boats.'

'Thirty-five knots. Once we get past them, we can outrun them.'

'Not with twenty-six extra people on board.'

'Um. Orders, sir?'

'We're here, and we go for it. Now Jamie, just remember: we have no time for talk. We shoot our way in, and we shoot our way out, with Mother. Just think of it as taking on an enemy U-boat. She might have a crew of seventy but you'd cheerfully send the whole lot to the bottom. Right?'

'Aye aye, sir. I just wish those bloody Leopards would go into action.'

He gunned the engine, drove on to the front, and then turned up the Pollet, which, at the top of a slight hill, led into the High Street, wheels skidding on the cobbles. 'There's the flag.' Duncan pointed at the drooping swastika on the staff outside a large building on their left.

'And there's a patrol,' Jamie muttered. 'Shit! With a bobby.'

'Go, go, go,' Duncan snapped.

Again Jamie gunned the engine and they roared down the street. 'Run like hell,' he bellowed as they passed the Guernsey policeman.

The unarmed officer dived to the ground. The two Germans unslung their rifles and were scattered by a burst from Duncan's tommy gun. Jamie braked, leapt from the saddle and ran up the steps. A soldier emerged from the doorway, alarmed by the gunshots. Jamie brought him down with a single shot, entered a large lobby, and encountered several more men coming down the stairs from the upper floor, most of them clearly only just waking up. He sprayed them with bullets and had them tumbling to and fro, heard the chatter of Duncan's gun behind him, and knelt beside a little man who he had hit but who was obviously not badly injured. 'The woman!' he shouted.

The man goggled at him.

'Ah . . . *La femme? Où est la femme?*'

Still no response.

'*Frau!*' Duncan snapped from above him. 'The *frau*?'

This time the man gabbled something in German, at the same time pointing at an inner doorway.

'The vaults,' Duncan shouted, and loosed another burst at one of the wounded men who was trying to get up. 'Bring her up. I'll hold here.' He retreated into one of the teller's cages, which had a high iron grill. Outside the bank sirens were blaring.

Jamie slung his tommy gun and ran for the door and down the stairs beyond. He half-expected to confront a time lock, but the huge outer door of the vault stood open. Beyond there were several more doors, and most of these were locked, but in the fourth room, lined with safety deposit boxes, there was a camp cot on which sat Kristin, fully dressed in skirt, blouse and pearls although lacking shoes.

'Jamie?!' she gasped. 'Oh, *Jamie*. I heard the shooting, but—'

'Let's talk later. Come along.'

He held her arm and pulled her up.

'But—'

'Later, milady.'

'They took my shoes!'

'Just come, for God's sake.' He half-carried her along the corridor to the foot of the stairs, and paused. The shooting had stopped, but there was a great deal of noise, not immediately above him, he estimated, but in the street, where men were shouting and whistles blowing. 'Can you walk?' he asked, setting her on her feet and unslinging his tommy gun. 'I'm going to have to use this.'

'But – you'll be killed.'

'I think that may well go for both of us. But we can't stay here.' Cautiously he went up the stairs, called, 'You there, sir?'

'Yes. Have you got Mother?'

'Duncan!' Kristin shouted. 'Oh, Duncan! My two knights in shining armour.'

'Are you all right?' Duncan asked.

'So far,' Jamie said.

'Well, I think you had better stay where you are for the moment.'

'What is happening?' Kristin asked.

'I think that's what Jerry is trying to work out. He doesn't know how many of us there are.'

'So how do we get out?'

'That's what *I'm* trying to work out.'

'That doesn't sound very positive,' Kristin remarked, severely.

The noise in the street had died down, so that a single voice could shout at them, apparently using a loud hailer. 'You in there,' the man called, 'come out with your hands up. You are entirely surrounded. You cannot escape. If you make us to force our way in, you will all be killed. You have one minute to comply.'

'What do you reckon?' Duncan asked.

Jamie cautiously looked out from the top of the stairs. The interior of the bank was in darkness, but there was a lot of light, mainly from torches, in the street, and by his own torch he could see several bodies sprawled on the floor, although his little friend seemed to have got out. 'Well, sir,' he said. 'We can hold them as long as we have ammo. They can only come through the door in twos or threes.'

'How much ammo have you got?'

'I don't know, sir. How much does this drum hold?'

'Maybe fifty rounds.'

'Ah!'

'Exactly. And you've used about half. And they'll have grenades, and bring up artillery if they have to.'

'This is their headquarters, sir. They'll hardly want to blow it apart.'

'It's a point. But they must get us in the end. Mother?'

'Let me get this straight,' Kristin suggested: 'there are just the two of you? – no back-up?'

'Well,' Jamie said, 'there should be back-up, around somewhere . . . Well, glory be. That's a Bren gun.'

There was suddenly a great deal of firing, some from the distance, but most close at hand, dominated by the chattering of the light machine guns, which was accompanied by the shouts and screams of the men in the street outside the bank.

Jamie got up. Kristin clutched his leg. 'Where are you going?'

'To see what's happening, milady.'

'You'll be killed.'

'We can't just stay here.'

As if in response a voice called, 'You in there! Let's get on with it.'

'Smith-Willoughby!' Duncan said. 'Come on, Mother.'

Kristin left the shelter of the steps, and Duncan caught her arm. 'Who is Smith-Willoughby?'

'Right now he is the most important man in the world. All clear, Jamie?'

Jamie stepped outside, and a shot whined past his head. Instantly the Bren gun responded and the firing ceased.

'Come on, come on, come on,' Smith-Willoughby commanded.

Jamie took Kristin's other arm and hurried her down the steps. There were a dozen Leopards waiting for them, four manning the Brens which commanded the far end of the street, to which the Germans had retreated.

'Where are the others?' Duncan demanded.

'Doing their own things, but hopefully they'll be on their way back to the boat by now. Who's this?'

'An English agent whom we have been commanded to get out,' Duncan replied without hesitation.

'Why wasn't I informed?'

'We reckoned you had enough on your plate. Look, old man, do you think we could get out of here?'

The Germans had resumed firing, although with great caution, but they could hear the sound of sirens as reinforcements arrived from various other parts of the island.

'Shall I bring the bike?' Jamie asked.

'Yes,' Duncan said. 'We may need it. Wheel it for the moment.'

Smith-Willoughby waved his arm, and his men withdrew towards the Pollet, broken glass from the various shattered shop windows crackling under their feet.

'My God! I'm cut,' Kristin exclaimed.

Jamie swept her from the ground and sat her on the bike. She swung her leg over to settle herself.

'Oh, Jamie,' she said, 'you are a treasure.'

'Shit!' Smith-Willoughby said. 'I beg your pardon, madam.'

Duncan, at his shoulder, saw what he meant. They had reached the turn-off to the front and could see that a large number of armed sailors were disembarking and being hurried along the pier to the Esplanade. 'We have to go up the hill,' he said.

'But our car is down there,' Smith-Willoughby complained.

'You have a car?'

'We found one with keys in it.'

'There'll be cars up the hill.'

'They may not have keys.'

'Jamie will fix that. Come on.'

The shooting had resumed from down the High Street as the Germans realized that their enemies were withdrawing. Two of the Leopards helped Jamie push the heavy motorbike up the steep slope of Smith Street, while Kristin clung to the handlebars. At the top they found four vehicles in Ann's Place, two of which were German command cars.

'Those,' Duncan said.

'We'll need them both,' Smith-Willoughby pointed out. 'Jamie?'

'No problem, sir.' Jamie got to work beneath the dashboards.

The firing from down the hill had now become general, bullets whanging off the various buildings and screaming into the night. The Leopards had set up their Bren guns again and fired down the hill, but now one of them gave a grunt and collapsed. Smith-Willoughby knelt beside him. 'How bad?'

The soldier coughed blood.

'Fuck it!'

Both engines were now running. 'Put him in,' Duncan commanded. Two of the Leopards lifted the wounded man into the back. 'I'll take one and you the other,' Duncan told Smith-Willoughby. 'The object is to get to Cobo just as fast as possible.'

'I'm not exactly sure of the way.'

'Then follow me. What of your other men?'

'They were operating at St Sampson's. They should be on their way back along the coast.'

'Let's hope they are. Jamie, don't wait for us. Take my mother on the bike and go like hell. You don't mind travelling by motorbike, do you, Mother?'

'I think that's a splendid idea. But are you going to be all right?'

'I intend to be. In any event, we can't all travel on the one bike. Here, take this.'

'My portrait!' Kristin cried, recognizing the cylinder.

'The cardboard is a bit crushed, I'm afraid. But the canvas should be all right. Jamie, tell Harris to wait fifteen minutes after your arrival and then cast off.'

'Aye aye, sir.'

Bullets were now flying all round them as the Germans cautiously advanced up the hill, and another man gave a grunt and fell, to be pulled up by his comrades, but Kristin was as calm as always. 'Do I sit in front or behind?'

Jamie threw his leg over the saddle. 'Behind, milady, and hold me round the waist.'

Kristin obeyed, and they roared into the night.

* * *

Although the racket from the High Street had definitely awak-
ened the town, and lights were appearing in some of the
windows, it seemed that no one was as yet willing to risk the
curfew, and the streets remained clear. They were passed by
a truck filled with soldiers, but Jamie was still wearing his
helmet and tunic, and the fact that he was going the wrong
way and had a woman behind him did not immediately seem
to register.

'Whee!' Kristin shouted in Jamie's ear. 'This is almost better
than riding your bicycle. Did you and Duncan really come all
this way to rescue me? And with soldiers too?'

'Well no, milady,' Jamie confessed. 'We were required to
bring the soldiers to attack the Germans, and thought we would
pick you up at the same time.'

'Oh,' she said, somewhat disconcerted. They raced out of
the Rohais and turned left for the Cobo road. Jamie cast a
hasty glance over his shoulder to see the headlights behind
him; he could only hope they belonged to Duncan and Smith-
Willoughby and not a German pursuit. As his face was in position, Kristin kissed his mouth and they all but skidded. 'Whee!'
she shouted again. 'I forgive you, because you are, after all,
my lion. My Leo! How did you know where to find me?'

Jamie regained control. 'The men at your house told us.'

'Oh, them! Did you kill them?'

'They had surrendered. We tied them up.'

'Thugs,' she growled. 'But you found my painting. Did you
look at it?'

'Well, no, milady. It was in the carton. Is it valuable?'

'It is to me. I'll show it to you when we have time.'

Jamie turned up the Albecq road and braked beside the
wall. 'We go over here.'

Kristin peered into the darkness. 'That's water. How deep
is it?'

Jamie looked at his watch: it was just one. 'Tide's about
full. Maybe six feet. Can't you swim?'

'I've never swum fully dressed before.'

'I'll help you. It's only a few yards. Look, there's the boat.'

Kristin stared into the gloom; the moon was just rising and
was not yet penetrating the various rock gullies, but the outline
of the MTB could be made out, if one knew where to look.
'Good Heavens! Is it supposed to be there?'

'Actually, no. But it's waiting for us. Come on.' He clambered over the wall on to the rocks.

Kristin followed, and gave a gasp of pain. 'My foot is in agony.'

'Slide on your bottom.' He entered the water, found that he was just within his depth, and turned back for her.

'The painting will be ruined.'

'Give it to me.'

She extended the length of cardboard, and he held it above his head. Kristin entered the water with a little shriek, and a voice spoke out of the darkness. 'Who's there?'

'Jamie, and Lady Eversham. We need a hand.'

He couldn't swim with the carton in one hand and Kristin hanging on to the other: she wasn't tall enough to stand. But a moment later a rubber dinghy was up to them, and Rawlings and another seaman were hauling her on board. Jamie handed up the carton and joined her in the bottom.

Harris was waiting for them with the rest of the crew. 'Milady? Good heavens! You're soaked.'

'Well, I've been in the sea, haven't I? I'll use the captain's cabin. And I need a drink.'

'Wilson!'

'Aye aye, Petty Officer.'

'Jamie, you'll come with me. You have to see to my foot.'

'Ah . . . yes, milady.'

'But where is the captain?' Harris asked. 'And the Leopards?'

'Right behind us, I hope,' Jamie said, and followed Kristin below.

She was already in Duncan's cabin, stripping off her wet clothes. 'I shouldn't be here,' he protested. 'The crew—'

'Bugger the crew. I'm bleeding.'

She gave herself a perfunctory rub with a towel, then lay on the bunk. Jamie fetched the first-aid box and peered at her left instep. There were three cuts, one of them quite deep and oozing blood. He wiped it clean. 'It should have something on it. But there's only iodine.'

'Well, use it.'

Tongue between his teeth, conscious of a lot of muted sound from above, he withdrew the applicator and stroked the open wound with the red-brown liquid. The leg jerked and he caught the ankle, looking up the long white limb. 'Milady?'

'Just do it.'

He covered the other wounds as well, and applied plaster.

Wilson appeared, carrying a glass of brandy. 'Oh, I beg your pardon, milady.'

'I need that.' Kristin drank deeply.

'Skipper's back,' Wilson remarked.

Jamie couldn't be sure whether he intended to reassure them or warn them. 'You should stay in bed, milady,' he said, and closed the door before she could protest.

Duncan and Smith-Willoughby were on the bridge, also dripping water, while the Leopards arranged themselves on the after deck as before – but there were still only a dozen of them, and one of them – the man hit in St Peter Port – was lying very still.

'Where is my mother?' Duncan asked.

'We put her in your bunk, sir,' Jamie told him. 'She has a badly cut foot. We've seen to that as well,' he added, continuing to include the entire crew in his account. 'May I ask where the other men are?'

'Hopefully they're on their way. I'd better see how she is.' Duncan went down the ladder.

'What do you reckon, sir?' Jamie asked Smith-Willoughby.

'We have to give them half an hour.'

'I meant, has the operation been a success?'

'If the rest of my people get here, I suppose so. Anyway, you got your agent out. Did I hear the skipper say she was his *mother*?'

'It's a small world, sir.'

Harris joined them. 'I'm afraid your man is dead, sir.'

'I suspected he might be. Shame. But it could have been a lot worse. Can we take him back to England?'

'Of course, sir.' He peered at the shore, increasingly bright as the moon rose. 'At least you weren't pursued.'

'I think we totally confused them, as to our numbers and our intentions.'

'And your other people, sir?'

'They'll be along. Look.'

The skyline to the north-east was glowing.

'That's a sizeable fire,' Harris commented.

'It should be the power station in St Sampson's. Oh, good show!'

Jamie wondered what the people of Guernsey would think about having all their electricity taken away, for no truly worth-while purpose; it wasn't as if this raid was a softening-up process prior to an invasion. And it had cost the life of at least one of the Leopards. On the other hand, but for the Leopards, they wouldn't have got Kristin back. In fact, he and Duncan would almost certainly now be dead. It was certainly a rum old world.

And now time was passing. The Germans in St Peter Port might have no clear idea of what was happening, of the numbers and intentions of their assailants, but they would have to be very dumb indeed not to know that those assailants could only have come by sea, and thus would intend to leave by sea, and thus had to have transport waiting for them. He kept seeing those three monster torpedo boats in the harbour. They would have to re-embark the crews they'd put ashore, but he'd be prepared to bet his next year's salary that they were already at sea, hunting.

Duncan returned on deck. 'She seems to be all right, although she's in some pain. You did an excellent job, Jamie. Any sign of your people, Smith-Willoughby?'

'Not yet, but there's no problem, is there? You said we had until 0245, and it's only just gone one.'

Duncan and Jamie looked at each other, and Jamie understood that the skipper was considering the same scenario as himself.

'Lights!' Rawlings said.

Their heads turned to look north, and see headlights racing down the coast road.

'Two cars,' Smith-Willoughby said. 'Same as us. That seems about right.'

'There are some vehicles behind, sir,' Rawlings pointed out.

'Shit!'

'Have the machine guns manned, Mr Harris,' Duncan ordered. 'They're not to fire at the two lead vehicles, but blow anything behind them apart.'

'Aye aye, sir.' Harris hurried forward.

Smith-Willoughby also left the bridge, to have his men set up their Brens.

'If those Jerries have a machine gun . . .' Jamie muttered.

'And we're still sitting on top of over a thousand gallons of petrol.'

'Well over.'

'So we have to hit them first. They don't know we're here, yet. Check the engine, Jamie. As soon as we open fire I'm starting up.'

'Aye aye, sir.'

Jamie slid down the ladder into the cabin, where Wilson was looking anxious, and then went down to the engine-room level. He had just opened the door when the night seemed to explode above his head as all four machine guns opened fire at the same time as the engine burst into life. He went inside, but everything seemed in perfect order, although he was terribly conscious of the huge fuel tanks to either side.

'What's happening?' Kristin stood in the doorway, wearing one of Duncan's shirts, which came down to her calves, and standing on one leg as she held on to the grab rail by the door.

'We're getting out of here, I hope,' Jamie told her.

'But . . .'

'Oh, yes, we have company. But we seem to be coping.'

As he spoke there was a crump as opposed to the general cacophony above them. Jamie spun round, half-expecting to see the flash of flame that would be his guide to eternity, but nothing had changed.

'What was that?' Kristin asked.

'A bullet hitting the hull. But it doesn't seem to have done any damage.'

The intercom crackled. 'Jamie, get up here.'

He had been holding her against him. He let her go and made for the ladder. 'I'll come with you,' she decided.

'But – you'll have to put something on.'

'I have something on,' she pointed out. 'And my clothes are all wet. Like yours,' she added, realizing that she was again damp.

'Oh – come on then.'

He climbed to the bridge and saw that the Leopards were wading and swimming towards them. The anchors had been taken in, and the boat was floating free. The machine guns were still blazing away, and at least two of the cars on the shore were burning, but it did not appear as if the Germans were armed with anything more than tommy guns, and the range was extreme for the lighter weapons.

'Get us out of here,' Duncan said, and then looked past him. 'Oh, really, Mother.'

'I feel like I'm in a coffin down there,' she told him.

'Take the helm, Jamie.'

Jamie grasped the wheel as the last man was hauled on board, put the throttle gently astern to gain deeper water, and then brought the ship round. The moon was now high, which made their situation look the more desperate, as they were surrounded by rocks. But Jamie knew it was the obstacles that were now covered by the tide and thus invisible that were the dangers. On the other hand, a breeze had sprung up. 'Could we have two men up front, sir?'

'Of course. Mr Harris?'

'Aye aye, sir. Looking for what, Jamie?'

'Any movement on the surface. Especially anything white.'

Harris went forward himself, accompanied by Rawlings, while Jamie himself stared into the suddenly bright night, keeping one eye on the bulk of the Hommet peninsular to his left. Smith-Willoughby stood beside him, breathing very deeply; Duncan was on his other side. Kristin was behind the men, holding on to the rail while her hair fluttered in the breeze. He did not dare increase speed above dead slow, and with the now fresh breeze had to work very hard, spinning the helm to and fro as the boat tended to yaw, while listening and reacting to the shouts from forward, 'Green twenty,' 'Red ten,' as his lookouts spotted suspicious movements.

'Will we make it?' Smith-Willoughby asked.

'Out of here, yes,' Duncan said.

'Well, then . . .'

'Keep your fingers crossed.'

'Clear starboard,' Harris called.

'Clear port,' Rawlings echoed.

Jamie looked over his shoulder. The headland was well astern, and the fires having died down, the coast was nearly invisible. 'I'd like to open her up now, sir.'

'Please do,' Duncan agreed. 'Course three five oh.'

Jamie pushed the throttle forward, and the MTB surged through the waves.

'When will we be quite clear?' Smith-Willoughby asked.

'When we see the Isle of Wight,' Duncan replied.

'You're not serious.'

'What do you reckon, Jamie?'

'They have the same distance to travel, up the Little Russel, as we do out here, sir. But I suspect they started sooner.'

'They?' Smith-Willoughby asked.

Kristin had got the drift of the conversation. 'There were three German MTBs in St Peter Port.'

'And you think . . .?'

'Oh, they'll be after us,' Duncan said.

'And here they are.' Harris had returned to the bridge, and now he pointed. As Jamie had opened her right up, they had been making fast time, and were already abeam of Grand Havre at the north-western end of the island. And coming round the Platte Fougère were the three German boats. They had been in single file to negotiate the narrows, but now they began to spread out in line abreast. Although they were still several miles away, they had obviously seen the British boat in the moonlight.

'Shit!' Smith-Willoughby muttered. 'I do beg your pardon, Lady Eversham.'

'I feel exactly the same way,' Kristin said. 'I also feel that at some time we should be introduced. If that time ever arrives. What is your plan, Duncan?'

'Ah . . .'

'Can't we burst through them?' Smith-Willoughby asked.

'Why are we slowing?' Kristin inquired.

'I think we should keep our distance until we decide what we are doing, milady,' Jamie said.

'We might be able to burst through them,' Duncan agreed. 'But it would be damn risky; they're more heavily armed than us. And even if we got through them, we couldn't outrun them, with the load we're carrying.'

'You mean you don't have a plan,' Kristin said disgustedly. 'It's surrender or drowning?'

The MTB was now virtually stopped. 'If I may make a suggestion, sir,' Jamie said.

'Go right ahead,' Duncan nodded.

'Well, sir, they may be faster than us, but not by much. If we were to run like hell, now, I believe we could make the Hanois Reef before they can catch us.'

'But that'd be going the wrong way, and they'd get us on the other side.'

'Not if they went round and we went through, sir. While if by any chance they tried to follow us through . . .'

'My God! You'd take us through there at night?'

'It's bright enough, sir. And if it's that or being sunk . . .'

'Jesus!'

'Will someone tell me what is going on?' Kristin demanded.

'Just hang on tight and keep quiet. Smith-Willoughby, will you tell your men to do the same thing?'

The captain clearly had no more idea than Kristin as to what was being planned, but he made his way aft.

'She's yours,' Duncan told Jamie.

Jamie thrust the throttle forward, and the MTB cut through the sea, now heading south. The Germans boats were still some three miles away, maximum range for their guns, but they opened fire anyway, their bullets cutting up the surface of the sea some distance astern.

Kristin was now clinging to the forward rail of the bridge, peering through the screen. 'Where are we going?' she shouted.

'You're looking at it, milady.'

The tide was still virtually full, and most of the rocks were submerged, but thanks to the fresh breeze their positions were delineated by flurries of spray, while on their starboard bow the light on the Hanois tower winked with unfailing regularity.

Kristin gulped. 'Isn't that a reef?'

'Yes, milady.'

She looked at her son, who grinned at her. 'We've done it before.'

They were rejoined by Smith-Willoughby. 'They've stopped shooting,' he said, unnecessarily. 'But I would say they're closing. My God! What are we *doing*?'

'Hopefully, getting away,' Duncan said.

Harris arrived, even more concerned. 'Sir?' He could have been speaking for the entire crew; even Wilson was on deck, staring at the approaching rocks.

'Relax, Petty Officer. We're in Goring's back yard.'

Jamie hardly heard the exchanges, although he was terribly conscious of Kristin standing beside him. But he was concentrating with every fibre of his brain as well as his body. The moonlight was brilliant, but even so there were shadows. He had to hope the clouds behaved, and didn't take away his light. He took his distance from the Pleinmont headland as he left Lihou to port and swung across Rocquaine Bay.

'They're following us.' Smith-Willoughby's voice trembled.

'Only two,' Harris corrected. 'The other bloke's turned off.'

'He'll be going round the Hanois, to cut us off when we come through,' Duncan said. 'Damnation!'

'One is a better bet than three, sir,' Jamie reminded him. He had the passage in sight, although approaching it at thirty knots was still a hair-raising prospect.

Several shots whined overhead to plunge into the sea. 'They're getting the range,' Smith-Willoughby commented, again unnecessarily.

'Holy Jesus Christ!' Harris shouted.

Jamie dared not take his eyes from the passage, but he heard the noise behind him as one of the German boats touched a rock, the ripping sound followed by the explosion as her fuel tanks ruptured. 'Where's the other one?' he asked.

'He's stopping,' Kristin said. 'He's not going to chance it.'

'He's picking up survivors, you mean,' Duncan corrected. 'And—'

'We're through,' Jamie said, and swung the helm to bring the boat round to the west. 'May I suggest, sir, that we prepare our tubes. The other bloke's out there, somewhere.'

'You heard the man, Petty Officer,' Duncan said.

'Aye aye, sir.'

'I don't see him,' Kristin complained.

'He's still on the other side of the tower, milady.' Jamie was aware of sweat trickling down his back and his legs; he had been more scared than he would have admitted even to himself. Now he just wanted to relax. But the third German was still there.

'Here he comes,' Smith-Willoughby shouted.

The Hanois tower was now wide on their starboard hand, and the German had clearly given it a wide berth, for he was still about two miles away. Jamie had been steering just south of west, also intending to stay well clear of the end of the reef. Now he altered course to head straight for their enemy.

'Shouldn't we steer north to get away?' Kristin asked.

'It's eighty-odd miles to England, milady. And he's faster than us. Will you take her, sir?'

He had never helmed a boat in combat, as Duncan understood. He took the wheel, watched the German turn towards him and open fire; the red flashes of the gun seemed continuous. 'Everyone hold on,' he shouted, and twisted the helm to starboard. *Seventy-Two* raced towards the lighthouse and the gun took a few seconds to follow. By then Duncan was racing back the other way, following the pattern he had practised so often. 'Range, Mr Harris?' he called.

'Three thousand, sir.'

'Isn't that close enough?' Smith-Willoughby asked.

'We can't afford to miss,' Duncan pointed out, again violently changing direction.

The German was holding his course, apparently confident that his gun would catch up with the elusive Englishman as the range closed. Duncan could see the three men on the gun, but no one was manning the torpedo tubes; the enemy skipper was not going to waste one of those on a small wooden opponent. He altered course again.

'Two thousand,' Harris called.

Another alteration, and a deep breath.

'Eighteen hundred!'

Just under a nautical mile. This was the crunch; he had to hold a steady course for the torpedoes to be accurate. He lined the ship up, brought the helm amidships. The next shot seemed to pass directly over his head.

Then Smith-Willoughby shouted, 'He's turning away! He thinks you mean to ram.'

'Just what we want,' Duncan muttered, as the S-boat presented his broadside. He made a hasty calculation as to the amount of deflection to allow, and altered course to port. 'Fire one! Fire two!'

The two torpedoes streaked away, just in time; the German was still firing, and a second later there was an explosion and the boat seemed to rear into the air.

'Shit!' Smith-Willoughby shouted, as he lost his grip and sprawled on the deck.

Duncan swung the boat to starboard and streaked to the north, maintaining as much speed as he could to push the stern down and keep the bow up. The twenty-millimetre bullets had struck the deck between the two tubes; the men manning the tubes as well as Harris were lying on the deck, and there was a lick of flame.

Jamie grabbed the extinguisher and ran forward, accompanied by Rawlings and Wilson, to dowse the fire. 'You all right, Mr Harris?'

Harris was bleeding from his legs, but he said, 'I am now.'

For the night was lit up by the glows of the explosion as a torpedo struck the S-Boat and exploded.

'Whee!' Kristin shouted, clapping her hands and all but going over.

'Casualty report!' Duncan called.

Harris struggled to his feet, aided by Jamie. 'Three wounded, sir. But none serious.'

'Well, gentlemen, and Mother,' Duncan said. 'Let's go home.'

'That was a most brilliant operation,' Rear Admiral Lonsdale declared.

Alison, standing beside his desk, had glowing eyes.

'I'm not sure what we achieved, sir,' Duncan protested. 'The Leopards lost three men killed and several wounded, and three of my people were wounded as well. All really to set fire to a power station, and as the flames were gone by the time we repassed the north of the island, that must have been extinguished pretty sharply.'

'Ah, but we shook them up, Duncan. Showed the Hun what we can do, eh? And you sank two S-boats. That was exceptional.'

'With respect, sir, one of the Germans hit a rock.'

'You are too modest, Duncan. There is going to be, at the very least, a bar to your DSC.'

'Again, with respect, sir, if anyone is to be decorated, it should be Engineer Artificer Goring. We wouldn't have made it without him.'

'Then I accept your recommendation, Lieutenant. Make a note of that, will you, Lady Eversham.'

'Aye aye, sir.' Alison wrote on her pad.

'And you'll give your men leave, Lieutenant.'

'Yes, sir. I have already done that. The ship needs some repairs.'

'Very good. And of course, the important thing,' the admiral went on, 'from our point of view, is that you got your mother home, safe and sound. How is she, by the way?'

'In the pink, sir, save for a cut foot.'

'And where is she now – in hospital?'

'Good Lord, no, sir. Knowing Mother, I would say she is wallowing in a hot bath.'

'Oh. Ah. I must telephone her.'

'I believe, sir, that when she has finished bathing and dressing, she is going out.'

'What? Shouldn't she rest?'

'I think she should, sir. But you see, we got the portrait back as well, and she seems to be very anxious to have it reframed. So apparently she has this appointment with this chap.'

'A framer?'

'Well, I supposed he must be, sir. I don't know him myself. Chap called Leo.'